YOU CAN'T OUTRUN YOUR ROOTS

YOU CAN'T OUTRUN YOUR ROOTS

MCGEE MATHEWS

SAPPHIRE BOOKS

SALINAS, CALIFORNIA

Editor - Heather Flournoy
Book Design - Christine Svendsen
Cover Design - Fineline Cover Design

Sapphire Books Publishing, LLC
P.O. Box 8142
Salinas, CA 93912
www.sapphirebooks.com

Printed in the United States of America
Second Edition – October 2022

This and other Sapphire Books titles can be found
at
www.sapphirebooks.com

Dedication

For Chris. Thank you for dragging me to South Carolina.

Acknowledgments

This story was inspired by my friend Pam Fowler, who asked me to write something set in her hometown, complete with the church signs at the city limit, with the line "There isn't enough Jesus in this town, and it shows." Translated, that means the place is beyond hope, which is the last thing we would say about South Carolina. We love this area, the people, the food, and especially the funny things we say. I want to share why, even with the myriad challenges of history and continued racism, people of a liberal leaning refuse to leave this red state. Pam, despite knowing me almost thirty years, is still my friend. I hope she laughs as she remembers Morris Jackson, who inspired the character Damion.

I want to thank my friend Heather Price, who as a native, patiently shared her knowledge of things like how to make sweet tea and why we don't plant before Good Friday. Ever.

Many hands touched this manuscript. Thank you to Kim Dyke, whose sharp eye and friendship mean so much to me. Ali Spooner kindly looked through the story to make sure I represented the South with humor and affection. Elle Bradford, Sue Green, Ellen Hoil, Allison Slowski, and my fellow students and the teachers of the GCLS writing academy all looked at pieces of the final product, and I appreciate their energy and kind words.

Thank you to the team at Sapphire Publishing for putting a shine on this book. Tara Young has again given the impression I know the rules of grammar and even laughed at the right places.

I appreciate all the readers who continue to give my stories a chance.

Chapter One

Awalkerblog

by Anna May Walker

M^{*y dear readers,*}

Does anyone else hate their hometown? Tomorrow I am headed to South Carolina for my father's funeral. His death was expected, and to be honest, I dread the next weeks. I apologize in advance, but there will be a delay before my next post.

Aside from the small minds and narrow view of the world, my life was so very boring before taking flight into the best city in the USA, Washington, D.C. My hometown is like many others in the South. There are three places to eat if you include the shaved ice hut and the store that sells fishing gear, live bait, and sandwiches. A worm deli. The scent of topsoil and salami blend in the air. It's as delightful as it sounds.

Every small town has limited shopping, a movie theater with one screen, and a single stoplight. Those annoyances are often discussed, but we all know the real reason we hate our hometowns is the people. Usually, one specific person. In my case, it's my mortal enemy since the first grade, Jimmy, the grandson of the town founder. Never fear, my wicked sense of humor and comedic timing are enough to keep the mental midget at bay.

It occurs to me that the deep-down reason I hate my hometown isn't about the person I despise, it's about the one that I adored. Maybe you have someone from your past that you hate that you loved, a handsome prince that turned into a frog after you had sex, the beautiful girl you cherished until she puked in your car after the prom, your one true soul mate. Or so you thought at the time.

For me, it's Gloria, my first girlfriend. We'd been best friends, and not the hang out and watch football kind of friends. Real friends. The kind of friend who becomes your first lover. Then I gave her the Judas treatment. I still feel terrible that I never apologized. There are some transgressions so egregious, you're ashamed to ask forgiveness. You trudge along pulling the truth with you, hoping she's forgotten, but knowing that's impossible because you haven't forgotten, so neither has she. No matter how many miles you drove, how much beer you drank, how many other women you dated, no, that memory was like a tattoo of your ex's name on your shoulder. Even if you cover it up, you know it's there, and so does she.

I don't mean to imply that I don't ever go home. I visit my momma and daddy for the usual holidays, but I get out of town as fast as I can to avoid reigniting the family feud. I'm not sure how I came from my parents. They are conservative, devout Christians and take offense if you disagree. And as far as I'm concerned, there is no middle ground when it is a moral stance. Listening to them rant is like listening to someone's baby cry on an airplane. You try to empathize, but then it just drives you crazy, and then you feel bad about that, too.

I'm sure I'm not the only one who cringes when

people ask where you're from, and I hesitate to share it here. Take a minute and post below to tell us why your hometown sucks.

Anna May stopped typing. Her fingers hovered over the keyboard. She chewed the inside of her cheek. The town of Chicora Point, South Carolina, was a painful reminder of the terrible person she had been. It was her own fault that she left town broken-hearted. Those other observations were true, but she wasn't quite ready to post about Gloria to the world. Anna May scrolled up to the paragraph about their relationship and hit delete. How did Gloria feel about their shared past? Maybe she didn't think about it at all. Anna May bit at her lip.

～～～～

Gloria Sinclair Montgomery Robinson folded the newspaper open to the obituary section and read the announcement of the death of Mr. Ellison Walker, aged ninety-three, a lifetime resident of Chicora Point, South Carolina. She would attend the funeral, of course, but would his daughter, Anna May? Her mind swirled around the memories from high school until the beep on her phone signaled time to load the produce for the food bank. Her worn boots knocked on the wooden floor as she crossed the kitchen. Outside at the greenhouse, she surveyed the partial load in the old Ford diesel. Over the faded blue paint, the bright bumper stickers practically held the sheet metal together. Jasmine, her daughter, must have loaded the truck. The produce, although deemed seconds, would all be edible but barely filled half the bed. She needed to bring more crates of food, even if it was all saleable.

Inside the greenhouse, she selected the most abundant varieties. Her back protested with a spasm that made her gasp out loud. Every year, the boxes seemed heavier. As she walked past the paddocks, multiple sets of soft brown goat eyes watched every movement, ever hopeful for a few morsels to head their direction. They would remain disappointed. With a snap, Gloria pulled the tarp over the end and fastened the bungee cords, her fingers starting to show the bends from arthritis. She grunted as she shoved the tailgate shut. With a bit of encouragement, the engine fired up, and she drove up the long gravel driveway. On autopilot, Gloria thought about Anna May as she drove. Poor Mrs. Walker must be just distraught to lose her mate of such a long lifetime.

At the roadside sales building, the bright neon shutters were propped open, welcoming all to share in the delights from the farm, whimsically named the Busy Beavers Farm. Her wife, Collette, named it when they first moved to the family farmstead. Collette's death gave Gloria more than insight into how Mrs. Walker felt. Gloria's chest still hurt when she woke up each morning and realized she was alone.

At the fruit stand, she put the truck in park and got out. She tugged her coveralls into place, the denim soft from many trips through the laundry. Her knee crackled when she stepped inside the back door. The dim light showed the racks of fruit and vegetable bins, a refrigerated section of cheeses, and a long shelf of honey jars and wax products. The young woman sitting near the front counter looked up from her notebook.

"Good morning, Mom. I've got an idea for a new backup system that won't need a ton of batteries."

Jasmine pushed a pencil behind her ear, her dark brown curly hair forming a cloud to her shoulders with the humidity. Her farmer's tan darkened her usually copper skin to sienna.

"What's wrong with the generators?" Gloria pulled her long hair together and slid on the hairband from her wrist.

"Nothing, except we have to keep filling them, and they're noisy."

Gloria held up her fingers to count. "And they smell awful. And the diesel fuel goes bad..."

"Right. Especially with the biodiesel. It's the organics, I would bet. Let me research if there are any additives to increase the shelf life."

"Stop, my young Einstein. I have to get to the food bank before nine, or I'll miss the opening, and Damion says things are surprisingly sparse."

"Surprisingly?" Jasmine's phone chirped as a message came through.

"Well, yes, people are usually eating from their own gardens this time of year."

Jasmine blinked a few times. "We could offer a class on the use of mini-plots for the city gardener."

"Great idea." Gloria kissed the top of Jasmine's head. "Love you, see you this afternoon."

With a puff of smoke, the truck lurched onto the two-lane highway. Gloria sang along to the radio over the hum of the cupped rubber of the tires chattering across the pavement. She waved as she passed a neighbor on a porch, Mr. Jackson, the man's white hair contrasting his black skin and navy coveralls. He lifted his hand in return.

The tiny homes created a sporadic pattern, the oldest house surrounded by a mix of former mill houses, their foundations shallow and cracked, and single-wide mobile homes. Not new mobile homes, the kind you got a deal on because the roof had leaked or some crime was committed, with stains down the siding under the windows, the paint faded and chalky. The neglected rusted swing set with a blue plastic seat dangling from a single chain was surrounded by bicycles and abandoned toy trucks, waiting for another cluster of children to discover the joys of a swing or slide.

Piney Grove African Methodist Episcopal Church, a huge brick building outside the town boundary, provided space at the social hall for volunteers to collect and disperse food. The church itself was in the area described by the old white people as the black neighborhood. Every Southern town had a black person or two who they tolerated in their village proper, usually a hairdresser or a cook. In this case, a gay hairdresser by the name of Damion Carter. His father was the preacher, and together, they worked to care for their community. Even though they had very different views on the world, they agreed everyone deserves respect and a full belly.

Putting the truck in park, Gloria called out, "Hey."

"Hey, Miss Gloria. Good morning." Damion's shirt was darker under the armpits as the heat radiated off the pavement. "Did you bring me any comb?"

"Of course." She held up the Mason jar with the wax surrounded by golden honey. "Just for you."

Damion tapped the rear window of the truck between the bright rainbow pride emblem and the Human Rights Campaign decal. "This sticker of the family being chased by a dinosaur. That's new."

Gloria nodded. "Yeah, it may be a statement about traditional families or more likely random foolishness. Either way, it's growing on me. It's better than the Hello Kitty."

"True. By the way, I just got off the phone with Daddy. He said Mr. Walker died. Anna May is coming home for the funeral. You gonna get up with her?"

"I don't know." Gloria paused. You never forgot your first love, but she thought her friends would have after all these years. "I didn't realize you two were still close."

"Oh, honey. I hadn't spoken to her in years until her momma gave me her number when we were putting on the addition to the church. She might not be a Southern girl anymore, but her pocketbook remembers where she came from." He lifted the tailgate open and took out the first crate. "Since then, we keep up."

She grabbed a box. "I better keep up with you."

He gave her a smug look. "As if." They both laughed.

After they finished unloading all the boxes, Gloria drove around the building. At the graveyard in the shadow of the church, she parked near the gardener's shed, which at first glance might be mistaken for an outhouse. The truck door creaked open, and she slid out. She walked through the oldest tombstones toward the newer plots by the fence, and the paper wrapped around the flowers crinkled as she carried the pink spotted lilies. At the name Collette Robinson, she adjusted the brass vase and put in the flowers.

A man carrying a water jug approached. "Miss Gloria, may I help you?"

"Hey, thank you so much."

He poured the water and then stepped back. "I'll

leave you to your thoughts. She was a fine woman."

Gloria smiled at him. "Remember me to your momma."

"I will. See you Sunday?"

"Yes, sir. Thank you again." With that, Gloria settled on a nearby park bench. "I had to split the lilies again, and they're still crowding near the porch. Jasmine added these pink ones for you."

A breeze rustled the ribbons on a nearby flower display. Although there was a perpetual care cemetery in the next town, and while Gloria knew she'd eventually reduce her visits, it was easier to have the memorial close. She bit at her lip and brushed aside tears. "I know it's selfish to want you with me. I guess I'm just tired. I still can't get Jasmine to go back to school. She wants to watch out for me. Every time I figure out a way to cut back, some other project comes up."

Gloria listened to the insects and the occasional scurry of some animal as the warm air caressed her skin. A cardinal flew over and landed on a tree branch. She whispered, "Hey, baby."

After three years, she'd hoped these moments would be less painful. Still the grief choked her. "I might ought to sell the place to some couple just starting out. Otherwise, Jasmine might never leave, or even if she does, she might try to come back. I want her to find her own place in the world." She paused. "I miss you." With a huff, she stood. She blew a kiss toward the headstone and turned toward the truck.

She put down the windows to let the heat out of the interior until the A/C got cold. An old Fleetwood Mac song started on the radio. "I know that's you, Collie. 'Seasons of my life.' Hilarious." She jammed the gear shift into drive. "My life's over. Can't wait to see you again." She held up a hand to the gardener as she passed by.

Chapter Two

A nna May hefted the suitcase into the trunk of the BMW 3 Series and slammed the lid. Sitting in the leather seat, she tapped on her phone screen and surveyed her list. Black clothes, check. All the shorts she owned, check. Chargers and laptop, check. Satisfied everything was complete, she set her phone on the charger. With the push of a button, the engine rumbled, and the screen flickered, indicating that the phone was now synced with the Bluetooth. She pressed the clutch, childishly thrilled at the power as she worked through the gears. At a red light, she surveyed the city lights of the U.S. Capitol. Her destination in South Carolina was, no doubt, dark at this hour. She mumbled to herself, "There's no place like home." Times like this, she missed a nicotine hit, but caffeine would have to do. Near the Metro stop, she pulled into a drive-thru and ordered at the menu sign.

As she rolled to the service window, the clerk smiled. "Good morning, Anna May. You're up early."

Clearly, she bought too many lattes. She passed the woman her debit card. "Trying to beat traffic."

The clerk nodded and in moments handed back the card and a giant pink and white cup.

Anna May carefully accepted the scalding beverage and set it in her cup holder. "Thanks."

With a heavy foot on the gas pedal, she popped through the gears, and the car roared down the ramp. Ignoring the speed limit, she headed south on the highway connector to pick up Interstate 95. With a tap on the display, she selected her favorite preset channel on Sirius and drifted away with the music. As she hoped, the traffic was light, so she made good time. The sun started to color the sky when she exited on Interstate 85, which would take her all the way to her childhood home. Everyone knew everyone. It was nothing like her life in the city. Exciting and anonymous.

In D.C., no one gave a damn what she did, certainly not who she dated. Not like her family. No matter how many times she brought a girlfriend home, her parents still asked if she wanted to meet some guy from church. It drove her mad. Not only did she grow up surrounded by racist homophobes, strangers assumed she was a red state Republican when she said she was from South Carolina. She hated being lumped in with people from the Bible belt. It had taken her years to reduce her Southern accent so that few recognized she wasn't from Virginia or other points north. Her breathing started to quicken. She wiped the sweat from her palm onto her slacks.

Visits home sucked. Whether she was forced onto her parents' sagging couch or a dingy room at the local no-tell motel, it was uncomfortable both physically and mentally. She couldn't possibly sleep on a couch more than one night, so she'd made a reservation at Whispering Pines Motel. On this trip, she had two objectives. First, her father's funeral. She had grieved the loss for years as dementia took him from her bit by bit. Saying goodbye to the shell that remained was more of a blessing. Second, she would stay long enough to convince her mother to move to Falls Park. She could live in the senior center not three blocks from her place. It was logical that Momma should be close to her. How long could it take to talk her into relocating? A week, tops. There was no doubt the house was too much for an octogenarian to maintain. It was a logical choice.

❧❧❧❧

Anna May pulled up to the only traffic light in her hometown and spotted the sign reading Chicora Point, South Carolina, population 872. That was inside the official boundary. Outside that imaginary line lived another thousand or so people, most of whom were black or shades of brown. At the edge of a flower bed of multicolor daylilies, the signs were still there. The markers pointed to the churches in town. Seven. Methodists, Baptists, and Presbyterians. The town was overrun with religion. They just couldn't put enough Jesus in the place, and it showed.

She started a mental running commentary about the village. Some minor things had changed but not the important things. Ending racism and eliminating poverty were as foreign concepts as finding the Statue of Liberty in the middle of town. The Buchanan Mill closed when she was in high school, and the town dried up but hadn't yet blown away. The chicken place was now a Mexican restaurant, and she could smell the spices. The train tracks, idle and weed-filled, ran along the road, rusting into dust.

The big yellow house on Second Street still flew a Confederate flag on one post without a hint of awareness that the war was long over, and they'd lost. Everyone knew it wasn't about the war at all, but rather an ugly sign of hatred—the kind not discussed in the local bar unless you had a shotgun in the rack of your truck, or a championship in running, or both. Jesus wept. That was what came to mind. It could be the town slogan. "Losing my Religion," a phrase meaning to be at the end of your rope, featured in the R.E.M. song to great confusion to Yankees, could be the town anthem.

At the four-way stop, Anna May stared as who should pull up but Gloria. She was still driving a truck, this one blue, and apparently held together with bumper stickers about world peace and clean water. The town hadn't changed her, but she showed signs of the struggle. Her long black hair was streaked with gray, her skin tanned as always, and there were probably a few new scars you could see and some you couldn't. I don't have to ask if she still sells honey at a flea market somewhere. I know she does. Anna May raised her hand in a wave.

Gloria lifted her fingers off the steering wheel and nodded. She drove through the intersection and then pulled into the parking lot behind the dry cleaner. Anna May was shocked Gloria didn't flip her the bird.

Anna May drove another block and parked in front of the motel office. She approached the discolored registration counter at the eight-room motel like quicksand in a jungle. She wasn't sure why it surprised her that she didn't know the clerk, although he had a strong resemblance to the guy who sat behind her in history her senior year. It'd been almost forty years since she'd lived here, things change and move on even in comatose towns like this.

"Hey, I have a reservation for a week."

The clerk nodded and began to type into a computer so old it could've been placed in a museum. A five-foot plastic plant drooped next to the tired couch. A rack of pamphlets promised everything from exciting river raft trips, an evening of delight at a dinner theater, and salvation at multiple churches. She spotted a familiar name advertising an oasis for swimming, fishing, and hiking at her brother's RV park. She shuddered thinking of spending a week in a tin can on wheels, which was scarcely an improvement over a moldy canvas tent.

The clerk's voice startled her. "Name?"

"Sorry. Anna May Walker." She slid a credit card across the counter.

"I'm sure sorry to hear about Mr. Walker. He was a good man."

Anna May lifted the corners of her mouth in a brief slight smile. "Thank you."

The clerk swiped the card. "If you'll just sign here." He put a paper on the counter with a bent pen advertising the local chiropractor.

Anna May scribbled her name and then picked up her card and accepted her room key. It was still a metal key on a large, green plastic fob. "I appreciate you."

Not even an hour in town and her vocabulary shifted to the girl she'd once been. She went to the car and took her suitcase from the trunk. Although it was less than a year old, the handle only came out with a jerk. She rolled it to number four.

The room was small but clean. The bed faced a new flat-screen TV, and a little card next to the remote explained the operating instructions as if this new style of television required complicated directions. She hung her garment bag, unzipping it the entire length before unloading the clothes, giving her something to do. The tall stack of white towels was good to see as she arranged her toiletries on the worn Formica counter.

In the mirror, she fluffed her hair, currently dyed strawberry blond, the exact shade of her father's in his youth. The early start to the day left purple circles against her pale cheeks. For a moment, she regretted not wearing makeup. Trying to cover the freckles left her face coated, and she couldn't stand it. The freckles were another trait from her father.

Her daddy. To be honest, he spoiled her. When she was little, he taught her to keep jars because you never knew what you needed to put in them, might be nails or buttons or even a ball and jacks. She still kept a cardboard box full of them in a closet. When she was a teenager, he patiently pretended to sleep as she practiced driving a stick shift, the gears grinding as she fought to find the right moment to let out the clutch. Her throat tightened, and a sniffle escaped. She seized the sink and cried; her head bowed until her chin pressed to her chest. How could he be gone? It was inevitable; after all, he was over ninety. He might be in a better place, but she would always miss him.

She splashed her face with cold water once the outburst passed and dried it with a soft fluffy towel. Her feet felt leaden as she shuffled back to the sitting area, if a table with two faded plastic chairs could be called a sitting area. She shut the curtain with a jerk and flipped her laptop open. A new blog about growing up in a small town might take her mind off her misery. She only managed a few paragraphs before her creativity stalled, and she gave up rather than staring at the blank screen. The mattress sagged when she flopped down and picked up her phone.

This was only delaying the inevitable. She tapped a number and waited.

"Hello." The voice sounded fragile.

"Hey, Momma. I'm in town and all settled. Can I bring you anything?"

"I sent your brother for more ice. I got more food than we can eat in a month of Sundays. Just you come on."

"All right, be there in a few."

Only a true Southerner realized the short exchange had no warmth or hospitality. They hadn't asked how the other was doing or offered any shocked words that she was staying somewhere besides her parents' house, and there'd been no mention of love. Anna May loved her parents, there was no doubt about that, but her family was the type hard to tolerate much less love. If you were willing to pretend everything was exactly how it was when she was ten, everything was fine.

The real test was coming, and it was always the same. How human rights became some crazy leftist idea was beyond her. It wasn't like she was still a vegan and shoved it in their face at every meal, but the constant complaining about liberals and how good things were in the "old days" drove her nuts. How long could she stay quiet? The odds she'd make it all the way to the funeral wasn't a bet she'd take. First, it was the stare, then little barbs, and finally, voices raised, although she had to admit that she usually got loud first. Her mother always weathered it like a lady, even when livid. The woman was Southern to the core.

Anna May put the laptop in a drawer as if that would dissuade a thief and grabbed her purse. It was time to face her childhood home and the people waiting for her to join in their grief. The next couple of days should last an eternity.

❧❧❧❧

Anna May drove through the neighborhood of cookie-cutter homes. The houses were first painted white by the mill, and even today, it was the rare owner who selected another color for the wood siding. Even the trim stayed white. Pretty much like the people who lived in Chicora Point.

Mill Hill was built in the late eighteen hundreds to house the families that worked at the textile factory. Some had a neat yard of flowers or a carefully tended lawn. Most not so much. In the driveways, older vehicles parked in front were faded. In the small yards surrounded by a chain-link fence, the grass withered to brown in the summer heat. At the corner house, a tireless truck was parked on cement blocks, unmoved for years, possibly decades.

Each house was about seven hundred square feet with a sloped roof, one window on each side of the front door, and had an identical four-room layout. Depending on the number of inhabitants, they might use two as bedrooms, one the kitchen, and a front combination sitting area and guest room. Originally, there was an outhouse out back, and many upgraded to have a sort of commode on the back porch.

Owners started the trend of adding an upgraded bathroom at the rear of the house, on a slab, which was lower than the original floor. This step down was not the usual seven inches, and even though one got used to it, visitors often stumbled. In order to match the original roof pitch, the ceilings were low in these new full bathrooms, and anyone taller than five-foot-six needed to duck through the doorway as they stepped up or otherwise crack their head. Like so many things about the South, they just accepted this as normal and would be shocked if someone mentioned this as an inconvenience. Using an outhouse was an inconvenience. This was the height of luxury, or so they thought.

In the sixties, the mills started to sell them to the occupants. To most families, this was deemed a financial "smart move" as they now owned property. It was really the first sign that the mills were in financial trouble, but no one seemed to understand that at the time. Many didn't now.

The Walker family Buick was parked under a carport, one of those aluminum-framed kits that you could build yourself, which her father had. This was an extravagance on their street. An A/C unit stuck out from a bedroom window, but the rest of the house was cooled by fans. Theoretically. It worked if the roof fan pulled the night air through the house and then you closed the windows in the morning. Most young people didn't understand the particulars of the old mill houses. When someone bought one with an eye on rebuilding or flipping the place, they were in for a challenge. The old rusty oil tanks in the yard still provided heat for the winter, and that was the first thing many new owners wanted to change. They didn't realize the electrical boxes were still only sixty amps and would not support a whole house HVAC unit. Then they gave up, and the houses became rentals and the occupants were unconcerned about such things as upkeep or even minor improvements.

Anna May wondered how long it would take before the local government started to condemn the places. She didn't understand how her mother thought she could stay here without her father. But then again, he hadn't been much help for the last few years. Her mother didn't even drive. Anna May's brother lived nearby. Franklin, who most people called Bubba, was two years younger but hit the school cutoff such that he was three years behind her in school. She doubted he could be bothered with helping their mother much. He and his first wife, Lisa, had a son, and he and his second wife, Stacy, had three kids, one hers, two theirs. He also had a business to run, such as it was. He owned an RV park near the river, which could accommodate up to twenty-five at a time by the water and another thirty on the hillside. Anna May was sure he drove around in a golf cart all day doing a lot of nothing.

With a flick, she took off her polarized sunglasses and got out of the car. Mrs. Wilson, the nosy neighbor, dashed out of her front door.

"Is that you, Anna May? I'm so sorry about your daddy. He was a good man."

"Thank you kindly." She kept walking toward the porch.

"Tell your momma the casserole is almost done, and I'll bring it right over."

"I'm sure that we all look forward to it. Thank you again." With that, she opened the screen door and stepped into the living room.

Her mother sat in her usual stuffed chair by the fireplace, her white curly hair falling around her alabaster face just as it usually did, but her eyes were flat and listless. "Hey, Momma." It wasn't a shock to anyone who knew her father that he'd passed, but to her mother, life would never be the same without him. As her own sadness gripped her chest, she realized she would never know the depth of her mother's loss. Was it Queen Elizabeth who said, "Grief is the price of love," or was that a myth? Words jumbled in her head. Instead of an eloquent turn of phrase about their loss, she mumbled, "Can I get you a tea?"

Looking up, she answered softly, "No. How was your drive?"

"Long but hardly any traffic until Charlotte. You alone?" She hugged the frail woman around the shoulders with a peck to her cheek.

"Franklin went to get more ice. The fridge is full already with food, and I need to get some in a cooler before we can't even get the door to close."

"Mrs. Wilson is bringing a casserole."

"I hope it's her country casserole. She adds a little garlic, you know."

Her father's chair, soft leather with a butt print in the cushion, was empty, but Anna May sat on the couch.

Her brother slammed the door open, a bag of ice in each hand. "Hey, Momma, I'll put this in the back." As he walked past, he said, "Hey, Anna May. Glad you could squeeze us into your schedule."

Anna May glared at him, the years of animosity between them coming to the surface faster than the races at the Anderson Motor Speedway on a Friday night.

He seemed oblivious to her upset as he thumped the bags out back. "I gotta go. Number fifteen has no power," he yelled.

Momma put her small hands onto the chair arms and sat upright. "Nothing serious?"

"Oh, probably just a breaker, but I'll be back with Stacy later." He leaned down and kissed her. "See you, sis."

"Not if I see you coming." Anna May stood and

hugged him. She whispered, "Truce until we get past the funeral?"

He nodded. "Bye, Momma."

Anna May turned her attention back to her mother after his loud diesel truck rumbled to life. After a long silence, she tried to sound cheerful. "I got a nice room at the inn, a middle one."

"Good. Did you eat? I put up dinner, but there's plenty of casseroles. Don't forget to jimmy the microwave handle so's it'll work right."

Anna May went to the kitchen and rummaged through the refrigerator. This place was falling apart around their ears. It's not like I don't try to send them money. Stubborn pride. Returning to the living room with a serving of a pasta something or other on a paper plate, she sat across from her mother. "Did you decide on a time for a viewing, or are we doing it before the funeral?"

"Tonight, at the mortuary, starting at seven. Not many coming from out of town."

Anna May swallowed more than her food as the biting quip was launched. Yes, she was the only one out of town except for her aunt Bessie, and she was in a nursing home in Georgia and couldn't travel. Anna May was the only one "up north," and after she got the call from Bubba, she'd dropped everything and left the next morning. Her mother, like most everyone else in Chicora Point, referred to the Civil War as the "war of northern aggression" and could not fathom what could possibly be of interest outside the borders of their little slice of paradise. The only large city outside South Carolina worth a mention was Atlanta, and even that was suspect with people who often forgot their manners and the hectic six-lane highways.

Anna May considered the flammability of the question: Should she go back and change? It was her personal failing, among so many others, to not know the appropriate clothing for a viewing, compared to a funeral. Her mother wore a simple flowered shift, and Anna May was certain she would change. Deciding it didn't matter what she wore, she asked, "Have you got any other errands before we go over? I'll carry you. Unless you'd rather go with Bubba."

"Uncle Dink is coming to carry me."

Anna May sucked in a breath. Uncle Dink, named after a character played by Jackie Cooper in a thirties film, was really named Henry, after her great-grandfather. He was eighty-nine or ninety, drunk as Cooter Brown more days than not, and could barely drive on a good day. No one could convince him to give up his keys. Momma said his independence was more important and believed people should watch out for old men. Not only did she reject Anna May's offer to help, but she also risked injury riding with Uncle Dink.

"You sure, Momma? It's no trouble."

"I'm sure."

Anna May hoped she'd only bury one parent this week. She picked up the small framed picture from the end table. A family Christmas portrait. As a child, it seemed a time of magic. As an adult, the strands of tinsel on the tree looked fake and cheap. "Remember that time we drove to the beach?" It was the only vacation she could remember.

"Why do you always bring that trip up?"

"It was so much fun just being together."

"You got so sunburned we almost took you to the hospital."

Anna May usually forgot that part. "I'd rather remember getting to eat pancakes for dinner."

After several moments, her mother whispered, "I remember seeing your father smile, he could light up a whole room. I guess he's smiling at Jesus now." Tears started to trickle.

"Oh, Momma." Anna May tried to hug her from the side, an awkward movement, but well-intended.

Just then, a knock at the door interrupted. Mrs. Wilson waved through the screen door. "I hope y'all are hungry."

Anna May shuffled her feet. "I'll put that in the kitchen." Standing at the sink, she could hear the women chat about almost nothing, and when the door slammed, she crept back into the small living room.

"Why you hiding from Mrs. Wilson?"

Anna May shrugged. "Last time we saw each other, she had a hissy fit because I parked too close to her rose bushes."

Her mother narrowed her eyes. She was not a stupid woman. The truth was Mrs. Wilson lit into her about her bringing her girlfriend into town to rub it in people's noses. It had been a rather heated argument.

Momma said, "She ain't got the brains to come in out of the rain."

"But she does make a good casserole." Anna May smiled.

"She does."

Settling on the couch, the women sat listening to the comings and goings of neighbors as the afternoon sun slipped lower.

After a long while, her mother said, "How about I ring up Dink and you just take me to the home?"

"Be happy to." There was hope after all.

Chapter Three

After the rare breakfast in town, Gloria laid the takeout carton onto the hood and pulled the box of not-quite-edible vegetables from the bed of the truck. With a thump, she dropped it onto the picnic table, and a collection of multicolored goats raced to the gate. The matriarch of the herd was Lulu, her brown coat mottled with white spots. The first goats purchased were Alpine for their good milk production, but over the years, abandoned kids from other farms joined in until there was every color of Nigerian dwarf, white Boer goats with brown faces, and the LaMancha with their nubby little ears. A few Angora goats timidly followed, their curly hair shining in the morning sun. Blending in were the fainting goats, most colored black and white. A stranger couldn't pick them out until a loud noise or quick motion rendered them startled and their legs stiffened. With a thump, they would hit the ground. This still amused Gloria every time it happened.

"Good morning, ladies. Who wants a treat?"

The bleating was loud as they pushed one another for access to the fruits.

Inside the barn, Gloria stopped at the sectioned-off pens for mommas and their babies, thankfully the last until next spring. She tried to stagger breedings to keep milk production steady, but often the goats had other plans. Not only did the studs get loose, sometimes the ladies went in search of the boys. Inside the barn,

Gloria let the babies nurse from momma before they were separated into the milk group. This pediatric area helped new mothers get used to nursing, and in a few weeks, they would go back with the full herd. She sang to the ladies as she distributed the chunks of melon. The kids watched their mothers briefly before going back to games of tag with their siblings. Twins and triplets were typical. Only one baby, a singleton, was unusual.

At the back of the barn, the last pen had a few teenage fainting goats that were having trouble with the pecking order of the herd. In the corner slept Petunia, the hundred-pound potbellied pig, her round stomach moving up and down as she snored. Visitors were surprised she wasn't smaller, but those tiny pigs were usually kept on starvation rations. And frankly, a regular pig weighed over a thousand pounds, so Petunia was small. Gloria tapped the fence, and the pig jerked up, her shiny black eyes blinking open under long lashes.

"Want some pancakes?" Gloria asked as she shook the box.

She dropped it over the railing, and the goats ran toward the box. Petunia screamed, like the proverbial stuck pig, and the goats all dropped to the ground. Petunia then ambled over, her round nose sniffing, and began to eat.

"You are so mean to them."

The goats began to stand and nudge toward the box, so Petunia screamed again. The poor goats could only watch her eat the last of the pancakes from the ground, their eyes glazed with jealousy.

Jasmine approached. "I wish you'd tell me next time before you feed them takeout. I want to get a video for TikTok."

"She only does that with pancakes. Besides, I'm not sure I want everyone to think we torture our goats."

"Mom, it's hilarious. Watch this." Jasmine picked up a striped umbrella. As the goats started to stand, she snapped the clip and popped open the fabric. Down went the goats. Jasmine chuckled. "Perfect for tours, right?"

Gloria rolled her eyes. "Until they get used to the umbrella."

"I'm just trying to change things up. People love the fainting."

"If you say so."

"You laugh every time they fall down. And people love to see the goats. You know I'm right."

"I'm thinking about cutting back on tours. It takes too much time."

Jasmine squinted. "What if we put a donation box on the sales barn? Then people will get the hint. Cash is always good."

Gloria hugged Jasmine. "Cash is good. Fine. Put up a box."

Her phone made a ding sound, and Jasmine pulled it from her pocket. "Look, already the spirit guides have answered. Some people want to bring their kids out next week."

"Before you go, can you schedule Hakeem to help with milking for a few weeks?"

"Why don't you just hire him full time?"

Gloria sighed. "I will when you go back to school."

"Part time it is." Jasmine tapped on her phone screen. "I gotta go."

"Sure, go Snaptweet."

"Snapchat, Mom. Really. Tweet is for Twitter."

"What's the difference?" Gloria asked.

"You don't need to know, honestly. Stay on Facebook."

☙☙☙☙

At Gloria's neighbor's farm, the mare stood idly in the pasture near the weather-worn shed, her attention on a new bale of hay. The afternoon sun danced off the kaleidoscope of wildflowers just out of the reach of hungry mouths on the other side of the fence.

Mr. Jackson limped from the front porch. "Thank you for coming so quick. I ain't heard from the doc yet, and Nutmeg hasn't let the filly nurse much, and these old hands don't hold the bottle so well." He smiled, and a gold tooth reflected from just the edge of his lip.

"Happy to help. Let's take a look at momma."

Gloria considered the horse's frame and the gray hair on her muzzle contrasting the snip between her nostrils. "She's getting a little old for breeding."

"You might ought to tell her and not me."

"All right, you little hussy, let me just feel. Nope, I think you're right. She's not going to produce this time." Gloria followed him into the shed. A beautiful paint lay on the hay against the wall, sound asleep.

Mr. Jackson whispered, "She seems good."

Gloria leaned over and lifted her eyelid, the rim bright pink. "You know, we could add another little bottle baby to the kids. Save you the special trip to the pasture."

He nodded. "That would be a great kindness.

Y'all don't know how I appreciate you. If you got a ball for your hitch, you can use my trailer."

She stared at the small two-horse rusting shell.

As if reading her mind, he said, "It's got a new floor last year. And the tires got a little life left."

"I got one under the seat." As long as the foal wouldn't push out the trailer walls, they might make it. She took the pin out and shoved it into the hitch box. Wiggling the pin back in, she forced the safety clip and stood. She climbed in the truck and turned it around, backing up to the garage and the trailer.

Gloria stopped and got out to check the height. The trailer jack was assisted by several bricks and boards. She'd have to raise it higher and then pull them out before she could mount it to the truck. Easy enough except there was no handle on the jack.

Behind her, Mr. Jackson said, "Hang on. I got another jack."

With the efficiency of a lifelong farmer used to having to make do, he tugged a floor jack from the garage and rolled it toward the trailer. He pumped the handle, and bit by bit, it raised toward the rusted metal. Soon the trailer was tipping upward. The creaking was ominous as they nudged the blocks out of the path of the trailer wheels.

He guided Gloria back with the precision of a flight deck marshaller, and in moments, they had the ball in the right position. With one hand on the tailgate, he lowered the jack handle, the truck creaking as it accepted the weight.

She called back, "Can you do the gate, or shall I call Jasmine?"

"I'm not sure who's slower, me or Nutmeg. You come on." He ambled to the gate while Gloria backed toward the pasture.

After she went through, he pushed it closed. Nutmeg barely lifted her head. Thankfully, the baby was small. It was all Gloria could do to lift her toward the trailer. They reversed the process to leave the pasture. Mr. Jackson held a hand up as she pulled the truck toward the road, the engine barely tugging at the extra weight.

Gloria eyed the trailer in the rearview mirror of her truck. Jasmine would think she'd lost her mind. There wasn't any other option. The neighbors were a collection of mostly senior citizens too frail to farm, unwilling to move away. Not that they could. The red loam was overplanted until it was just dirt, devoid of nutrients, and unable to retain water. She popped the brake, and the gears clanked as they lurched forward.

A few town planners held out hope for a revitalization from new development. There hadn't been a major housing project in thirty years. Or more. Gloria was sure the key to rebuilding their community was resurrecting the dirt from its current wasteland into rich farm soil. People were starting to notice her success at her farm. She planted a complicated schedule of mineral-providing crops, mostly beans and peas, and a rotation of her milk goat herd to fertilize as they mowed the grasses. The short stems and their roots developed the intricate network of organics that supported the fungi and worms busily healing the soil.

She drove past a McMansion, built on a small parcel of five acres or so. Like the other huge houses, it was obscene, populated with people who wanted the view, but not the smells of animals or the dust of tractors or the noise of harvesters. It infuriated her as the monoculture of grass did little to help the dirt and nothing to feed people or animals.

At her farm, she eased the truck into the turn, the trailer groaning as the axles protested the movement. There was no telling how long it had sat in the pasture, and honestly, she was surprised the tires held up.

Jasmine rolled up in the side-by-side UTV. "What's in the trailer?"

"Funny story," Gloria said. "Mr. Jackson's mare didn't have any milk."

"Well, she's older than I am."

"Shouldn't matter. Anyway, the little thing was pitiful when I got there."

Jasmine leaned toward the side of the trailer and peered into the opening. "Cute, nice markings. How often do we have to feed it?"

Gloria got out of the truck. "Just like the kids. Every two hours for the first several days. The goat milk is better than cows for horses."

"Is his momma okay?"

"It's a filly. And momma needs more than I have on hand. Mr. Jackson put a call into the on-call vet network. Might take hours to hear back."

Jasmine put her hands on her hips. "I'll go get the colostrum out of the freezer. Can we put her with the goats?"

"I don't see why not. She's not sick as far as I can tell." Gloria sighed. "I know we have plenty to do. I just couldn't leave him in a lurch. And he said we can hold on to the trailer until she's ready to go home."

"Never look a gift horse in the mouth?"

"Yeah, something like that." Gloria rubbed her forehead, the sweat rolling toward her eyes. She rummaged in the cabinet and found a tarp. "Hey, Jazz, come help me lift this baby."

Jasmine's voice sounded close. "I'm right here, give me a second."

The trailer door swung open. Gloria looked up. "If we each hold a corner down with a foot, maybe we can slide her over and carry her out."

"Maybe." Jasmine put a shoe on the tarp. With a grunt, she lifted. "Why do I always get the butt?"

The foal swung her head, and Gloria narrowly missed a hit. "Because I always get the black eye."

With a practiced grace, they carried the horse into the barn. The goats stood on the railings seemingly to get a better view. At the last stall, they urged the baby up.

Jasmine put her hands on her hips. "Maybe she's too dehydrated to stand. The milk should be defrosted by now."

Gloria watched the baby. "I think you're right. Hurry."

The bottle still dripped water from the warming bucket. Gloria bent down and urged the nipple into the baby's mouth. After a few false starts, the baby figured out the process and leaned into the bottle. Near the end of the milk, the filly abruptly pulled her mouth off.

"I think she's done." Jasmine tapped her phone. "I hope she can use a bucket soon."

"My back is too old for this," Gloria agreed.

"I don't know why you take on these projects."

"That's rhetorical, I assume."

"Of course."

"You know, if you went back to school, you wouldn't have to feed ungrateful babies."

Jasmine pointed. "Look, she's going to get up."

They never tired of the magic of a new baby walking only hours after it had been born. The filly was determined to stand. Her legs quivered, and she nearly fell several times, but soon she was wobbling across the stall.

"Come on, little one," Gloria said.

The baby took a few quick steps toward them.

Jasmine grinned. "Look at her go."

"She needs to find her way. Just like you." Gloria brushed back her hair. "Have you sent the letter to the college?"

Jasmine pressed her eyes closed for a moment. "Momma, this is where I belong. I don't see why you keep pushing me to leave."

"Because you will be alone here. You need to find those forever friends. Maybe a partner."

"Momma, honestly. That's not important to me now. You are."

"I won't be here forever, and then what will you do?"

"Start a commune."

The women giggled together, the joyful noise echoing through the barn.

Gloria took off her gloves. "Just go for a semester at least. I'll show you I can manage myself, and you can show me how smart you are by getting on the honor roll."

"The honor roll? Mom. Honestly." Jasmine took out her phone and began furiously moving her thumbs over the screen. She stopped and held it toward Gloria. "See? Friends."

"Yeah, yeah, Instachat. Not real friends."

"Wrong. Real friends, just not ones I can touch. And it's Snapchat."

Gloria looked into Jasmine's eyes. "Touch is nice, too. Maybe you'll meet a special someone."

"Ah, stop, I know. I know." With that, Jasmine turned and marched toward the door. Over her shoulder, she yelled, "Love you."

Gloria answered, "Love you more." In the quiet, she leaned against the wall. She wasn't quite sixty yet, and her life spiraled to extinction. They had built their dream farm, the soil was producing again, and every day brought a new challenge. Together, they seemed unstoppable. Alone, she wasn't up for any more trials.

Chapter Four

At the funeral home, Anna May pulled the car under the awning near the front door, and an employee rushed to help her mother out of the car. Her navy dress matched her shoes and small hat; she insisted on hose, even though it was hot as Hades.

Her mother stopped. "I forgot to change earbobs."

"No one will notice." Anna May gritted her teeth. "I can take you back if you want."

The tiny woman folded her hands. "Please."

Anna May waved to the man. "Be right back."

At the house, she helped her mother out of the car and up the steps. She paced the floor, a fine layer of sweat coating her face. The grandfather clock gonged at the half hour.

Her mother appeared at the doorway. "You ready?"

Anna May bit her tongue and simply said, "Yes."

Retracing their route, Anna May blasted the air conditioning. At the funeral home, she dropped her mother off and went to park the car. Only a few spots remained open. Before she got out of the car, she popped in a mint and stuffed a few tissues into her pocket.

The Wilkins family mortuary was now in the third generation. The white building was large and majestic, the columns in front reaching the second story. Inside the lobby, two men in black suits greeted visitors with a solemn smile and a gesture toward the back rooms. Anna May thought they looked like Secret Service, and when a third man appeared in the same uniform, she realized it felt more like the movie Men in Black.

At the lectern outside the room marked WALKER, Anna May paused. Two rooms had been opened, and both were packed with people. Pretty good showing for a nonagenarian. Florists were still bringing in arrangements, Bubba supervising the chaos. Her mother was surrounded by a group of distant relations, cousins she couldn't remember by name but by sight. Her kin. Her blood. Unnoticed by her family, she made her way to the coffin.

Approaching the steel blue box, she stared into the face of a man she could picture wearing a set of coveralls, instead of the pressed dark suit, nudging dirt in a garden with a hoe. His tanned, gnarled fingers were folded together, the left over right covering a missing fingertip on the middle finger from a long-ago mishap. His thick white hair gave his age away under the glasses his blue eyes wouldn't need any longer. She held back the sob in her throat but let the tears flow with no effort to stop them. The tissue in her hand disintegrated as she wiped her cheeks.

Bubba said, "He looks good. It was like herding cats to get Momma through it all, but we did it."

She knew the short statement was also about what he didn't say, which was that he didn't get his way and that he alone had to help Momma with the details. Truth be told, Anna May couldn't care less, as long as it was how Momma wanted things. "He does look good."

That was as much of a thank you as she could muster.

"I tried to get her to just do a service at the cemetery, but she wouldn't hear of it."

"I suppose she wouldn't." Anna May picked up a paper fan printed with the Last Supper and a small card with the likeness of her father on one side and the Lord's Prayer on the other. She slipped the card into her pocket and opened the fan. Waving it in front of her face, she decided some traditions were worth keeping.

Her sister-in-law, Stacy, approached and slid in close. With one hand, she took Bubba's hand and the other she put on his chest, claiming him as her property. Anna May sighed. It wasn't like someone was looking for a phone number at a funeral home. Maybe they would. Almost nothing would surprise her.

Bubba said, "We tried to talk Momma into a memorial with a cremation."

"I have no idea why you would. I bet Momma said cremation is tempting the devil, didn't she?"

Stacy whispered, "Yes. You're already halfway to H-E-double hockey sticks if you're cremated."

Bubba rolled his eyes. "You wouldn't believe how expensive this all is. There won't be any money left at all by the time it's finished."

Anna May took the opportunity. "Maybe Momma can move in with me."

"And leave Chicora Point? This is her home. It's a struggle, but we can take care of her. We always have." He lowered his voice. "Of course, you could move home and do your share."

Anna May bit at the side of her cheek. Better to keep the peace, for Momma. She nodded and looked for her, speaking of the woman. Glancing around the room, she spotted her mother, still ringed by a swarm.

She slipped toward the back and took a chair near a window, the last bit of sun blocked by a canopy. Flowers of every color blended into a garden at the front of the room. A line of people waiting to pay their respects wound around the lobby. Would she be expected to join a line to greet them all? Maybe if she stayed quiet, she could avoid the worst of it. She hadn't seen these people in decades, and they were not there to see her.

Momma touched her shoulder. "Come on, they're getting the line up."

Anna May took a position after Bubba and Stacy, before her mother. It was a good spot because her brother would greet everyone by name, so she didn't have to admit she forgot most of them. It was a bad spot because as each person spoke to her mother, they all would move on with a word or two about how Anna May needed to be there for Daisy now that Ellison was gone. She would nod and smile, but it would be a cold day in hell before she moved back to Chicora Point. Momma needed to move near her.

She wasn't quite sure what started the ruckus, but a loud thump echoed through the room, knocking everyone silent. Her daddy's niece Julia Elizabeth was nose to nose with her momma's niece Ella May.

"You know that teacup belonging to my great-grandma Walker. Uncle Ellison said I could have it someday." Julia nudged Ella May.

"That's rich. Aunt Daisy ain't even dead, and you're taking the cup that was her mother's."

Uncle Dink raised a hand. "Let us pray for the soul of Ellison with a peaceful heart."

Both women dropped their heads as he mumbled his words. Anna May shook her head. I should have brought popcorn.

It was then her brother's ex-wife, Lisa, paraded in, wearing motorcycle leather, clutching the arm of a very tall, muscular man.

Bubba stiffened as Lisa approached. "Thank you for coming out."

"Of course, I loved your daddy. Trey, you remember Franklin?"

The huge man clutched Bubba's hand, then pulled him into a hug. "I'm so sorry for your loss, man."

Ella May's daughter Paula's voice echoed to the front of the room. "What kind of douche wears leathers to a freaking funeral home?"

Anna May watched in slow motion as Lisa pushed forward through the crowd. She couldn't hear what was said, but it was obvious Paula wasn't too happy with the words. When Paula swung, Lisa ducked and grabbed her in a headlock.

Bubba raced across the room. "Son of a sea biscuit, we're at a funeral. Y'all got no sense at all. Stop that. Right now."

Lisa twisted, and Paula stooped over, clearing out a row of folding chairs as she flailed her legs. She tugged at Lisa's arm. "You hussy. Let me go. I'm gonna kick your ass."

Lisa leaned, and they both fell backward. "The hell you are."

Bubba tried to catch them and ended up on the bottom of the pile. Paula swung and cracked him in the head.

Anna May snapped into action and grabbed a box of Kleenex to stem the flow of blood down his face. "You always had a glass nose."

Lisa was crawling away.

Paula said, "You should have stayed away, Bubba.

She ain't your wife, ain't your life."

Lisa rose and adjusted her leather vest. "I just tried to give my respects, and y'all can't even respect the dead."

Anna May retreated as the preacher stepped between the ladies. "Emotions are high. Let's all just go on home now, ladies. Come on now, I'm asking nice. Come on."

Lisa's hair straggled out of her hair tie. She brushed it back. "I'm sorry some people can't behave."

"Bitch, you can't be talking about me." Paula's face glowed red with anger and exertion. "We can finish this in the parking lot."

The flash from blue lights pulsed through the front windows. Bubba sat on a chair with his head hanging down with a wad of paper at his nose. In a muffled voice, he said, "Sheriff's here. Y'all act right."

The man was covered in tactical gear like he was entering a war zone. "Hey y'all, I'm sure sorry for your loss. You okay, Bubba?"

Bubba said, "I guess people were carried away with grief. Sorry to have been a bother."

"No bother, your father meant a lot to me. He was a good man. Where's your momma?"

As the sheriff shuffled toward the casket, Anna May hissed, "You tell those women to get the hell out of here."

Bubba handed the gob of papers to Stacy, who was hovering. "Fine. Come on, y'all clear out."

The women marched out, separated by the funeral home staff. The shouting started again in the parking lot.

The sheriff dashed past them. "Excuse me for rushing out. My condolences, Anna May." He pushed out the door. "Hey now, I'm arresting the first one I get to, go on now. I'm not kidding."

Lisa drove off, her arm extended out the window with her middle finger up.

Anna May said, "Your ex is a classy woman, Bubba."

"Shut up, Anna May Elizabeth."

She pointed toward the front of the room. Their mother leaned on the coffin, her shoulders shaking as she sobbed. "You better get Momma before she crawls in there."

"Jeesh, or knocks the whole thing down." Bubba rushed to her side and gently nudged the tiny woman into a chair.

At that moment, Anna May suddenly felt like this was an alien world. She knew all the characters and even the setting, but the plot line was unfamiliar. She may have been from this town, but she sure didn't belong here anymore. She accepted a bottle of water from the staff. She would leave the very minute Momma was settled. Kinfolk or not, these people were all insane.

෴෴෴෴

Anna May settled into the motel room, the slightly moldy smell turning her stomach. She cranked the A/C to high, and after a high-pitch whine, the unit created a constant squeak as some belt protested working in this heat. A blast of cool air streamed out, dueling with the stagnant air. Sweat droplets rolled down her back, tickling until they soaked the waistband of her pants. With a sigh, she turned her cellphone back on and found a message from her boss. Before she even listened to the words, she tapped the screen to return the call.

"Hey, Sho."

Shoshanna answered, "Anna May, I'm so glad you called. How you doing?"

"Well, not much has changed. A fight broke out at the funeral home. The sheriff had to come and everything."

There was a long silence. "Are you kidding? I hope you're kidding."

"I wish I was. Redneck as hell." She sighed. "My brother's ex-wife showed up in motorcycle leathers, and my cousin from Momma's side thought it was in poor taste. They started going at it. And knocked a bunch of chairs over."

"You aren't kidding. Was everyone okay?"

"Bubba got clocked in the nose."

"I'm so sorry. Do you expect trouble at the church?"

"Our little church doesn't hold that many people. Not like Six Flags over Jesus. We'll be crammed in too tight to get a good swing," Anna May stated matter-of-factly.

"Wait. What is a Six Flag Jesus?" Sho asked.

"Six Flags over Jesus? It's what I call those mega-churches. Six Flags, like the amusement park. Six Flags over Jesus."

There was a hesitation, and Shoshanna asked, "Any idea when you're headed back?"

"It depends on how things go with Momma. I hate her being so far away from me, but I'm not sure I'll be able to get her to move."

"In that case, I thought maybe you could do a piece on the old cotton mills." Shoshanna sounded hopeful.

"What about them?"

"We've all seen the pictures of barefoot kids standing by machines, something about that?"

"So you mean the obvious capitalistic abuse of a targeted population for financial gain?"

"Yeah, sounds about right. I have a call coming in. Be safe."

"Thanks. Bye." Anna May tapped the screen and then rested it under her chin. By the time she and her classmates reached high school, the first consolidations shifted the mill work. Not that she wanted to climb onto that treadmill for life, but the jobs were few and far between. She left for college and never moved back home. First Atlanta, then D.C. The excitement of city life with fascinating people, the concerts, the plays, the museums, all those things were like living in Disney World, albeit a dirty, chaotic variation.

What if there had been plenty of jobs at the mill? Would that have lured her? Her parents and all their siblings, both sets of grandparents, they all worked at Buchanan Mill. Didn't she have an uncle who died in a car crash before she was born? Yes. Did he work at the mill? She would have to ask Momma.

～⁓⁓⁓

Restless and exhausted, Anna May knew she'd never get to sleep without something to relax her. She grabbed her keys and drove around the small downtown until she found herself at a small pub. The Weary Hiker. Inside, a large chalkboard described the latest concoctions and offerings. To her surprise, there was a microbrewery in Chicora Point. She sat at an empty table and cheerfully read through the menu. After selecting the darkest from a row of samples, she took out her reading glasses and began to tap on her phone.

A voice startled her. "As I live and breathe, I can't believe it. Anna May Walker." Damion Carter stood in front of her, his soft brown eyes twinkling against his dark skin. He put a hand on her arm. "I'm so sorry about your daddy. He was a good man."

Anna May put a hand over his and squeezed. "Are you here with friends? I don't want to keep you, but I'd love to catch up."

He pulled out a chair. "There is only one person in this town who sticks out more than me in this place, and that's you." He waved at the server, who brought over a pitcher of light ale and a bowl of chips. "How've you been holding up?"

She said, "To tell you the truth, I'm a little shaky. I've already seen two fights, and we haven't even gotten to the funeral."

He patted her arm. "Don't you worry. I'll protect you from the hot mess that is the population of this town. They try, but they can be trying, too. How are you?"

"I'm good. I mean, Daddy had dementia. On the phone, he hasn't known me for years now, and in person, he thought I was his sister. I only want to get past the funeral and settle Momma near me."

He took a long drink. "You ever think of moving back?"

She laughed until she realized he was serious. "No. I mean, not much has changed, and I can't exactly pull up all my roots." She refilled her glass. I could. In a second. I just won't. "This place is like a time warp."

"It is changing. There are lots of good things happening."

Anna May studied his face, perfect, with just the tiniest lines near his eyes. "Not enough. Just one example, I can walk down the street at home holding a woman's hand and barely get a glance. I wouldn't dare do that here."

Damion said, "Do you have a woman's hand to hold?"

"Not at the moment. How long have you been with David?"

"Oh, we've been together more years than I can count. He's at choir practice. One day a week of church is about all I can take."

"You never think of leaving this place?"

"How can I fix things if I just up and go?" He shrugged. "If not me, who?"

Anna May took a long drink. "I admire you for that. How about another pitcher?"

"Girl, you can still drink me under the table. Why not?"

After polishing off the beer, Anna May leaned toward Damion. "Honest, how do you manage here? I mean, I love the big city. Nobody gives a crap what you do."

He smiled. "That's exactly why I love this town. People take care of each other. Don't mistake that for accepting their old ideas."

"This place is beyond hope."

"Do you really think so?"

She nodded.

He sighed. "I got to try, though. This is the prettiest place in the whole country, and I'm not abandoning it to the white trash." He pushed away a half-full mug. "Girl, I'm glad I can walk home. You driving?"

She fished out her keys. "Yeah. No problem. It's just a few blocks."

He hugged her. "Be careful. See you tomorrow."

The night air had cooled to a comfortable level. The street was abandoned. She unlocked her car and sat in the seat for a moment. "Damn. I'm not even drunk. Maybe I should cut back." At the motel, she bumped against the door to open it and gracelessly flopped on the bed. If she couldn't find a girlfriend in D.C., how would she ever meet someone here? She wouldn't.

When she woke, she realized she was still dressed and on the comforter. Even though it was four a.m., she took a long shower and then crawled back into bed.

Chapter Five

As she parked in the little remaining shade near First Baptist Church, Anna May adjusted the air vent in the dashboard, the car's compressor struggling to push the temperature back down into double digits. Her blouse was plastered to her back, and for a moment, she wondered if a skirt would have been cooler. It didn't matter. She hated the shoes that were expected to be worn with the skirt, so it was out of the question, even for her daddy. Her mother would be disappointed. Nothing unusual about that.

With a lazy glance, she studied the plain structure; the building was a simple rectangle, a cross high at the top of the steeple. There was no bell tower like the Presbyterian church, nor a copper encasement like the other Baptist church. The white clapboard building was freshly painted, appearing exactly as it had when she was a little girl. Across the parking lot, ladies from the Methodist church carried covered dishes into the recreation hall, the green tin roof contrasting against the white metal sheeting on the walls. There would be quite a meal after the service. Banana pudding was guaranteed and a fitting reward for good behavior.

Anna May wondered if she should feel sadder. Did that make her a bad daughter? Even more than the whole lesbian thing? Maybe. The bald truth was she was relieved he was at peace. Heaven gained another angel, or something like that. Assuming there was a heaven. Maybe this was it, and we were just worm food after we died. No, there had to be somewhere...other. She sighed and then closed her eyes. She was already sweating like a sinner in church, and she wasn't even inside yet.

A little tap on the window startled her. Damion said, "Get out of that car and give me some sugar."

She opened the door and straightened, the air like a blow dryer in her face. Reaching around his broad shoulders, she rocked side to side as they hugged, his Paco Rabanne Invictus cologne strong on his shirt, the fabric damp but soft against her fingertips. "You look fabulous."

He waved a hand in front of his face. "It's as hot as a goat's ass in a pepper patch."

"You aren't kidding."

"Kidding, how punny."

"Don't goat me started. You know I'm the queen of puns."

"Girl." Damion smirked.

Anna May glanced around the nearby cars. "Have you seen my momma?"

"She's already up front. Come, I'll shield you from the evil glares of the saved people of Chicora Point."

She chuckled. "And I'll protect you from the throngs of women who covet your scarf."

Arm in arm, they climbed the steps and pushed through the heavy wooden doors. The blast of cool air was a relief, the floral arrangements casting a light fragrance even at this distance from the display at the altar. The pianist played the song I'll Fly Away on the Hammond organ with running scales and added beats, the original tune barely recognizable even to those familiar with the old-time hymns.

Her cousin Heather stood at the doorway; a fitted black dress barely covered her assets with her bottle blond hair swept under a black hat with a tiny matching veil. With a flourish of her wrist, she handed Anna May a pamphlet. "Shame we hold our family reunions at funerals."

"Is it?"

Heather stared at Damion. "I see you haven't improved your choice of companions."

He took the flyer with a pinch. "Always good to see you, Heather. Delightful weather. Hot as the hinges on the gate to hell. But I'm sure you're used to it." His eyes crunched nearly closed as he smiled, dimples popping.

Heather opened her mouth and closed it without speaking.

Most of the pews were packed. Damion whispered, "You go on up front. I'll sit by that tall drink of water in the back row."

Anna May smiled. His partner, David, waved. "Get his number by the altar call," she teased.

"Oh, I accept the challenge." He sashayed along the back wall toward the folding chairs jammed between the pews.

Abandoned to face her kinfolk, she marched toward the ornate casket holding the remains of her father. At the front pew, she turned and reached to hug her mother. After a quick pat, she trailed past Bubba and Stacy to the empty spot at the end of the bench. Her sister-in-law was very near a dramatic swoon, rocking in her seat. It was going to be a good funeral if someone screamed and fainted before the service even started.

From behind her, her maternal aunt whispered,

"I reckon his baby brother will be next. One foot in the grave and the other on a banana peel."

Anna May turned around. "Nancy, honestly."

Her aunt shrugged. "Your daddy looks good, though, real natural."

Bubba whispered, "He does, now hush. Show some respect."

Respect for whom? Momma? The church members? God? Anna May watched as the preacher approached the lectern and opened his notebook. If I had any self-respect, I wouldn't even be here. She was here for Daddy. Even if he wouldn't know. Or maybe he did. His little Katydid. Not because she was little and cute as a bug as a baby, oh, no, it was because she had colic and cried at the top of her lungs all the time. While the preacher rattled on, she wondered if he said the same things at every funeral. Her father was quiet and practical, rarely raised his voice, and could fix anything with a screwdriver and duct tape. If she was to say, her favorite memory was when she came home from elementary school soaking wet. Bubba and his friends used to swing out over the river on a rope tied to a branch. She wasn't supposed to go near it, but she tried and, as predicted, fell in. Her mother lit into her, and her daddy looked up from his paper. "Dear, she's already walked home looking like a drowned rat. Let her be."

She pressed her lips together, and tears welled in her eyes. Her daddy was gone. The music to Rock of Ages began, and the choir sang. Anna May broke down and sobbed.

✿ ✿ ✿ ✿

The preacher adjusted the mic and gripped the lectern with both hands. "A relationship with Jesus shows what God has done for us. He loves us fully, freely, and completely. He loves us without reservation, unconditionally. That love sets us free to share the love of Jesus with others. So many have religion, oh, yes, many have religion, but they do not know Jesus." He wiped his brow. "Jesus is not your momma's pie. You do not need to keep it all to yourself. You can keep sharing that love, and you will get more for yourself, not less."

Anna May bit at her lip. The church of her childhood rendered St. Peter to no more than a bouncer at the gates of heaven. Religion tied them up in rules and bound them. Obedience. Yet they selected which rules to obey. The good people would wave their hands, smiling, feeling the joy, and still not understand how or why they themselves could possibly be a better person. They spouted the phrase, "I'm not perfect, just forgiven."

The preacher thundered, "If you want to see Ellison again, you must get right with God. Without Jesus—"

Her ears heard the message a hundred times, if not more, and she felt the anger growing in her throat. The grace of God meant they didn't need to follow even the commandments. Love thy neighbor. They did not seek any more for themselves. Good enough as-is. Scrutinizing their lives was not required, even if they found it abundantly easy to scrutinize others. Like Anna May. Heat rose in her chest as she became angrier. She was angry at the people in this town for making her feel less than and furious at herself for allowing that to push her away.

Insulating herself from them and their religion was easier than confronting them. Any of them. Her friends. Her family. It was easy to face the hypocrisy, but she couldn't turn the mirror to herself. It was too hard to face her own spiritual void. She would have to admit her shame grew from her mental judgment. And as with all things, she was the most brutal on herself. She had to forgive herself, love herself. She shifted on the hard bench anxious to run. She could try to change if she wanted to, but there was no hope for Chicora Point. As they say, there was not enough Jesus in this town, and it showed. Amen.

Outside, Damion stood waiting at her car. "Hey, you want to ride with me?"

"Thank you, no. I'll be okay."

"You won't mind if I go on?"

"Of course not, I appreciate you just coming out." Her chin started to wobble. The double meaning of the phrase stung.

He reached around her, pulling her close. "Don't be brave, Anna May."

She leaned her head against him, trying to pull herself together. She sniffed. "Thank you."

He released her once she relaxed. "I expect to see you before you leave town."

"I promise." She unlocked her door, needing a moment of solitude to face the rest of the day.

Even though the cemetery was only four blocks away, the caravan outside of the church was carefully arranged. Immediate family. More distant family. Friends of the family. Little orange flags with the funeral home logo on them had been attached to the hoods. Each car they approached pulled to the side of the road, and a few drivers got out and stood holding their hat, even though he wasn't a veteran.

At the Walker family plot, folding chairs were arranged by the open grave. Anna May took the last seat next to Bubba, secretly relieved to not have to lug the coffin in the heat. Momma would never allow a woman to be a pallbearer. She peered down at the concrete vault. What about that? She thought that six feet under referred to the amount of dirt over the body, not the depth of the bottom of the box. She glanced around, suspicious now that she knew how close the deceased were to the surface. Once the casket was arranged on the rollers, the staff completed the interment while her cousin played music on a boom box. She wasn't surprised that her cousin had one, just that it still worked. And that she had a cassette tape.

Anna May took one last look at the casket before it was lowered. "It was a nice service."

Bubba touched her arm. "I guess I'm the man of the family now."

Anna May blinked. Was he being serious? From his expression, she could guess he was, and it was unbelievable. She recovered. "I guess."

☙ ☙ ❧ ❧

The air conditioning of the social hall was cranking its heart out as the crowd gathered for the celebration lunch. The noise from dozens of conversations buzzed. Anna May collapsed into the metal folding chair. The good ladies of Chicora Point did not disappoint, and her plate was mounded with assorted dibs and dabs of the best Southern cuisine. She could smell the heat in the pulled pork from a foot away.

Damion sat across from her. "Ooh, you have to

try the corn pudding. Mrs. Yetty made it."

Mrs. Yetty was the only other black person who worked in Chicora Point proper. She cooked at the King Café, a local meat and three, where one picked a protein and three sides, and with luck, it might include pudding as a choice. They served a familiar, comforting list of entrees: fried chicken, meatloaf, fried catfish, pot roast, hamburger steak with gravy; with sides like mashed potatoes, creamed corn, collard greens, green beans. Simple country food right from the garden, always served with tea. If you had to ask if it was sweet, you weren't from around these parts. The same white people who fifty years prior wouldn't drink from a water fountain used by a black person were happy to eat meals prepared by black hands.

"Give me a bite." She reached her spoon over and scooped a taste.

Bubba sat. "Couldn't get enough on your own plate, you gotta eat his, too?"

Damion shrugged. "A little Anna May spit don't bother me, but for the record, she did use a clean spoon."

The hot red burn slid up Bubba's neck. "And I suppose your spit don't bother her. Disgusting."

Anna May snapped her head. "Is that so?" At a certain time in her life, she would have let such an overt display of racism just waft away. The burden of women raised in the South was to avoid conflict. Not any longer.

Stacy sat next to her, unfazed by her tone. "He's really become a germaphobe."

Anna May considered this for a moment. It was true he could be both a racist and a germaphobe. She looked at Damion, who calmly ate. If it didn't bother him, why did it bother her? Because maybe it did bother him, and he didn't dare show his anger. Not here. Not even now, fifty years after the Civil Rights Act. It was bullshit, but she held her tongue.

Damion swallowed and wiped his mouth. "Must be a real burden in the hospitality industry."

He owned and operated an RV park, so in the loosest terms, that was true. Bubba shifted in his chair. "Yes."

Falling into silence as they ate, Anna May glanced around the room. Across the far side of the hall, there she was, marching toward the far doors. Gloria. The blood drained from her head. It was too much to hope that Gloria would speak to her, but she was too dizzy to stand. *What would I say? Please don't hate me. I'm sorry.* After so long, an apology seemed a pathetic offer compared to the trespass. It was ridiculous to worry after the amount of time that had passed. Gloria looked about the same, a little rounder, but that was not how she recognized her. No, it was the walk. She'd know that stride anywhere. The sway of her hips lured her like a bee to a sweet flower.

"Earth to Anna May. Come in, Anna May Elizabeth." Bubba nudged her.

"Sorry, what did you say?" Anna May asked.

"I said that you need to come see the row of cabins along the river." He picked up a second chicken wing, sweat starting to bead on his forehead. "These have a little heat, y'all."

Stacy gushed. "It's up to five now. People just love them. Each one has a different name, but they ain't that different except I made the curtains different colors."

Anna May looked back, and Gloria was gone.

The crowd in the hall started to diminish, and she spotted her mother. "Hey, you want a ride with me home?"

"Dink will carry me."

Anna May nodded. She didn't have the strength to argue. As she trudged to her car, she barely had the energy to unlock the door. She slid onto the seat and cranked the engine. The blast of air from the vents slowly cooled. Holding a hand to her forehead, she looked up at the cross reflecting the sun. "Goodbye, Daddy." She dabbed at her eyes. After just two days, she was considering her life in a new way. Maybe there wasn't enough Jesus for her, either.

She drove the long way around town, past the high school. A sharp pain started in her chest. The doctor told her it was anxiety and not some heart condition. At her age, she'd worried, but her people lasted a long time. She might live another thirty years. She pulled over. With a slow breath, she did her relaxation meditation, certain a mixed drink would be more effective. Her pulse slowing, she put the car in gear and drove to Momma's house.

The simple mill houses stood in the same place for over a hundred years. They looked as exhausted as she felt. She couldn't get out of here fast enough.

Anna May parked in front of the house in the center of the block and dragged to the front door. "Momma, it's me." She leaned down to kiss the woman shrunken into the recliner. "You need anything?"

"No. I know this sounds wrong, but he's in a better place, and I wish I was with him."

Anna May sat. "I'd rather he was with us."

Her mother didn't respond as she dabbed at her eyes. She wrung her hands around the paper, the blue veins visible through her pale skin.

Anna May pushed on to her main goal of getting her mother to move. "I was thinking, there's a lot for one person here, what with keeping up the house and flower gardens and all. I wonder if it's too much work for you."

"Who do you think has been doing it? The man on the moon?"

"Right, I just wondered if you might want a new place."

"Could you just let me be? I just buried my husband. I don't want to leave our home. Unlike you, I hate change, always have. Why are you so keen to have me move? I'm staying right here."

Anna May went to speak but stopped herself. There was no point today. "Let me get you a drink." That's just what I need, a real drink. She got the tea.

Chapter Six

The next day, Gloria waved as she pulled up to the fruit stand. Jasmine was chatting with an older couple with two children. No doubt they were here for a tour of the farm. "Good day. Ready for a ride?"

The family clamored into the plastic seats of the side-by-side. The man smiled. "I'm Joe, this is Lucy. The kids are visiting us from Columbia, and we thought they'd enjoy seeing where food comes from, besides the Piggly Wiggly."

Both already had a game console in their hands, staring at the small screens, their thumbs flying across the buttons.

Gloria nodded. "Great. Welcome to our farm." Driving to the back tree line, she pointed to the fruit trees and stopped by the grapevines. There was one surefire way to get the kids engaged. "Let's get some grapes."

The kids looked up when the cart stopped.

Gloria led the group to the closest row. "This won't be picked for another few weeks, but the darkest ones are ready. If you pull like this, they pop right off."

The kids yanked, fruit falling. She demonstrated again, popping a grape in her mouth. That was all the encouragement they needed, and before long, both had purple grins.

Gloria offered them wet wipes. "Shall we go see the animals?"

The kids ran back to the seats.

Joe said, "Thank you for that. I haven't seen them smile in two days. I'm afraid we can't compete with the games."

Lucy nodded. "All they want to eat is crap from fast food places. I don't know how their parents afford eating out all the time."

Gloria drove past the gardens, explaining the various vegetables and the story of how Native Americans planted the three sisters—corn, beans, and squash—because they thrived, just like sisters, clinging together.

At the chicken coop, she parked. "If you move slowly, you might get some fresh eggs." Holding cardboard cartons from the back storage bin, she led them to the nesting boxes. "Gertie, be sweet." Gloria eased her hand into the hay. Gertie clucked as she popped off the nest, and Gloria handed a warm egg to each child.

"Look, Grandpa! It's a whole bunch of them."

Gloria grinned. She loved sharing farm life. "Carefully fill up the carton, and I'll watch for Gertie."

Lucy held an egg toward the sun. "I don't see a rooster."

"No, we get new layer chicks each spring, and these girls will be retired to a back pasture to keep the bugs down."

"Let's go see the goats." Driving past the hives, Gloria pointed. "See the bees hanging out the front of the hive? They call it bearding. They're hot and waving air toward the inside of the hive."

"They won't chase us?"

Gloria said, "Oh, no, there's plenty of space between us and them."

At the goat pen, she took some paper cups from a cupboard and gave each child some cracked corn. The kids squealed as the goats pushed toward them to reach the snack.

Gloria warned, "Hold your hand flat so they don't think your fingers are french fries."

Each child nodded solemnly and clamped their fingers together. Lucy snapped some pictures.

Returning to the front lot, Joe put cash into the tip box nailed by the stand door. "I thank you kindly for the gracious tour. Brings back my days of home-grown tomatoes."

Gloria handed each child a tie-dye T-shirt with "There is no planet B" printed on it. "My pleasure. Thank you for visiting with us."

～～～～

After another morning unloading crates at the food bank, Gloria hugged the volunteers goodbye. There was a task for anyone willing to pitch in. Some loaded paper bags, and others would deliver packages that afternoon. For decades, the members of the Piney Grove AME Church worked to feed the hungry. If someone asked for food, it was cheerfully given. No explanation was necessary. Black, white, purple, it didn't matter.

Some people didn't appreciate the effort.

In the parking lot, Gloria froze with her hands on her hips. Every car had the same yellow flyer shoved under the windshield wiper. She read the three K's from ten feet away. Bastards. With a sigh, she yanked out the paper and then wandered around the lot repeating the process. She didn't see who had put the papers out but had her suspicions. Cursing under her breath, she unlocked her truck and stuffed the papers into the pockets of her door panels. She would destroy them somewhere besides the church it was meant to intimidate.

She slid into the seat and took a deep breath. Waiting for the glow plugs to heat, she flicked through the local radio channels, settling on a classic rock channel. Finally, she started the engine and rolled out toward the street, her blood still boiling about the flyers. Then she saw the sports car. A pretentious foreign model, the paint perfect and shiny. It had to be Anna May.

To her surprise, the car whipped through a U-turn and parked next to her truck. The car was beautiful, even if it lacked the chrome of American tastes.

Anna May rolled down the window. "Hey, look what the cat dragged in."

Gloria took off her sunglasses. After all these years, that was her greeting? Anna May wore a checked blouse over a tank top and khaki shorts. Her hair curled over her ears, not a gray strand in sight. Gloria ignored the fluttering butterflies in her stomach. There were so many comments that could be made, but she went with the usual expected response. "I'm so sorry for your loss. Ellison was a good man."

Anna May fidgeted. "Thank you."

"I'm sorry I didn't get to speak to you after the funeral. A neighbor had a horse in labor."

"I hear that excuse all the time. How're you doing?"

Gloria realized the music was blasting and turned down the radio. "Sorry, I still like to listen to loud rock. I'm surprised I'm not deaf by now."

"What?" Anna May cupped her ear with a hand.

"I said…" She paused. "Funny. I see you still have a sense of humor."

Anna May looked down and dropped her hands into her lap and picked at a fingernail. "It's been a long time."

Gloria couldn't quite place the look on Anna May's face, crow's feet distinctive by her blue eyes, dark circles underneath. After a few awkward moments, she said, "Maybe we can catch up while you're in town."

Anna May's face tightened. "Maybe."

Not surprised by the rejection of the offer but still disappointed, Gloria cut the conversation short. "Please remember me to Daisy. I guess I'll see you around."

Anna May said, "I guess so. Bye."

Gloria nodded. She rolled up her window and put the truck in gear. The sports car zoomed away as Anna May left the parking lot. Gloria resisted the urge to drive after her and demand they have some sort of conversation, if not about the past, at least the present. It would be a waste of time. There was no future.

The blasting horns from across the street called attention to the parade of trucks flying Confederate flags. Instantly, she forgot all about Anna May. Gloria flipped them the bird, which Jimmy Buchanan returned. She seethed all the way home, thoughts of Anna May buried as she plotted various ways to get revenge. As she drove around the barn, her gaze settled on the beehives. She immediately thought of a perfect plan. A hive wouldn't miss a few hundred bees, and if she played her cards right, she could trap them and bring them home herself.

Chapter Seven

The next morning, several empty beer bottles stood on the table, and Anna May was disoriented at first. Chicora Point. Funeral. Shit, I have to get to Momma's. What time is it? She stumbled to the shower and felt her energy rise as the water washed away the sleep.

She had driven a few blocks when she spotted Gloria's truck. Like it was on autopilot, her car swung into the parking lot. When she finally had the chance to ask her for coffee or something, she blew it. They talked about nothing, and worse, when Gloria offered to get together, she panicked and wavered.

Anna May took a long breath and blew it out slowly. She'd cross that bridge another day; it was a small town, and she was bound to run into Gloria again. She needed to focus on getting some work done. She hadn't even made so much as an outline. No topic gripped her. Yet.

A visit with Momma would spur some ideas for a story on the mills. Of course, there were factories worldwide, as well as mistreated, underpaid workers. That wasn't special. No, this story was more about the South. As if that was just one topic. So far, it felt like someone talking about your sibling. You could call them names, but if someone else did, you'd clean their clock. Maybe the focus should be on Mill Hill. Who moved there? Why did they stay?

When Anna May pulled into the driveway at her

mother's house, the morning sun already baked the air. She got out of the car and struggled with her computer bag.

Mrs. Wilson's voice came through the bushes. "Hey, glad to see you."

Anna May froze. Just her luck, the woman was weeding the flowers at the side of her house. There was the potential to just get past with a few niceties, but the odds were not good. "Hey, Mrs. Wilson."

"When are you moving in with your momma?"

Anna May pretended that she hadn't heard the question. "How's everybody doing?"

She cleared her throat. "Jeremy started grad school, and Alicia is fixing to have the second baby at the holidays. I assume you're still, uh, single."

"Yes, still a lesbian. I am single. Know anyone looking?"

Mrs. Wilson straightened. Her eyes narrowed. "I'm sure I don't."

Anna May shifted the computer bag. "It's been nice catching up. I should go."

"If you'd have been my child, I'd have beat that smart mouth right out of your head."

"I'm glad you find us all so entertaining. I'd suggest you mind your own beeswax."

Mrs. Wilson turned red, and she pointed her trowel at Anna May. "Well, somebody should keep an eye on your momma. God knows Bubba tries, but a daughter knows what needs to be done."

Anna May seethed. She put on her best manners. "You have a nice day, Mrs. Wilson." Carrying the computer bag on her shoulder, she held the strap in place and strolled to the porch.

"I'll pray for you."

She stopped on the steps. "Bless your heart. You do that, ma'am."

Her momma snapped open the door. "Do you have to pick a fight with the neighbors every time you visit?"

Anna May shadowed her mother back into the living room. She set her computer bag on the floor. After she looked at the outlets, she realized none of them had a grounded plug. "How do you even plug in a vacuum cleaner in this place?"

"Not that you really care, but Bubba broke off the extra part. Works just fine."

Anna May nudged the bag over, hoping her computer battery wouldn't need a charge, and plopped onto the couch. It was a miracle they hadn't electrocuted themselves years ago. "I'm glad. You want to go get breakfast?"

"I ate hours ago, but we got enough food for an army in the icebox. I'll get you something."

"I got it. You have a seat. You want a drink?"

"Yes, please. The paper is on the table if you want to see it. I doubt you'd recognize any of the names."

Zing. The first verbal arrow of the day was launched. Anna May didn't take the bait, but she did take the paper. She tucked it under her arm and carried a plate of cold pasta to the living room. They sat in silence, which was probably for the best. Scanning the paper, she searched for any interesting tidbits. There was a zoning meeting coming up soon for the old lot by the Methodist church, and it seemed unlikely to pass as the congregants were opposed. The football coach was predicting a rebuilding year for the team. In decades, nothing had changed.

A door slammed outside. She peered out the

window and saw Bubba slide out of his ice white truck. This morning couldn't get any better.

Bubba hollered as he stomped across the porch, "Momma, I brought you biscuits."

Anna May folded the newspaper, all eight pages of it. "Ain't nobody's biscuits better than hers."

"She shouldn't have to cook at a time like this."

Anna May squinted. What does he want? It's always something.

Momma hugged him like she hadn't seen him in years. Anna May frowned. The favorite child, right from birth. There was something unexplored there, but instead of opening that box of memories, she wrapped it with more psychological duct tape and shoved it to the back of her mental shelf.

He asked, "Momma, where's Daddy's ring?"

Her mother's gaze shifted to Anna May. That don't-you-dare-say-anything glare. Anna May pressed her lips together and reopened the newspaper. This was going to be good.

"What ring? He never wore a ring. Good way to get your hand caught in a machine."

"Papaw's ring. With the red stone."

She repeated, "With the red stone?"

Anna May watched her mother, who absently twisted a gold charm on her necklace.

Momma said, "You mean his old Dragon ring? I haven't seen that in years."

Momma never lied. It had been years since her father had it melted down into the block bauble all the women were wearing twenty years ago. The one she was twirling. "You go look if you want."

Bubba ambled toward the bedroom, and the rattle of drawers opening and closing echoed toward the front room. Finally, he reappeared. "I can't find it. Momma, you keep an eye out."

Anna May said, "I don't see why you want that thing. Just a hateful—"

"Don't start it. It was grandfather's, and I want it."

Momma said, "If I see it, it's yours, honey. Would you like his watch? He got it when he retired."

"That old pocket watch?" His face reddened. "Yeah, I guess I would. Thank you." His phone made a dinosaur roar. "That's Stacy. I gotta get back to work."

After he'd pulled away from the house, Momma said, "If you ever tell him, I'll beat you into next week and smack you again on Tuesday."

Anna May laughed as the old expression tickled her ear. "I won't, Momma. Not ever." She made a cross sign over her heart.

"I'm just glad he didn't ask for his old robe. It's still hanging in the back of the closet. I'm burning it with the trash."

"Papaw was skinny as a stick, it would never fit Bubba."

Her mother's face twisted. "It was your father's."

"What? Why did he still have it?"

"Oh, he didn't use it in years. I just hate it hanging there. Besides, Bubba probably has his own by now."

"Momma, please tell me that he's not in the Klan."

"How would I know such a thing?" Momma's face began to change from coral to scarlet.

"Momma."

"Don't ask me again."

"Fine. Is it more like a Moose Lodge now, where they drink beer and listen to bluegrass music, or do they still terrorize black people?"

Her mother opened her mouth and shut it again.

"Never mind." Anna May pressed her eyes closed. Move here to take care of her mother. Ridiculous. She couldn't possibly live in this town again. "I wanted to ask you some questions about Mill Hill for a story I'm working on, but I'm getting a headache."

She heard the footsteps to the kitchen. "I got aspirin. I don't know anything you don't already know."

"Why did you move here? Why did you stay?"

"I was a child. I went with my parents. Then I met your dad. We worked in the mill, just like our parents. Not very interesting, if you ask me."

Anna May accepted the pills. "I'll think of some questions, maybe we can talk later."

"Sure. I got no secrets." She winked at Anna May.

ॐॐॐॐ

Inside the safety of her sports car, Anna May breathed in the scent of leather and rocked her head back and forth to the music blaring from the high-end speakers. A drive around twisting two-lane roads satisfied her in a way shooting down a six-lane highway could not. She glanced at the gas gauge and noticed the countdown on the remaining miles was only eighty. In D.C., that would last her a week. Here, wherever exactly here was, it might not get her back to Momma's again.

She pulled up next to a station with two pumps. Small towns. She pressed the gas cap door, and it popped open. The premium gas was probably stale, but she knew her baby would protest lower octane. The card reader beeped when she ran her card through. See manager ran across the screen.

"Oh, for fuck's sake." She took her wallet from the passenger seat and marched inside.

One side of the store had the typical refrigerated beverage selection. There were several aisles of snacks. The other side looked like a Confederate museum with assorted Southern pride designs on bumper stickers and a disgusting but impressive assortment of T-shirts and caps.

Anna May turned her attention to the clerk's station. An uninterested teenager sat on a stool jabbing at a cellphone. "Excuse me, the pump didn't read my card."

He looked at the car outside and then back at her. "Dope ride. You from out of town? Mr. Buchanan makes us run those cards inside."

She extended her arm, and he accepted the plastic. "I want to fill it up. I'll be back to sign."

"You don't gotta sign. You use your PIN code. We got the new machines last month."

Anna May smirked. "Welcome to the twenty-first century."

Unfazed, the clerk snapped his gum and went back to his phone.

When she returned to her car, the numbers were set to zeros so she could start the pump. It had to be Jimmy's place. She seemed to recall his sister married a lawyer in Atlanta. James Dale Buchanan was a descendant of the original mill owners. In high school, he led Gloria's tormentors. Her face warmed as the shame roiled her stomach. The pump clicked off, and she went in to retrieve her charge card. She wanted a Coke but was loath to give him one more penny of her money.

The clerk didn't acknowledge she'd come in.

Anna May cleared her throat.

He slid her the card. "Okay, boomer."

"Bless your heart." Anna May stomped out. She wasn't sure what pissed her off more. That he said it or that it was true she was a baby boomer.

Chapter Eight

That night, Gloria sat with Jasmine on the front porch. Each had a large bowl in her lap and, between them, a bushel of green beans. Jasmine tossed a stem toward the small box for compost.

In her mind, Gloria kept replaying the chat with Anna May. Gloria thought they might at least get a drink, but Anna May only said maybe. She still twirled her hair when she was nervous, and Gloria could only speculate why.

Gloria said, "I saw someone today I haven't seen for a very long time."

Jasmine rocked forward in her chair and picked up another big handful. "Oh?"

"It seems silly to mention it, I mean, we barely spoke." Gloria paused. "We went together in high school."

"Went together?"

"Dated."

"Wait. Hold up. I mean, I assumed you dated other people besides Momma C, but I don't remember you talking about a girlfriend from high school."

"It seems so long ago, honestly. I'm sure she barely remembers."

Jasmine cocked an eyebrow. "Two things. One, you always remember your first sweetheart, and two, she? Tell me."

Gloria shrugged. "Well, we had known each other since kindergarten. She was my first girlfriend. It was all pretty innocent. I mean, it was until it wasn't." She hesitated. "We were together most of our senior year. The other kids found out, and she wasn't cut from that kind of cloth to stand up for herself. So that was that. And then in college, I met your mom."

"You've only dated two women?"

"I didn't say that, I'm just saying that there were two women I loved." Gloria dumped pieces into her pan and picked up another handful.

Jasmine asked, "So are you fixing to see her?"

"I did see her."

"Stop it, you know what I mean. Are you going to go out with her?"

"First, I don't think she wants to see me. I've been here thirty years, not exactly hard to find the town lesbian. Especially the town lesbian with a black partner." Gloria did some math in her head. My God, it's been forty years. She exhaled.

"Is she single?"

"I don't know, even if she is, she doesn't live anywhere near here. Seems pointless."

Jasmine shrugged. "Do you want to talk to her?"

"I thought I did, but now I don't know." Gloria rose. "Let's get these put up."

"Do you have her picture?"

"Of course not," Gloria lied.

※ ※ ※ ※

Anna May no longer noticed the roar of the A/C unit as she hunched over her computer in the hotel room. The beep startled her, and she answered her phone.

Shoshanna said, "I had an idea for a story for you

as long as you're still in South Carolina. There's a farm that's doing permaculture to reclaim the dirt worn out from overuse growing cotton. She's not too far from you."

"She?"

"Yeah, cool, right? Her name is Gloria Robinson. I'll email you the info."

Gloria. How many Glorias could there be around here? It wasn't an uncommon Southern name, but it wasn't exactly common, either. Robinson. Nope. That wasn't her. She wouldn't have married, a man anyway. Or maybe she did.

"You still there?"

"Yeah, sorry, I was just thinking," Anna May drawled.

"Well, if you stay there much longer, I may not understand you at all. You're already talking biscuit gravy."

Anna May snickered. "You ain't right for that."

"See what I mean? How's the Wi-Fi?"

"Slow, but I can set up a hot spot."

Sho said, "Good, I want you to send a few pics with the stories. I got another call coming in I have to take."

"Sure, bye."

Anna May touched the glass to end the call and stared at the image. If she hated her Southern roots so much, why was a picture of a sunset over Lake Hartwell her screensaver? She refocused on the new story and Googled the farm Sho mentioned. The webpage was slick and full of bright colors. No doubt a hired professional. She scrolled through several pictures of goats and then clicked on the email button. After pecking out a short message, she searched for information about Buchanan Mill. There was a story there, she could sense it. Just not online. With a sigh, she flipped the laptop shut. It was time to go ask Momma some questions.

Chapter Nine

Anna May knocked as she went into the house. "Momma? Do you have a minute?" She went into the kitchen, hugged her mother, and sat at the table.

"Sure, what do you need?"

"I've been working on an assignment, well, an idea, for a story. About the mills. And it got me wondering. What happened to Uncle Tillus?"

"Honey, that was so long ago. He died before you were born."

"I know that part. I mean before his accident. Did he work at the mill?"

Her mother's features froze. After a long moment, she pressed her lips together and nodded.

"Was he married?"

"Yes, but she left town after he passed. We lost touch."

Her mother folded her hands in her lap and looked away. She was being very vague. She was hiding something. But why?

Anna May said, "Was there something wrong with the car or bad weather?"

"What are you talking about? He died at the mill." Her mother clapped her hand on her mouth.

"That's terrible. What happened?" Anna May waited. Who knew how many ways there were to be killed by moving machinery? It would an interesting angle for a story, even if gory. She just had to wait her mother out. Given enough uncomfortable silence, her mother usually started to share. "Let me get us some tea."

Taking the pitcher from the refrigerator, she was careful not to upset the stacked pans of food. After filling the glasses, she took out saucers and added some slices of cake. This might be a long discussion. Or not, and they could at least enjoy the food. She took out the glasses and returned for the plates. Finally settled in, her mother took a sip and exhaled.

"As you are surely aware, there were attempts over the years to unionize the workers. Your uncle was involved at one point."

"Good for him. Unions fight for fair wages and safe conditions. Did he have an accident?"

"Not exactly. Remember, he was the oldest, and I'm second to youngest. It was a long time ago." She took a bite of cake, seeming to consider her next words. "There was an incident."

Anna May felt her journalistic nerves light up. "Oh?"

"Daddy used to say that if he had just gone along with how things were, it never would have happened." She pulled out a Kleenex and wiped her glasses. "I guess Tillus was willful, even as a boy. Momma always said, 'Tillus is stubborn as a mule.' Anyway, the story is one day at work he handed out flyers, and they had a big rally outside the mill. Then all hell broke loose."

"How come you never told me?"

"It's not exactly the kind of thing you tell a child. Besides, he's gone. The whole story doesn't change that. It's ancient history."

"But it's our history."

"No, it's his. We don't have anything to do with

it."

"But—"

"Stop. How about we go to Yetty's and get some dinner?"

Momma called the King Café by the cook's name, the irony not lost on Anna May. She knew that this was the end of the storytelling. For now. She helped her mother descend the steps, holding her elbow. In truth, she could have just heaved her on a shoulder, and it would have been faster. With a click of the remote, she unlocked the door and then pulled it open so her mother could sit. She waved to the neighbor as she hurried around to the driver's side of the car.

Her mother startled when Anna May pushed the button to start the car. "There's no key?"

"No, well, yes, it's electronic." She held up the boxy fob. "See? It won't start unless this is in the car with us."

Her mother clapped her hands together in delight. "What will they think of next?"

The drive was blessedly short. The building was plain yellow brick, like a warehouse or a manufacturing building of some sort. Inside, long tables ran end to end, the same as a school cafeteria, a few booths filling the space carved out for the restrooms. Nevertheless, it was the hub of local politics, and many state and even national candidates visited this restaurant if they had any chance to win an election. Anna May made a mental note to add that to her blog.

Out of the car and settled into a booth, her mother studied the menu through cloudy eyes. "The pulled pork is always good, but the fried chicken is better."

Anna May could feel her heart clogging as she

ordered. "Chicken, mashed potatoes, green beans, and a side of corn bread."

The server scribbled on her pad. "It comes with tea. You want banana pudding or the chocolate cake?"

"Cake."

Her mother listed the same, except, of course, the banana pudding. "After, would you bring a coffee?"

"Sure." The waitress disappeared.

Momma said, "She's a little rude."

"Momma, she's just busy. She doesn't have time to chitchat with everyone."

"That's the problem right there. People don't take time to really talk to people. Always got their phones to their faces."

"They are talking, well, texting, to people." Anna May thought about her shorthand and the brief messages she sent. No greeting. No closing. The texts just stopped when she was finished with her topic. Maybe Momma had a point.

࿇ ࿇ ࿇ ࿇

After lunch, Anna May dropped Momma off and went to the courthouse, intent on finding more on the story about her uncle's death. At the dark red building, she skipped up the steps, the stones slightly worn from a century of shoe leather rubbed against them. Inside the lobby, she emptied her pockets into the plastic bin and stepped through the metal detector. At the elevator, she studied the signs and pushed the button. The brass trim was so old Otis could have installed it himself. Inside the tiny box, the polished wood gleamed even as the carpet smelled moldy. She listened to the ticks as the box slowly rose.

At the third floor, the bell rang, and she waited as the doors crept open. "Thank God." She pushed the door at 3B and walked up to the clerk's counter. She patiently waited until the man finished typing something and sauntered to the window.

Anna May said, "Hi, I'd like to inquire about the way to get a death certificate."

"Are you related to the deceased?"

"Yes, he was my uncle."

The man squinted at her. "How long ago are we talking about? It's got to be seventy-five years."

"I'm not sure exactly. His name was Tillus Chapman. Can you check for me?"

He shuffled to his computer and started to click the mouse, swinging his hand around. He tipped his head to align his bifocals to read. "I'll just see what we got here." He tapped the keys, then scratched his head. "I can make you a copy. Do you need it certified?"

"Um, I'm not sure."

"Some people get copies for research, like family trees and stuff. Some people need them for insurance, and that kind of thing. Costs extra for the seal."

"Oh, well, then just a regular copy. Like for the genealogy."

He hit a button, and the printer across the room began to whine as it shifted paper between the wheels. "That'll be fifteen dollars. Cash. An extra two percent for a credit or debit card."

She fished a credit card out of her wallet. "That's fine. Thank you very much for your help."

She heard the familiar voice behind her. Jimmy Buchanan, the grandson of the founder of the mill, had regularly harassed her since grade school. There was no mistaking that ugly tone.

Jimmy said, "Well, look what we have here."

Anna May turned. "I thought I smelled you."

"What are you doing here?"

Her Southern manners dictated that she answer his question. "Getting family records on the Chapman side."

"I thought you had no appreciation for tradition and history."

"Not usually. I'm looking up my uncle Tillus, if it's of any concern to you."

Jimmy's eyes narrowed. "It's not. I can save you some time. I know the story. My grandfather built this town, and those that challenge a Buchanan live to rue the day."

"So he challenged a Buchanan?"

"Yes. And it's still true. If you know what I mean."

Anna May tipped her head. "Is that a promise or a threat?"

"Both. You still a dyke? I suppose yes. We don't take kindly to your kind around here."

"That's rich coming from a guy living in a single-wide trailer."

He stepped closer. "You don't know who you're messing with, missy. I suggest you skedaddle back to wherever you come from now."

She could smell the minty chewing tobacco on his breath. The hairs on her arm stood up. "I'm not staying long. Just getting Momma settled."

"Good." With that, he yanked off his sweaty Confederate Sons hat. "I'm sure sorry about your daddy. He was a fine man."

"Thank you." She nodded and went past him. He was the perfect example of the polite Southern boy wrapped in a rebel flag, plus he was batshit crazy. She skipped the elevator and hurried down the stairs, her Mace in her hand. With any luck, she could make it out of town before running into him again.

Her heart still pounding, she tried to walk confidently to her car. She got in, the dark leather scorching her legs. Before the car started to cool, she jammed the clutch in. Jimmy was an ass in high school, parading around the halls like a king. That was a long time ago. Ancient history. She didn't need to be afraid of him, did she? Her gut told her yes.

☙☙☙☙

Back at the motel, Anna May returned to the mystery of her uncle. She flicked on the table lamp and studied the document. It listed the name as Tillus Jackson Chapman, and his parents' names—her grandparents—birth date, and place. On the right side, it listed his death date and location. The cause of death was scribbled. She angled the paper as if it would clear the image. Blunt force trauma to the head. That was all. No explanation. Did he fall? Hit by a car? Punched in the face? This was no help at all. There was no story unless somehow Jimmy was right, and the Buchanans had some role.

Anna May mumbled, "How will I prove that? I won't."

Anna May flipped open her laptop and began to search. The online newspaper sites were subscriptions, which she was willing to pay, but the files only covered the biggest towns or regional newspapers. She would have to visit the library. She wasn't sure newspapers were on microfiche. Sho would want some column inches soon. Tomorrow, she'd go explore the mill for inspiration for her article. In the meantime, she had an idea for another blog.

She opened a new file and began to type. "I continued to the records office, intent on finishing the miserable task and getting out before the preacher caught sight of my truck, or worse, my brother. Clutching the folder, I scampered up the steps. Inside the tiny lobby, I glanced at the sign indicating myriad departments. Before I could move, I heard the voice. It was too late. Only Jesus could save me now."

Her finger hovered over the delete button. Too dramatic? She hit save. The Weary Hiker was only a few blocks over. She grabbed her wallet and headed toward the bar on foot. There were no cabs in Chicora Point, and by the end of the night, she planned to be drunk enough to need one.

Chapter Ten

It had been a long week, and Gloria hadn't checked emails for the business. Smokey the cat curled on the desk next to her computer keyboard, watching intently as her fingers started and stopped as she answered messages. She skipped over several promotional emails, and then one caught her eye. The tagline said, "Hoping to schedule a tour," and the name was awalkerblog. How many A. Walkers could there be? Anna May had been in town since the funeral, although Gloria assumed she'd scoot right out. In all these years, she'd only caught a glance of her passing in her car once in a blue moon. After their brief chat in the parking lot, there had been radio silence. Why would she come to my farm? And why now?

Gloria scrolled down through the formal message asking for a guided tour to write about permaculture. Then Anna May wrote about herself. Ha! She doesn't know it's my farm. Are the stars aligning to bring us together, or is this just an ugly random coincidence?

Gloria flipped through her phone calendar before she hit reply and suggested the day after and early afternoon when things were usually quiet around the farm. She hit enter and sat back. What should I say to Anna May Walker after all these years? Hear any good stories? She cackled. She reread the section about her award-winning articles. Big deal. She was in high cotton but not good enough at research to know this is my farm. She doesn't even know who I am now, but I know her kind. Fancy clothes and an expensive car. Small-town girl makes it in the big city. "You can't outrun your roots, Anna May."

In the professional picture, Anna May's hair was three shades lighter than when she was young. That crooked smile was still sexy as hell after all this time. No ring on her finger. Any of them. Gloria's muscles tightened in her belly, her pulse raced, and the stagnant air in the office forced her to breathe harder.

ॐॐॐॐ

In a moment of nostalgia, Gloria carried a step stool to her back closet. Two steps up, she could reach the top shelf. The shoebox from Montgomery Ward was at the far end, and Gloria had to take another step to reach it. Not quite. Balancing on one foot, she weaved her hand past the other boxes, a pile of sweatshirts, and a knit afghan before she could touch the lid. She squiggled her fingers to inch it forward. With a twist, she pulled it loose and climbed down.

She sat on the bed, her heart starting to pound. Of all her possessions, why did she know right where she stored this box? She hadn't opened it once since high school, but she didn't throw it out, either. The dry tape on the sides fell away as she lifted the top. Held together with a rubber band, an inch-thick bundle of letters was tucked toward one side, a T-shirt rolled against them with dried flower petals scattered over it all. She nudged the shirt and picked up the shot glass decorated with a pastel palm tree and Myrtle Beach printed in black. A small envelope crinkled from the sand inside. A tiny conch shell, not even complete, fell as she unrolled the shirt, a winged shoe in their school colors. It had been Anna May's from track. Gloria loved to watch her run, those legs muscular and leading to a great ass. It was so long ago.

For a moment, Gloria hoped maybe there was still a flicker of interest between them, then the idea vanished. It would never happen. The childhood story about the city mouse and country mouse did not end with the mice together again. Anna May wouldn't even agree to meet for coffee. What would they talk about at the farm? Only business. She shoved the items back into the box.

Gloria shivered as a chill of loneliness overcame her. With Collette in her life, she felt invincible. Now? The tears were unexpected, pooling in her eyes before they dribbled. She reached over to her bedside table and picked up the picture of her and Collette on a whitewater rapids trip in North Carolina. They both wore wet suits, and their hair clung to their faces from the splashes of the ice-cold river. That smile. "Oh, Collette. What the hell am I going to do? I miss you so much. Some days, it feels like I'll never be happy again. We sure had us some fun, didn't we, baby?" She touched the glass. "You aren't going to believe who flit back into town. Yep. Anna May. Part of me still wanted to throttle her, and part of me, well, I don't know how to explain it. It was like I was sixteen again."

She gently set the picture back down. "You know how I hate change. I just want what we had. I know you understand. I'm afraid to try, and I'm afraid not to. Damion is always trying to set me up. Maybe I should let him." She opened the side drawer and took out a shirt, spritzed it with a bit of Collette's perfume, and pulled it close. Drifting to sleep, she could almost hear the river rapids crashing against the rocks morph into waves falling onto the sandy shore.

Chapter Eleven

The next morning, Anna May regretted the last beer at the pub. After a run through Hardee's for black coffee, she took two aspirin and drove across town. The mill structure was the tallest by far, even after a hundred years. She stared at the remnants of the walls in the distance, imagining the magnificence when it was new. She lifted her phone and took a picture. Her mouth was as dry as the cotton they used to spin. Something about the place made her anxious. Even though she went slowly, the car bounced down the neglected road, weeds as high as the windows grew on both sides. Grasshoppers popped on her hood as they leaped from the startled animals racing away from the intrusion. At the foot of the tower, the five-story brick section with huge arched windows remained the most intact. Of course, all the glass was long gone. In each direction, the foundation of the exterior walls still stood, although the entire roof was missing. The charred window spaces confirmed the fire, or fires, that likely consumed any remaining wood in the building. Watching for snakes, she stepped into a gap in the wall and considered the cavernous space, once packed with clanking machines, flying lint, and sweating humans attending to the looms and whatever particulars one did in a mill.

When doing her research online, she found black and white pictures of children in coveralls crawling under and over the moving mechanicals, picking up stray bits of cotton. Young boys stood unsmiling, their arms around the bobbins of thread. Ladies in dresses looked to the camera across spinning threads and shifting levers. Men in long pants and sleeves must have melted tending the machines, or was that image from winter and they froze?

She'd found a doctoral thesis filled with stories of aged retirees. They described how everyone breathed the lint as it filled the air because the windows were kept shut to protect the precious threads. It must have been brutal in the summer. Near her foot, the grasses shifted as some little critter scurried past her feet. Probably a mouse. Or a rat. She sprinted across the floor before the vermin could attack.

Passing through the back wall, she watched the water still flowing down the river that powered the machinery from the last century. Her grandparents talked about how Duke Power put in electricity after World War II. She made a mental note to verify the date. She moved toward the shore. The smooth water-worn stones were arranged such that, if so inclined, she could have stepped her way across the stream and not gotten her shoes wet. She wondered if the workers had meals at the riverside, a bright spot in their day. Maybe they couldn't even hear the splashing over the noise of the mill. She strolled back toward the abandoned loading dock. She needed to find some additional historical papers, maybe at the library. She spotted a broken crate that had a faded BUCHANAN on the side. Perfect. She took a picture. Sho would think it was artistic.

Ambling back to her car, she couldn't fathom what would draw so many families to a life of work in the cotton mills. Just about her entire family had been "lintheads," and she was the odd duck who had no interest in the drudgery, no matter the salary. Which, while low by national standards, in truth, it wasn't bad for the area. Why did people stay, besides just money? That was a curiosity. She would have to ask Momma.

The few photos wouldn't be enough. On her way to the motel, she swung by the town sign. She took a picture, and the church signs caught her eye. She took a few more shots.

Back in her room, she studied the image of the seven church signs. There was more story to be found behind that shot. Why so many in a small town? Why two different Baptist congregations? It was like an electric fence. She knew she shouldn't write about religion, but it was so tempting. So very tempting. Momma would say that when you pointed at someone else, three fingers pointed to you. Anna May wasn't ready to think about her own spirituality, or lack thereof. Any day now, Momma would ask her about Jesus, worried for her soul. It made her madder than a wet hen. Why? The arrogance? The blind faith? Anna May considered herself a small-c christian. Jesus, save me from your followers. That would be a good bumper sticker. Maybe that was where she'd seen it.

This train of thought needed to stop. She had research to do on farming in the South before she went to the hippie place tomorrow afternoon. What did people grow, besides cotton? Maybe that was another article subject. Readers might not have seen the short plant or even a cotton boil for that matter. The fall harvest was before Halloween if memory served. Too bad it was only August. She opened her laptop and tapped in "permaculture."

Chapter Twelve

A nna May drove slowly, her tires crunching on the gravel at the side of the road, watching the GPS logo spin on the phone in her hand. Was there only one cell tower for the entire county? The signal finally came back, and the map popped onto the screen. It showed that she would arrive in one hundred feet. She looked up to see the fences around the pasture and a wildly colorful sign indicating that this was Busy Beavers Farm. What a stupid name. These granola eaters were too much. Still, she had a job to do, so she snapped a picture.

She put a hand to her forehead as she peered, as if it would improve her vision. The farm stand was shuttered. A farmhouse stood in the distance, but a red barn was nearer, and several trucks were parked at the side. She chose to head toward the barn first.

She put on a wide-brimmed hat before she got out. Her chalky skin didn't tan so much as the freckles overlapped after a sunburn. As she slammed her door shut, a huge white dog threatened, and she leaped back inside.

A woman in her twenties approached the car, her skin tanned a tawny brown and her shoulder-length black curls pulled into a bandanna.

"Luna won't hurt you. Unless you're a coyote." The dog pushed against the woman's legs, demanding attention. The dog stood taller than her waist, menacing teeth peeking through the black lips, the huge mouth slobbering as the woman scratched behind her ears.

Anna May opened the door, watching in case the dog should lunge. "Hi. I'm Anna May Walker. I'm here to interview Gloria about the farm."

Hazel eyes peered over sunglasses. "Related to Ellison Walker?"

"Yes."

"Sorry for your loss. He was always kind to my family. I'm Jasmine Robinson." She reached to shake her hand. "Welcome to the farm. Gloria had something come up, but she'll be back in twenty minutes or so. She asked me to show you around. Follow me."

Jasmine, in a well-worn set of green cargo pants and a hot pink tank top, led her to the barn and slid open the large door. Stepping into the cool, dark aisle, Anna May took off her sunglasses, and her eyes adjusted to the dimness. The structure was similar to horse barns in Virginia. She'd been to wine tasting events in the country. Those barns smelled better. This space had a long path through the middle with assorted rooms to the left and fencing to the right separating multiple stalls. A huge fan pulled air through the barn, fluttering her shorts. It felt at least ten degrees cooler inside. She jumped when oodles of multicolored goats raced to the closest rails. The largest pushed through the crowd and lifted above the rest, her hooves stepping on a rail. She emitted a noise not unlike a scream.

Anna May stepped backward until she pressed against a wall.

"They won't hurt you." Jasmine turned to the pen, then reached over and scratched the white goat between her ears. "Cupcake, it's not dinnertime. All y'all go on, I'm giving a tour."

They passed a steel door. Jasmine said, "That's

the cooler-slash-cheese room." She pointed to some wooden contraptions. "That's where we milk the goats."

"So this is a goat farm?" Anna May took out a small notebook and slid the pen out from the metal coil, scribbling questions for later.

"Yes and no." Jasmine slid open the back door. "Come on before they sense the escape route. They shouldn't be able to get out, but goats are little Houdinis."

Anna May hurried through the door and looked around the dirt paddocks. A dusty four-wheeler was parked next to a golf cart on steroids. Jasmine got behind the wheel.

"The side-by-side is the easiest way around. Have a seat. Wear the belt if you want to." Jasmine did not put her seat belt on.

Anna May looked at the dusty holster and risked death instead of staining her pants.

Jasmine turned the key, and the gas-powered machine shot forward.

Anna May reached for the hand grab on the a-pillar to brace herself.

Jasmine began her pitch. "Permaculture is about everything working together. In this area closest to the barn, we consider it zone one. Everything that takes daily attention is clustered around here. The milk goats, baby animals that need care, the food gardens."

Anna May asked, "Is that a little horse in with those goats?"

"Yes, her momma was dry, so we're bottle feeding her."

Anna May assumed that meant the momma didn't have milk. Why? Do they know these things or just deal with them? She searched the other paddocks. With a little dread in her voice, she asked, "Where is her momma?"

"She belongs to the neighbor. We're just helping out with the filly." Jasmine's muscled arms flexed as she turned the wheel toward a large greenhouse. "This is the area where we grow food year-round."

Anna May flipped over the page and jotted down questions about zones. With all this to take care of, why on earth would they take on a neighbor's baby horse? Lunatics.

Jasmine said, "This is our zone two. It includes the pond for irrigation, the chicken tractors, and the beehives. It borders zone three with assorted berry bushes, and the orchard is behind that."

Anna May asked, "Chicken tractor?"

"A movable hutch. Those little boxes with wire walls allow free range with some protection, and there's a laying box so we can find their eggs. There's no floor, so the chickens can eat bugs and scratch around in the dirt. The tractors have tires, and you lift the handles and move them around like a wheelbarrow. Keeps the ladies from eating all the grass, and since they fertilize, too, it makes a nice symbiotic relationship."

As they whizzed past the rows of gnarled trees, Anna May wondered what grew on each variety, but it wasn't important to the story, and she'd look like a city slicker unable to distinguish an apple from a peach tree. Why it bothered her, she wasn't quite sure. She made a note to ask what fruit trees they had. Clutching her pen and pad in one hand, she reached for the grab bar as they bounced across the rutted path.

"The outer perimeter of zone four is hardwood trees surrounding the cereal pastures. It seems counter to have a monoculture, but we rotate it regularly. The grasses are just a cover to protect the soil, and what we don't cut off, the goats clean up and fertilize as they work."

Anna May released the frame. "Cereal pastures?"

Jasmine said, "Rye, wheat, or barley that we plant in winter to help avoid the need for more hay."

Anna May smiled. "So not corn flakes for people."

"No, but I did think it would be cool to grow Froot Loops when I was a kid."

Anne may wasn't sure if she should laugh at the joke.

Jasmine stopped the cart and pointed across a paved two-lane road.

"The farthest out is natural forest areas that surround the main branch of the creek that two other creeks feed into. There are several rain gardens that filter the runoff and the mushroom logs. On the other side of the big creek, we just Bush Hog a few times a year to keep out trees and let the meadow grow. We add clover on occasion to help the soil, but given enough time, it will come back."

"Bush Hog?"

"It's a brand of pull behind mower, like a Kleenex."

Anna May asked, "And what are mushroom logs?"

"Just what it sounds like, it's how we grow them. On rotting logs."

Anna May wrote several lines and put a big question mark next to the word mushroom.

Jasmine took a path around the farm and stopped. "Can you open the gate?"

"Of course." Anna May hopped out and

approached the latch. She'd never seen a catch like the one holding it closed. It seemed like a shepherd's crook in miniature. "Maybe not."

"Push the ring up, then pull it open. It'll automatically catch once it shuts." Jasmine drove through the gate and waited while Anna May watched the gate to make sure the latch did, in fact, relock. It did.

"I guess as a millworker's daughter, I never learned farm gates."

"Huh. Gloria is a millworker's daughter." Jasmine watched her settle in and hit the pedal. "Where are you from?"

She'd almost forgotten about the mystery of Gloria. "Here. I mean, not now. First Atlanta, then D.C."

"Ah. Hotlanta."

"Yes. There are two Georgias, Atlanta and all the rest." Anna May rubbed a hand over her sweaty forehead. Usually, she was good with strangers, but Jasmine seemed distant and cool. She was a tough nut to crack. "How long have you worked here?"

"A lifetime." Jasmine giggled.

Anna May wasn't sure why that was funny. This tour left her with more questions than answers.

Jasmine steered the side-by-side toward the large two-story farmhouse. The building was painted light yellow and contrasting accent paint with a vaguely Victorian style. If not for the little additions here and there attached to the original box shape, one might expect a lady in a hoop skirt to step out the front door any moment. She turned off the key under a shade tree near the long front porch. "I'm kidding. I love it here. That set of solar panels runs all the water pumps for the pastures. We might get a third cut of hay this year."

Anna May wrote down third cut and another question mark. "Goats eat a lot?"

"Oh, no, we sell most of it. Another income stream. Like the mushrooms and goat cheese. Gloria can tell you more about that, I mostly fix stuff."

Anna May raised her eyebrows. "An engineer?"

"Not by degree."

A familiar form appeared at the side porch. Anna May stared as Gloria approached them. Her head spun. The worn set of coveralls and a yellow T-shirt didn't flatter the rounder body, but it highlighted a bigger chest. Anna May caught herself staring. Her breath caught in her throat. High school was a lifetime ago, yet at this moment, it was yesterday. She'd had this conversation in her mind a hundred, no, a thousand times, and now she went blank.

Gloria waved. "I do apologize for being late. A neighbor got a tractor stuck and needed a tug out of a ditch."

Jasmine stood and turned. "I'll leave y'all to catch up. I'll be in the study if you need me, Mom."

Anna May said, "Thanks for the tour."

Gloria. Mom? Gloria's husband was black? Up close, the familiar face had wrinkles near the eyes, laugh lines. Those eyes still twinkled with mischief, and that smile still made her heart skip a beat. Maybe I can leave with the notes I have already. Anna May peered toward the barn. It must be a half-mile away. She used to be fast, but that was before the knee surgery. Help me, Jesus. Now why did I think that? One week in town, and she was her sixteen-year-old self. She stumbled out of the seat and dusted her clothes.

Gloria reached out both hands toward Anna

May. "It's good to see you again."

Anna May froze. Take her hands? Step into a hug? She decided to at least shut her mouth first. She touched her fingertips to Gloria's hands, and a familiar, distant memory jolted to her mind. A cool fall night, walking back to the truck after a football game, and Gloria took her hand for the first time. Forty-odd years later, she had the same reaction. Thrilled. Terrified. Her mind reeled, and she couldn't find her words, a mighty crisis for a writer.

Gloria broke the silence. "Come inside. Let's have a cool drink."

Anna May dropped her hands to her sides and staggered after her, almost tripping up the steps.

"I was surprised to see your name in the email to set up the tour." Gloria put out two glasses, the ice clattering as it fell. She poured the tea from a large pitcher. "I'm sorry I was delayed."

Anna May shuffled, still mute. She knew it was me! If she wanted to avoid me, why show up at all? I'm the idiot that said maybe to coffee. Her breath was rapid, and she clutched at the glass to wet her dry mouth. "No problem. Jasmine gave me a tour." She paused. "You weren't trying to ditch me?"

"No." Gloria peered at her like she was studying her soul. "I'm hoping to get an honest review of the farm, not influenced because we were friends."

Anna May noticed the past tense. "Influenced in a good way or a bad way?"

"Either I suppose. Are we still friends?"

Ever the flirt, Anna May used her most sultry voice. "I don't know, are we?" Immediately, she wished she hadn't, but judging by the color rising on Gloria's cheeks, she'd hit the target.

"Let's sit in the living room, shall we? I'll get some cookies."

Chapter Thirteen

Gloria fidgeted as she watched Anna May move around the room. She'd seemed surprised to see her. No, more shocked. When their hands touched, the spark was still there. After all this time. She wasn't the same, the question was, who was she now? A big-time author and way out of Gloria's league. She was the kind of woman who wore white shorts to a farm. The running shoes looked brand new. Red clay stained forever. The Southern Anna May should know that.

Anna May strolled the room, evidently still unable to just sit. She stopped briefly to consider each of the family pictures, then studied the large overhead image of the entire farm.

Gloria said, "That's before we added the second greenhouse."

Anna May leaned closer. "Is that a third creek down here?"

"No, a ravine. Once in a blue moon, it rains hard enough to run water, but it's dry about all the time." She had so many questions for Anna May, and here they were chatting about a creek. "How's your momma?"

"Good as can be expected. I haven't got her convinced to come live by me. Stubborn as a mule."

"You think she might move?"

"I don't know what's keeping her here. Bubba complains about having to do everything for her. There's a nice senior center three blocks from me."

Gloria furrowed her eyebrows. How far was three blocks? Did it matter? Was Anna May going to walk? She couldn't think of anything worse than having to leave her home after Collette died. It was hard enough just losing her. True, every nook had a memory, but most were very good. She would never leave their farm. "It'd be hard to leave all you know." Instantly, she regretted saying it. Wasn't that exactly what Anna May had done thirty, no forty, years ago? Just up and left?

Anna May turned and sat across from Gloria. "There's much better medical care in D.C. And she wouldn't have to worry over the house. I bet they built those things over a hundred years ago."

Gloria shrank into the chair. That was that. It was foolish to think anything might rekindle between them. Anna May hadn't considered ever coming back to live. "How's work? I saw your name on that article about the next generation of electric vehicles."

"Ah. It's good. For work."

"Writing is what you always wanted to do."

Anna May seemed to contract and shrank toward the window. "I was surprised when you pulled up, you know, that it was your place. I mean, when I got the assignment to learn about this permaculture farming, I didn't recognize the name Robinson." She paused as she turned to face Gloria. "It's been a long time, hasn't it?"

Gloria folded her hands. For a writer, she sure had trouble finding words. "Yes. Literally a lifetime ago."

Anna May turned scarlet. "Your daughter is really smart. Pretty girl, too."

"Thank you. I wish she'd go off to college, but

she's been reluctant since it's just the two of us now."
Gloria wondered if she'd take the hint.

Anna May looked toward the office. "It's good to see you."

Gloria asked, "Do you want more tea?"

"No, I should be going. I've taken up enough of your time." Fidgeting with a loose thread on the arm of the chair, she said, "I'm not sure where to begin exactly, but I want to apologize. For what happened. In high school."

"Why would you apologize?" Gloria realized her hands tightened, and she forced them to relax.

"I just left you taking all the heat."

"Ah. Water under the bridge." Gloria stood. "I hope we can visit again before you head home."

"I'd like that."

At least it was a step up from a lukewarm maybe. And then Anna May was gone. Gloria waved from the porch as the sports car rumbled to life. Anna May stuck out a hand when she reached the end of the driveway, and then she zoomed away. Just like before. Poof. Gloria wasn't even sure why it bothered her to see her go now. What had she expected?

She sat on the porch swing and read a farm catalog until it was too dim to see. The sky was dark with a distant summer storm creeping close. Lightning snapped and lit up the tree line, the thunder rumbling moments later.

She sipped her tea, and her mind wandered to the trip she and Anna May took to Myrtle Beach in high school. They walked the sand that night, the stars hidden by clouds then, as well. The water crashed into the shore, each wave threatening to soak their shoes. Time stood still as Anna May touched her fingers to

Gloria's, the conversation stilted and full of giggles until the chilly air on freshly sunburned skin drove them closer together, and lightly, their lips touched. Who kissed whom first was open for debate, but in her mind, Gloria was sure it had been Anna May. They simply held hands and walked most of the night, both surprised by the morning sun sliding up along the water.

The plans for another day in the sun were abandoned for an afternoon spent naked and exploring, the air conditioner blasting but unable to cool the room. Sweaty from heat and nerves, they pressed together, discovering the joy that could be. She would never forget the thrill of knowing she was the one who caused Anna May to cry out with pleasure. The perfume of Noxzema on red skin mixed with the musky scent of sex. With the slider cracked open, they could hear the waves crash as they drifted to sleep. Gloria would never forget the wave of sorrow as she woke, watching Anna May breathe, her blond hair scattered over the pillow. She knew this magical time would end and they'd be back at school. She didn't have to ask what would happen. They would hide. They would sneak notes, maybe a long glance, but there would be no announcement of love. There was no room for them in Chicora Point.

Secrets had a way of making things seem awful and eventually filled Anna May with shame. The blowup was sudden and nuclear. Complete devastation.

Gloria pushed the swing into motion, the rain starting to fall. Unlike Anna May, she found her strength. She demanded a place here for her and Collette. And their wonderful daughter. Tears slipped out. What if Anna May had stayed? Would they have been together? No. There would have been no reconciliation. Her stomach churned, and she clenched her teeth. With a flick, she brushed the tears off her cheeks.

Chapter Fourteen

The engine jumped to life as Anna May stomped the gas pedal to the floor. Her heartfelt apology barely registered in Gloria's expression. The soft lines around her sky blue eyes tightened. That was it. Clearly, the apology didn't matter to her. Anna May's hand shook as she turned the knob for the A/C. What did she expect? Tears? A thank you? Forgiveness? Yes. That was it. Instead, there was practically nothing. What did she say? Water under the bridge. Anna May parked at the ABC liquor store, Aunt Betty's Café. Local laws prevented any word related to spirits on the shop sign, so a large red circle marked it as such. Do kids still call it the Japanese Embassy like they had back in the day?

She went inside. She loved liquor stores. All the possibilities. Passing the wine, she paused at the little jars of moonshine. Cute. But four dollars. Forget it. She sorted through the flavored vodka, relieved to see they carried Tito's. Conveniently, they also sold orange juice. She would need food first, or her stomach would churn all night.

Circling the parking lot, she spotted the familiar yellow sign of the Waffle House.

❧❧❧❧

The corner table afforded Anna May a view of the door without it seeming too obvious that she was studying the patrons. Maybe it was nosy, but she considered it potential inspiration for her story. The notebook was stuck to the table with syrup. She scribbled as ideas popped into her head, hoping to find that nugget that led to an actual byline. Her mind kept returning to Gloria and those sultry pouty lips.

The waitress slid a plate on the table. "You need ketchup?"

"No, thanks." She took the cap off the Texas Pete and shook it over the potatoes. Smothered, covered, chunked, and diced. Translated, it meant onions, melted cheese, ham, and diced tomatoes, and likely some antacids in the near future. You might find grits in D.C. but not the hashbrowns like at Waffle House. She shoveled in a scoop and sighed as the hot sauce hit her tastebuds.

She'd spent years agonizing over that moment of betrayal, and Gloria didn't give it a second thought. If the situation had been reversed, Anna May was certain she would have planned a counterattack and a lifelong effort for revenge. Gloria was still amazing. She was relaxed and confident. An opportunity squandered in her youth. Maybe there was still a chance. For what? Companionship? A true love? At her age, a lifelong relationship only had to last twenty years. She stabbed the eggs, the yolk spilling across the plate.

Tidbits of conversation floated to her ears over the sizzle of the grill and the clank of dishes in a sink. The usual—how's your momma and them, how you been, remember me to your daddy—all repeated around her until a short phrase caught her ear.

"The rally is at ten. They ain't taking down our statues."

"That's for dang sure."

Anna May turned her head. The man speaking had his back to her, and his companion was unremarkable. She half expected a Confederate flag or some Nazi emblem. There was just a cotton shirt, a little worn, with cigarettes in the pocket and a ball cap with a seed company logo and a salty sweat line an inch up from the brim. She strained her ears, but nothing more of their conversation rose above the din around her.

The waitress startled her when she refilled her coffee cup. "You need anything else?"

"No, ma'am, thank you so much."

Anna May added more sugar. Watching the liquid swirl, she drifted back to the day she discovered her father's Klan robe in her parents' closet.

She had been about five or six. It started as a game of shoe store, carrying everyone's footwear to the living room and arranging the pairs across the floor. She was in the back of the closet, fetching her momma's church shoes when she noticed the silky fabric. The crimson red trim against the white was striking and irresistible. She touched the soft cloth, sliding her hands into the folds. The crack on her backside shocked her.

Momma said, "Get up outta there, Anna May, you're crinkling everything, and you're gonna knock my good dress off the hanger."

She backed out, still holding the hem of the cloak.

Momma slapped her hand. "Let go of that. It don't belong to you. Now go pick up all those shoes before someone trips and busts their ankle or something."

It had been years before Anna May realized what the cloak was for, not that she ever saw anyone wear it. To her knowledge, it never left the closet her entire childhood. She couldn't remember exactly when she first understood what Klan meant, but it was long after she knew it existed. Previously, she assumed it was like the Moose Lodge, a social club for men with a thin thread of charitable work. Then she saw the images on TV of a flaming cross with men circling around in white hoods. On a color screen, it would have been terrifying. In your own front yard? She shuddered. Momma had swooped in and told her to cut off the boob tube and get outside so she could run the sweeper.

She couldn't imagine her sweet daddy out in the night like that. Her grandfather? Yes. He unabashedly believed in "white superiority" and made no secret of his views. Oh, he was polite to everyone. He did his ranting at home about the Communists tearing at the fabric of our country, the Catholics and Jews, well, they knew better than to step in this town. His town. He would be spitting with each word by the time he brought up the homosexuals. He'd spin in his grave to know his granddaughter was a lesbian. He was the leader of the local group, the Grand Dragon. Like a fraternity house with secret handshakes and code words. Except the secrecy hid the bombings and shootings. The Knight Riders of the Ku Klux Klan. The bile came up in her throat.

She looked down at the cold food on her plate and took a sip of the lukewarm coffee. Maybe Daddy was pressured to join. Did he quit after his father died? She was in high school when Daddy took Papa's ring and had it made into a charm for her mother. Ever practical, he recycled. And now her brother was on a rampage to find the ring. How long should she wait to tell him? He would be furious that the ring was gone, and then Momma would be furious that her secret was told. She should wait until after Momma passed. She winced at the thought.

The Tito's vodka waiting in her car called to her. In line to pay her bill, a tall elderly man waited before her.

He turned and said, "I guess it's hot enough for you."

Anna May had many variations of this conversation as a young person. She answered, "They say it'll be cooler next week."

"We won't know how to act, will we?"

"Sure won't."

"I can't hardly get my lawn mowed when it ain't hot." He accepted his change. "You have a good day."

"Y'all too."

This place was like a record with the needle stuck in a groove. Did kids even know what a record was? She felt every bit her age bending into her car.

Chapter Fifteen

The next morning, Anna May drove to the cemetery, a fresh bouquet of carnations on her passenger seat. Her family plot was near the west fence, under a giant magnolia tree. Lilies bloomed around many of the oldest tombstones. A huge azalea bush leaned against the only bench. If you looked closely, you could see a family name on one edge. They weren't allowed to plant trees or bushes anymore as so many grew, and twisting roots nudged the interred closer together and sometimes right toward the surface.

She parked toward the side of the narrow gravel path. It would have been helpful to bring a vase. Instead, she laid a bouquet of multicolored flowers on the sod; the fresh squares of green sharply contrasted the surrounding brown blades dried out in the summer sun. She wandered to the bench and sat, stretching her legs. Thank God it was in the shade. The breeze carried a hint of charcoal and slow-cooking meat, making her mouth water. While some preferred a dry rub, in her opinion, pork slathered in sauce was the best. She had tried a lot of barbecues, but there was no comparison to the local hot sauce.

In the corner of her eye, she spotted a dark, mossy statue from momma's side of the family. Was Tillus there? She went to investigate. The features of the figure wore away years ago, but the lettering faintly hinted at Chapman. The grass nearly covered the flat marker, and she had to kick with her heel to dislodge the roots. Tillus. Her uncle. As a child, the family went to the cemetery on Decoration Day, but she couldn't recall ever seeing this stone. But did she honestly ever read any of them? Momma would hand her a flower with a ribbon, and she'd stick it in the dirt and move on without any fanfare.

The rumble of a truck broke the quiet. She turned her head. Jimmy Buchanan. Could her luck get worse? At least his family was near the front. The statue of his grandfather with one arm raised was prominently featured inside a short iron rail fence. She wouldn't have to speak to him. To her dismay, he kept rolling until he was close.

Raised to be polite at all costs, it pained her, but she still lifted her whole hand. Would he just complete the circle and move toward his family plot? The truck thudded into park. He needed to get that transmission looked at, but with the jacked-up tires, it wouldn't surprise her if the drive shaft was wrong. Why did she know this? Her brother? She would bet he had the engine modified to blow black smoke at will, making some political statement by destroying the environment.

Jimmy rolled down his window. "Hey, Walker. Still a Communist?"

She didn't answer.

"You picking out a spot?"

She pressed her lips together. "I brought flowers to Daddy." She hoped that would be enough to appease him.

"Rest his soul." Jimmy paused, then spit. "Maybe you should go right next to your yellow-bellied uncle."

Anna May stiffened. "I don't know what you mean."

He hissed, "Buchanans know what to do with people who are trouble. Trust me. I know what to do with you." With that, he rolled up the window and drove off.

That same cryptic message. What did he mean by that? Did his grandfather have something to do with the death of Tillus? They owned the mill, obviously, but it was a car accident. That's what Momma said. Or did she? She said incident. There was a story in there somewhere begging to be set free.

☙☙☙☙

As Anna May stopped at the traffic light, she looked to the right and noticed Jimmy's truck. He sat watching her. A "Don't Tread on Me" yellow flag blew out as he passed in front of her, his arm extending her the middle finger. She didn't need to hear the sound to know what words he spoke in her direction.

Swearing might be lazy, and she knew dozens of better phrases, but instantly, she responded under her breath. "Not if I fucking see you first, you bastard."

Chapter Sixteen

It had been two days since Anna May visited, and Gloria couldn't quite stop from mulling over the what-ifs. This morning, she had work to do. Many people were still out of work as the economy adjusted to the new normal after the pandemic.

The food pantry was low, and she watered plants as she waited for Damion. One of the overhead mister heads must be clogged as an entire section was dry.

Damion parked next to the greenhouse, the bass from his music audible through the truck windows. He got out, adjusted his shirt, and pushed the door shut. His face shined with sweat.

Gloria watched him for a moment, then went to greet him. "How do you do it? I know you're my age, and you're still shockingly handsome."

He smiled. "You know the answer, my dear. As Whoopi says, black don't crack. And just for the record, you're shockingly beautiful."

She reached and squeezed his hand. "And you are a shameless flatterer. Come on, let's get you loaded."

"I don't mean to question you, but this stuff looks like prime to me. Shouldn't you sell this?"

"I've sold enough. People are hungry. I have food. It's simple."

He grabbed the top box. "I wish it was."

Once the back of his truck was full, she helped him cover the load with a cargo net. "I appreciate you coming all this way."

He waved his hands. "No, thank you. This is wonderful. You shouldn't have to bring it to us all the time."

"You have time for a drink?"

"Tea or otherwise?"

"Yes."

"Of course."

The air conditioner was ancient but still managed to cool the air in the house. In the kitchen, Gloria opened the fridge and took out the pitcher of tea. With one hip on the door, she pulled out a package of pimento cheese.

With the familiarity of a longtime friend, Damion took out glasses from the cupboard.

Gloria said, "There's crackers in the right lower cabinet." She set down the items and took the glasses, pressing them into the refrigerator door to get ice.

"Aren't you fancy?" he said, a lilt to his voice.

"I don't know how we lived with ice trays. Although I miss them when I want vodkasicles."

He laughed; his whole face crinkled with joy. "I have to drive, or I'd say we should make cocktails."

"I wish we could. I have to get out on the tractor later. You shouldn't drink and mow with a Bush Hog." She sat and then filled the glasses.

He flipped the lid off the plastic tub, opened the box, and shook some crackers into his hand. With one, he scooped the orange dip. "Mmm. This is almost as good as my momma's, and you better not tell her I said so."

She crossed her heart. "I would never break that woman's heart."

"Good." He took a drink. "Ah, that hits the spot." After a beat, he asked, "Have you seen Anna May?"

Gloria froze a moment. Slowly, she answered, "Yes."

He leaned in. "Spill it."

Gloria twisted her glass on the tabletop. "She came out to the farm for a tour, you know, for a story."

"And?"

She shrugged. "That's it."

"You know I love David dearly, but when I saw my old flame at the bar in Spartanburg, I almost died on the spot. And he didn't look half as good as Anna May does."

Gloria shifted as the heat rose up her chest. She was sure she was pink and headed toward crimson. "She does, I guess, look good, I mean."

He tipped his head. "You noticed."

"I'm not blind. I'm just not interested."

"The woman who shattered your heart in high school shows up on your porch and you're not interested? Not even a teensy bit?"

She fidgeted.

Damion squealed. "I knew it."

"Come on. Be real. She'll head back to D.C. in a week and won't even see us in the rearview mirror."

"Or she could stay."

His words echoed in her head. "I suppose."

"If she had a reason to, stay I mean." He took a drink. "Would you want her to?"

Gloria sprung to her feet and paced. "Sure, why not? Orphaned horses, stray kittens, just bring them to me, I'll fix them all."

Damion scooped more dip and held the cracker up. "She is a little broken. We all are."

"She doesn't know me. She thinks she does." Gloria frowned as she heard the sting in her voice.

"You have changed. She has changed. But under all that, we are the same people."

Gloria dropped into the chair. "I just can't, after Collette, all the plans we made for someday."

Damion rose and went to her. He wrapped his arms around her shoulders and held her tight. "I miss her, too."

Gloria wiped at her eyes. "What would you do if something happened to David?"

"Crawl in the box and die next to him."

"You do understand."

Damion hugged her tight and then let her go. He sat and said, "And I know I might find another love. It will never be the same, doesn't mean it can't be nice, too."

Gloria bit at her lip. "I don't need Anna May."

"It's okay to want her."

"I don't know that I do." Gloria tapped her fingers on the table.

"I should go before those crates cook in the back." He put his hands on her shoulders. "If there is anyone in this world that deserves to be happy, it's you." He let go, and she stood.

"Thank you."

"Always. Love you."

"Love you more."

At the door, she watched him stride toward his truck and waved as he drove off. What if Anna May did stay?

❧ ❧ ❧ ❧

After a long hot ride on the tractor, Gloria sagged into the porch swing as the first cooler breeze of the evening wisped from the creek. Rocking back and forth, she realized she was as firmly rooted in Chicora Point as a kudzu vine. After her grandfather died, she'd come out to the farm to stay with Grandma until she passed, puttering around the acreage and dreaming. She kept up Grandma's garden and Grandfather's beehives, still not really having a direction, like a compass swirling, centered, uncommitted. Until there was Collette, beautiful, charming, smart, driven to change the world.

It was a chance meeting of the state beekeepers. Or was it fate? Collette was presenting a lecture on the uses of beeswax, her dark eyes flashing with energy and poise. Her hair, braided into neat rows across her head and hung past her shoulders, swung as she moved, hypnotizing. Gloria was smitten, and after a lunch to discuss the merits of a nine versus ten frame box, she had Collette's phone number and a plan to meet for dinner. It turned out her aunt lived thirty miles from Chicora Point, and their next visit led to a discussion about their dreams, which became plans. It had taken a lifetime, but they finally built their own better world, the Phoenix from the ashes, a bountiful farm out of dirt worn out by years of cotton.

Jasmine sat next to her on the bench swing. "Can I ask you something?"

"Always."

"Are you going to date Anna May?"

Gloria shifted on the wooden seat. She cleared her throat. "No. She's not going to stay, honey. No reason to think she would. No reason to waste my time."

"I didn't say forever. Just have some fun for a change. I wondered why you wouldn't. I mean, it's hard to meet people here. Everybody already knows everybody."

"I used to know her. I don't now. I'm not sure what the point would be." Gloria let the words get soft and then added, "Are you interested in someone?"

Jasmine shrugged. "No."

"You never know when Cupid will strike."

"True. But there's not even anyone here I would date." Jasmine turned to look toward the picture window. "I don't know. I love the farm, but I just..."

"You getting restless?" Gloria reached over and brushed back a strand of hair.

Jasmine picked at a fingernail.

Gloria said, "Let's go for a ride and get some shaved ice."

Once in the safety of the truck cab, with both women staring out toward the road, Jasmine found her voice. "Why did you and Momma C stay here?"

"In many ways, it was foolish to bring a lesbian interracial relationship here. The reaction in town was polite. Most people didn't call us names to our faces. They waited until we left the room. But this was home."

Jasmine snorted. "Home is where you hang your hat."

Gloria pressed her lips together. Maybe they were past the days when her advice was useful. She knew nothing of the pansexual, alphabet soup of letters kids used today. If pressed, she couldn't even say for sure if Jasmine preferred men or women. Or both. The silence begged to be broken. She forced herself to wait.

Finally, Jasmine said, "Why did you come back to Chicora Point? The farm you inherited. You could have just sold it. The real reason."

Gloria chose her words carefully. "I loved being in the big city, the nightlife. But I felt invisible there."

"I'm invisible here."

"Maybe you are. I'm sorry I can't understand."

Jasmine huffed. "I'm not saying it right."

"We knew the child of two women would have some challenges. We hoped we could love you enough to insulate you."

Jasmine got louder. "It's not that. I mean, sometimes it was, but it wasn't a big deal. Although it was annoying every queer kid in the county came out to me."

"You were safe."

In a monotone, Jasmine said, "Yeah. Terrific."

Gloria parked at the grocery store lot near the Brain Freeze Ice hut. "Get me a lime?" She watched as Jasmine went to the line, her movements graceful like a dancer. Maybe this was about her birth parents. The adoption was closed, but they could get one of those DNA test kits. She startled when Jasmine opened the door.

"Here you go." She slid into the seat and tackled the paper cup of red slush with a tiny spoon. "This is called a volcano. Kind of a stupid name for ice, but it's tropical flavors."

Gloria smiled. "This lime would be better with tequila."

"That may be marketing genius. Wait. Isn't that a margarita?"

"Nothing gets past you, does it?"

Jasmine snorted. "You're weird."

Gloria started the truck, and they chatted about nothing all the way home. Whatever was on her mind would come out when Jazz was ready. One thing was clear, Gloria needed to convince Jasmine that she could manage the farm without her.

Chapter Seventeen

The sun crept over the tree line, casting a shadow across the lawn as the first light of the day spread, the pinks and oranges. Gloria stepped out onto the porch wearing her robe. Holding her mug in one hand, she eased the screen door shut. Some preferred a romantic sunset, but she loved the sunrise, the fulfilled promise of light after dark. The magic of Apollo bringing his chariot across the sky, chasing away the stars.

For all the memories of Anna May, there was one that overshadowed them all. It was easy to say it didn't matter and childishly fun to watch Anna May struggle to apologize. Somehow, it opened the wound she thought long healed.

Surely, it had been an accident, but the sting was as fresh as the day Anna May betrayed her. The soaring high of first love left her dangerously close to the sun. They had been in the biology lab washing trays when Barbara Sue came in. Over the clinking of the glassware and the splashing of water, Gloria hadn't heard the entrance. She just leaned toward Anna May and pecked her cheek. That was it. Barbara Sue screamed like she'd seen a bear lunge into the lab.

Anna May pulled away, and the look of terror in her eyes crushed Gloria more than the words that followed. "Gross, Gloria, keep away from me."

It didn't take long for the story to spread, and by the time she got on the bus, the whispers of her supposed attack on Anna May were barely disguised. Gloria ignored them as best she could. There was nothing to debate. It was true she kissed Anna May, and it was true that she was a lesbian. All the less kind names, well, her mother would say there was no reason to dignify the teasing with a response. In truth, her mother might have joined them in disgust, but she didn't. The conversation between them was blessedly short.

Gloria had stomped up the back porch, her fists clenched. Momma looked up from her dishpan. Gloria said, "Why do we have to live in this hateful town?"

Momma wiped her hands on her apron, smoothing invisible wrinkles. "Wherever you go, there you are."

Gloria moved to leave the room.

Momma asked, "What's got you fit to be tied?"

Stopping, she said, "If I had my druthers, I'd rather not say."

"Gloria Sinclair, I'm waiting."

"Yes, ma'am." She looked away.

"Come on, I was fixing to make tea."

Gloria pulled out the kitchen chair, the legs scratching on the worn linoleum. Her chin dropped to her chest. What she wanted to say was that her heart was shattered, and she was not embarrassed she loved Anna May, and if people would just shut up, maybe they would still be together. Instead, she muttered, "People been saying things about me, and now Anna May ain't my friend anymore." The ridiculousness of the understatement was laughable.

Momma put down two glasses and sat quietly for a long time. She wiped at the condensation beading on the glass with a thumb. Softly, she said, "There ain't no pot so crooked that a lid won't fit."

Her heart leaped. Momma knew. And she didn't care. Where Momma'd heard it was irrelevant, gossip in a small town moved fast. "I got homework."

"Supper's at seven tonight. Daddy is working late."

That was the only time they ever discussed it. Momma died the next spring and her father not long after. Gloria spent a year studying agriculture and then returned to her grandparents' farm with enough knowledge to be dangerous and enough attitude to succeed. Thank God for Collette, who had been raised in the country.

She looked up. "We did good, baby."

Anna May had up and left for journalism school without so much as a look back. In almost forty years apart, Gloria rarely touched the memories. They were like a fragile dry flower found in a scrapbook, gently nestled away in the past, seldom brought out for examination. Yet here Anna May was again. Gloria couldn't deny that just the sight of her made her heart pound, and the wave of nausea hinted that their history was demanding her attention. But who was she now? Did it matter? Damion said she lived just outside D.C., a city Gloria visited once with Jasmine on a school field trip. It was an exhilarating and exhausting tromp around the history and pageantry of the American government. The smells of exhaust and food carts and perfumes. She was quickly tired of the many people everywhere they went. Noisy, pushy, not at all like home.

Gloria thought herself about the same as always. How had Anna May changed? "Do I even want to know?" The answer was yes. Now what was she going to do about it?

~~~~~~

Gloria watched as Jasmine tucked some clothing into a waterproof duffel. "But you've been in canoes since you were four. You must have five kayaks in the barn. Why do you need to take lessons?"

Jasmine shrugged. "Kim insists there's a difference between river kayaks and open water."

"Kim?"

"Coffman."

"Right, she always wore that leather jacket."

Jasmine raised an eyebrow. "As I was saying, we're planning to go up to the campground on Lake Jocassee, you know, that you have to boat over to. They want to make sure I can get back in if I fall out."

"Or I could hire one of those pontoons to follow along. I could bring all the gear." Gloria shrugged.

"Right. Since when do you do anything new?" Jasmine challenged her. "Come kayaking with us."

"And who's going to help me out of the thing when my shoulder seizes up?" Gloria pictured herself in the middle of a lake clutching the paddle in one hand and the boat with the other, hopelessly stranded. "Out of curiosity, how do you get back on if you fall out?"

"There's a deck mount where you kind of throw yourself up and wiggle in, or the cowboy mount, you know, like getting on a horse. Or a cowboy." Jasmine winked. "I wonder if there's a reverse cowboy."

Gloria tried to ignore the sexual reference but failed. The heat crept up her neck. Jasmine grew up on a farm and had full knowledge of babies since she was knee-high to a grasshopper, but still. Gloria found discussing it with her a challenge even now that she was an adult. "I'm sure I have no idea what you're talking about."

Jasmine smirked. "Nice red. Someone should get lucky around here once in a while."

"I don't want to hear about anyone getting... lucky. Good or bad."

"Mom, there's only good sex and great sex."

"Stop. I don't want to hear it." Gloria shoved her fingers into her ears. "I just assume things, don't tell me."

Jasmine slid the bag on her shoulder. "I didn't figure I'd have to come out in reverse."

"I know, I'm sorry. Collette was better at these things."

"That's only because you couldn't see her blush. She stammered like Professor Quirrell when we talked about girl stuff."

Gloria said, "I'm sure I don't remember any such thing. What time will you be back?"

Jasmine smiled. "Depends on if I get that cowboy thing right." Her laughter followed her out the door.

Gloria rubbed her temple. She was good with little kids, but trying to find the line between parent and friend was a pain in the butt. Collette was better at it. Her life would be forever split into life with Collette and life without. What if she did meet someone? She wouldn't replace her, just add to Gloria's life. What if she had already been a part of her life? Did that count? Luna barked. Gloria pushed back from the table and went to see what the ruckus was about.

A goat had its head caught in the steering wheel of the side-by-side. Gloria ran down the steps. "Damn, you are short a few cards from a full deck."

Gloria grabbed the horns and twisted. The goat screamed.

"Oh, stop."

The brown eyes blinked at her as she carried the buckling to the pasture, now content to taste the strap on her overalls. Gloria opened the latch with one hand. The goat hit the dirt and sprinted across the grass. "You're welcome. And you got my shirt wet, you little monkey."

Luna pushed against her leg, her tongue hanging out as she panted.

Gloria rubbed her ears. "You're a good girl, Luna, thank you."

Chapter Eighteen

Anna May hunched over the microfiche machine, her gaze flicking across the images as she scrolled. She loved this library. The kids' section still had an adult human-size Cat in the Hat painted on the wall. The copyright holder was unlikely to sue the small library for infringement. The distinctive scent of damp carpet permeated the place. Each patron had on earbuds, which she had forgotten. The desired article slid into view. She studied the story about the disgruntled employees and the alleged threat of unions to the workers' way of life if organized labor was to infiltrate the mill. A grainy image of Mr. Buchanan, standing on a platform with a fist raised in the air like a fascist leader, took up three columns. He was quoted as saying, "There is nothing I will not do to protect the workers from the Communist influences trying to infiltrate this town."

Even murder? She shuddered. One image at a time, she turned through the reel. There it was. Local man killed in single-car accident on Anderson Street. The man supposedly left the road at a high rate of speed, into a tree. She imagined an old-fashioned Model T rumbling along as other cars chased down some narrow path with twists and turns. But this man was her uncle. Her mother's brother. Only twenty-three. It was a shame. Anna May was certain that Momma said he died at the mill. Did they fake the scene? Was it criminal?

A creepy chill inched up her back. She glanced behind her. Jimmy stood near the window staring at her. She turned back to her papers, arranged her notes, and resisted the urge to challenge him. She'd bet money his grandfather had plenty to do with the car crash and double the odds Jimmy not only knew but was quite proud of the story.

She took her phone and scrolled to the number for Damion. His dad would know the truth. She texted, "Hey, Damion, do you think your dad would talk to me about the old days at the mill for a story I'm working on?"

Little dots danced and then a response. "I'm at the office with him right now. I'll ask."

She scrolled on Google until her phone dinged.

"He says Thursday either after three or at ten a.m."

She whipped her thumbs across the electronic keyboard. "Let's do ten so I can take him to lunch. I hope you'll join us."

"I'll clear my schedule. Looking forward to seeing you again."

She tapped the calendar and added the appointment. She dropped her phone into her satchel.

༄ ༄ ༄ ༄

After she returned the boxes to the wheeled cart, Anna May took the stairs to the entry hall. She stopped short. Jimmy blocked the doorway with his portly frame, casually smoking under the No Smoking sign.

She steeled herself. "Why so mad? Chevy stop making trucks?"

He raised a lip into a snarl. "You think you're

funny."

"It was funny. Excuse me." She shifted to the right side of the door to pass.

He flicked the cigarette butt and ground it out with his boot. "There ain't no excuse for you. I been thinking I might get some of my friends up to come visit and remind y'all who is in charge around here."

Anna May froze. Surely, her brother would stop him from parading around Momma's house. Would he hassle her at the motel? Unlikely. Her heart went to her throat. Maybe he had seen her with Damion. Words failed her.

His smile belied his words. "I'm watching you. Don't start no trouble." He stepped to the side.

She ducked her head as she passed, her hands trembling.

๑ ๑ ๑ ๑

Momma stood in the kitchen. "Are you still here? I haven't seen you in almost a week. I was starting to wonder if you'd gone home without saying goodbye."

"I'm sorry. I've been working on a story, well, two actually."

"Come sit. I got grits enough for two." Momma ladled a large serving into a bowl. "You want butter, or do you do some fancy D.C. thing to it?"

Anna May usually added hot sauce. "No, ma'am, just butter, please."

Momma handed her the bowl and shuffled to the living room. "You can get a tray. I'd rather sit in this chair. My hip is flaring."

"Sure." Anna May approached the topic with care. "Momma, would you tell me about when you moved to Mill Hill?"

"Oh, I can't hardly recall. I wasn't but four or five. Why do you ask?"

"I'm writing a story about the old mill. I just wondered what the community was like, you know, why everyone stayed here."

"This neighborhood was our entire lives, we worked together, we played together. All the parents kept up with the children on the street. If you needed food, a neighbor just happened to show up with something extra. We took care of each other."

"But the mill owned you. All of you. If you quit, you lost your home and everything."

Her mother's face froze. "All the more reason to be on time to work."

"It was dangerous and paid low wages. Look at this house, Ma, look at it."

A red darkened her mother's face, and her voice quaked. "Yes. Look at it. It's kept you dry through every storm, and that stove kept you warm with wood your father cut with his bare hands until we got the oil burner. You never went to bed with a belly aching with hunger. You never had to leave school to care for your siblings." Tears started to roll down her cheeks. "You think you know everything, Anna May Elizabeth, but you're nothing but a spoiled brat."

Anna May knew that she'd gone too far. "You want a tea? I'm fixing to get one."

She went to the kitchen, opened the fridge, and took out the pitcher. She peered over the curtain, down the street of identical houses, where the mill still stood, casting a shadow over them all. The mill was the town. No matter how far away she went, she was from here. She carried over the drinks. "I'm sorry, I didn't mean to belittle this house."

Her mother accepted the glass, set it on the coaster on the side table, and then folded her hands in her lap. "Of course you did. I know you don't see this place as much, not compared to your big city. But think about what a job meant to people living on a farm, poor as a church mouse, scraping by just enough to feed themselves if they were lucky. This was a blessing to have a house and a steady wage. We were glad to have it."

"Wouldn't you have rather lived in the country somewhere?" Anna May forced her voice quiet. "On a farm, you work by the season. At the mill, it was six days a week for life."

Momma set her jaw. "You don't know because you don't have children. You would sacrifice for them."

Anna May slouched. She did not know. And she never would. You could bet that she wouldn't risk their injury or death to feed them. Or would she if there was no other choice? "You're right, thank you. I need to rethink this story."

"I reckon." Her mother took a gulp. "This hits the spot. Hand me the clicker. I assume you don't want to watch the news."

"Faux News. Not a chance."

"Don't start with me, Anna May Elizabeth." Her mother pointed the remote.

The conversation ended with the music of the Andy Griffith Show blasting from the TV. If only life was as simple as Mayberry. It might be if she let it.

Chapter Nineteen

Anna May tried to concoct a reason to see Gloria, but a visit to learn more about the mushrooms was a bit contrived. To her surprise and delight, Gloria called her first and offered an extended tour to make up for her late arrival. Now Anna May was sitting in the side-by-side, this time with her high school sweetheart. The heat was tempered with a steady breeze. The sweat running down between her breasts was all nerves. She tugged at her shirt collar.

Anna May studied the rows of plants in assorted shapes and sizes and wondered what grew on the plants. The tall ones were corn, but the rest? She had no clue. At least she recognized the peach trees. Or probably peach trees. Short, gnarled. "Peach trees?"

"Yes. And apple, nectarine, plum, pear. Behind them are the berry bushes. There, the native trees provide shelter and soil retention for the creek."

Gloria spun the wheel, and they rounded under an evergreen tree line, and she could hear the water tumble over the rocks. "Those short logs are all inoculated for mushrooms. They won't be ready to harvest until next spring."

Anna May thought there might be dozens, no hundreds, of logs leaning against a low fence of some sort. She took out a notebook and pen. "Inoculated?"

"Injected with the mold spores. They eat the wood. Then grow mushrooms." Gloria pointed toward a small cabin. "The tools of the mushroom trade are in there. Cut the logs. Drill holes. Stuff them with spores. Paint it with wax. Not terribly high-tech."

Anna May said, "Sounds like a lot of work."

Gloria shrugged. "All farms are a lot of work."

Anna May wrote work and underlined it twice and then looked up from her notes. A rusted box stuck out of a mound of dirt. "I'm curious about that truck trailer."

"Ah. It's an old container we use to force mushrooms early in the season. The dirt helps keep the temperature more even." Gloria tooted the horn, and a raft of ducks crossed the path. "These ladies clean up the vegetable gardens and leave fertilizer everywhere."

"Where do they go in the winter?"

"They have a shelter near the main pond. They can fly off if they want to. Sometimes, we get visitors flying south or north, and a few of ours will join them, and sometimes, a few travelers stay here."

For a moment, both their hands rested on the bench between them. Inches between them might as well have been miles. Anna May pulled her hands into her lap.

✖ ✖ ✖ ✖

They didn't speak much on the trip back to the barn. After the vehicle stopped, Anna May got out and wandered toward the goats. The question burned in her mind for days ever since she learned that Jasmine was Gloria's daughter. Anna May would have to be more direct since Gloria still hadn't mentioned anything about former partners.

Anna May asked, "How long were you married?"

Gloria stopped in her tracks. "Married? You

mean like to a man?" Her laughter echoed in the large barn, maniacal and musical at the same time.

Anna May scrunched her eyebrows. "But..."

"You assumed since Jasmine is biracial, her father was black, and he was married to me. How heteronormative of you. Frankly, I can't believe you would think I'd sleep with a man after we—"

"Yes," Anna May interrupted. "It was lazy thinking."

"You didn't notice the family pictures? Collette and I were together twenty-eight years. You didn't consider that she might have been Jasmine's birth mother?"

"Yes, no, I mean, I didn't really think about anything." Anna May could taste the lie.

"Clearly." Gloria put her hands on her hips. "And off the record, she's adopted."

Anna May wanted to ask by whom but sensed that was going too far. "She's a terrific young lady."

"Thank you."

The conversation lagged, and the sunlight filtering in cast a warm glow over Gloria's face. Anna May ached for the familiarity they once had. She reached over and brushed a lock from Gloria's forehead. "Do you ever wonder what would have happened if Barbara Sue hadn't seen us?"

"You would have found another time and place to run like a scared rabbit. You weren't ready for all that pressure."

"Sometimes, I think about it."

Gloria sighed. "I'm an Aquarius. You're an Aries. We get along well, but we aren't star matches. We weren't meant for a lifetime together."

"We could have been. It was my fault." Anna May

dropped her hand and found her courage. "For years, I've avoided you. I mean, I've wanted to say I was sorry that I ruined your life. I just didn't know how."

Gloria threw back her head and cackled, a hard edge to the tones. "You're kidding me, right?"

Anna May mumbled, "I abandoned you, and I didn't stick up for you."

Gloria waited for a beat. "I did miss you. But did anyone lie? No. I am a lesbian. And I did kiss you."

Anna May clenched her fists. "I was a coward."

"Maybe you're upset with yourself, but don't push it off onto me." Gloria leaned against the rail, and several goats rushed for a snack but accepted a pat instead.

Anna May blinked back tears. "I'm trying to say I'm sorry for the worst thing I've ever done my whole life."

Gloria spun around. "You really think the worst thing that happened to me was in high school? Please. I lived in Chicora Point with a black woman for nearly thirty years. Think about how that went over. Right after high school, I buried my parents two weeks apart. They worked themselves to death. I dropped out of college, which I loved, to stay with Grandma after my papaw died. I held my wife when her family shut her out for being a lesbian. I've had strangers at Walmart tell me to stay to my own kind when I was shopping with my sweet, beautiful child. I've had parents refuse to stay with us on field trips. We worked our asses off for years to bring life to worthless dirt. And then I watched her shrivel away. You, my dear, don't even make the top ten."

Anna May deflated like a balloon.

Gloria softened her voice. "I was right here. You

never came to see me. Not once."

Anna May shuffled her feet. "I did want to visit you. I just thought, you know, that you wouldn't want me to. That you would still be angry."

"Oh, don't misunderstand me. I was devastated at the time. I lost my first love and my best friend all at once. I was lonely, but I could sleep at night. It seems you couldn't."

"Fine. I was guilty."

"So you deal with that, not me. My forgiveness doesn't help you forgive yourself." Gloria swept back her hair. "And from what I understand, you abandoned the whole town, not just me."

"Hey now, I came to see my parents all the time."

"Maybe. But it's your brother that took care of them."

"Frankly, I'm pretty busy, and I don't see what Bubba has to do with this."

"We sit on the county council." Gloria put her hands on her hips. "He's trying to keep the town going. I don't agree with him on many things, but at least he takes good care of your momma."

"And I should because I'm the daughter?"

"Your words, not mine."

A long silence fell between them. What had she expected? A tearful profession of a life of longing for her? The shame burned at her for forty years, and Gloria barely thought of it. Of her. The other day, for a moment, she thought she saw a flicker of interest from Gloria. She had clearly misinterpreted Gloria's signals.

Gloria took her hand. "Look. I've heard the rumors about your fights with your parents. Not much is a secret on Mill Hill. We could have been friends. We could have supported each other. But that's not what you wanted. Obviously. I'm not sure what you want now. To be forgiven? It don't amount to a hill of beans, but fine, I forgave you years and years ago. If you gave half a shit about me, you would have said it way before now."

"I did care about you. I'm not the type meant for a long relationship. They all crashed and burned in less than a few years. And every time, it was a replay of the same hurt from high school."

"Oh, come on, this is still all about you. See, the thing is, I've grown up. I had a family and a business to run. You had parties and a wild life in the city. I don't even know who you are anymore. And if you're pining for the child I used to be, well, she's long gone."

Anna May dropped her head. I don't know who I am, either.

"It seems to me you ran as far as you could from this place. You abandoned your family and friends to find that nirvana you thought was out there. So go on back to your life in the big city. We don't need you."

"Well, I sure don't need this. I don't need to live in a place that's so backward stores still don't open on Sunday because some pastor said they couldn't. Life isn't all about church and then treating people like shit because you're saved." Anna May choked on the words.

"I agree. But if you looked a little deeper, you would see people who bring you food when you're sick. People who stop whenever they see a car broken down on the road. People who hand you a five if you're a little short at the grocery store. You would see people who are not perfect, yes. That's true. But you dismiss us all, and you're wrong for that, Anna May. You're wrong for that."

"You could have left, too. You were too afraid.

Instead, you settled for life in this shit town. I feel sorry for you."

Anna May ran back to her car. She slammed the door and spun the tires, sending gravel flying behind her. What did she expect? A second chance? She cranked up the radio and cried as an old country song played and her heart broke.

Chapter Twenty

Gloria watched the dust rise behind the car. "Goodbye, Anna May Walker. You can leave town, just like you always do. Wherever you go, there you are." The cat wove around her legs and purred. "I know who loves me. Come on." She picked up Smokey and went inside.

With a meow, the cat leaped down. "Fine. Abandon me." She went into the kitchen and made a hot tea. With a heavy hand, she dumped in sugar but skipped the brandy. The yellow flyer stuck to the calendar with a push pin taunted her. The Ku Klux Klan was more of an annoyance, but this felt different. Hostile. The usual troops were easy to rally to protest. But at what cost? The victims of violence she saw on TV were bad enough, but her own people injured or killed? She took out a pen and a notebook. Bubba Walker was the grand poobah, or whatever they called him, but it was Jimmy Buchanan, with all the flags on his truck, who took every opportunity to intimidate people of color.

Gloria doodled notes on her paper, uncertain of the best way to disrupt the Klan rally in her own town. There was power in numbers. She marked a few names to email. She stared into her teacup and remembered the night long ago when she learned what the KKK was about.

❧ ❧ ❧ ❧

Gloria woke when her father shook her shoulder, his hand warm and rough, calloused from hours of holding tools.

His brown eyes soft in the dim light, with a crew cut starting to gray, he spoke in a slow drawl. "Come on up out of that bed. I have something to show you."

Slipping her shorts on under her nightshirt, she and her sister, still barefoot, followed their daddy to his light blue Chevy pickup truck, the dirt in the yard still warm from the heat of the day. He opened the door for them and retreated to the driver's side. Cranking the eight cylinders to life, the half-burnt gasoline burping a cloud of the distinctive odor of oil and creosote, he popped the clutch, and they rolled off into the black of the night. There were a few stars, and the moon was just a sliver glowing behind the clouds. Over the horizon, a yellow glow started from Old Man Jackson's place. Her dad parked some distance from the bonfire and took the girls and lifted them into the bed of the truck.

He whispered, "Stay quiet."

They sat and watched as the scene before them came into focus. Maybe a dozen white-robed men walked around the fire. Gloria thought the hoods must have been hot in the summer night air. I don't know why they're having a bonfire party so late. Nobody brought their kids or anything. Her knees pushed against the metal as she shifted on the truck bed; her feet tucked under her body were pins and needles.

Her father winced as the form of a cross burst into flames, the combustion audible from their location several hundred yards away.

"That right there, that's what hate looks like." He

spit his tobacco onto the ground. "You look real good, so whenever you see it, you'll know right away."

Gloria squinted her eyes. "Why are they doing that?"

"They're cowards. Too afraid to even show their faces." He gestured as the men started to leave the field. Quietly, he carried them to the front seat, his cotton shirt damp in the heat, the smell of Old Spice mixed with the acid of his sweat. Gloria craned her neck to watch the flames flicker and pop. Slowly driving, he left the lights off until he turned toward town.

Gloria tried to figure all this out. He'd never driven in the dark like this before. Was he afraid? He was never afraid—even when that big snake crawled out from under the outhouse. Maybe he was. "Daddy, you scared?"

"I ain't scared. There's more of us than them but no reason to poke a sleeping bear."

"I ain't going to be scared, either."

"That's my girl."

Gloria said, "Those were bad men, Daddy. They shouldn't be mean to Mr. Jackson. He's always sweet to me. I'm gonna be extra nice to him next time I see him."

"Extra nice sometimes is as bad as the mean. Just be polite like you would to everybody else."

She repeated the words in her mind. Extra nice is as bad as the mean. "I don't understand, Daddy."

"You will someday, honey."

He pulled into the driveway and cut off the engine. "You be quiet now."

"Yes, sir."

Smokey rubbed against her leg, pulling her from her memories, still so vivid she could smell the Old

Spice. "Daddy, what am I going to do?" Truly, there was nothing she could do to stop the rally; however, she might be able to give Jimmy some grief. As she scribbled on the edge of the paper, a little hive took shape. Bees. Brilliant. One time in high school, he'd run clear out of the classroom when a bug blew in the window. She reconsidered her idea about the bees. Most people were nervous around bees. She could deliver a special surprise for Jimmy, and if she played her cards right, she'd be the one they called to clear the insects out. She wrote "Operation Stinger" on her paper. Just like Muhammad Ali, she would float like a butterfly and sting like a bee. It was genius.

꧁꧂

The next afternoon, the beehives were decorated with the workers fanning at the entrance. On a sunny, still day, Gloria started Operation Stinger when most bees would be harvesting the beginnings of the fall pollen season. Sweat rolled down her legs into the socks poking above her work boots. She could have taken a frame from a hive box and just shook some bees into a carton, but she wanted flyers that would buzz around. In the shed, she poured a bit of the liquid from her special bee lure concoction into the bottom of a Mason jar. She regularly caught bee swarms with it, and enough ladies could be caught quickly. She just needed enough to frighten someone scared of bugs, not enough to start a hive. With one hand, she put on the bee hat with the mesh. She set the jar down near the apiary. The bees quickly found the lure and began to explore. When a few dozen had landed, she twisted on the lid.

At her truck, she lowered the box over the tailgate. A new sticker caught her eye. Save a horse, ride a cowboy. "Damn it, Jasmine, that's not funny." She smirked. Yes, it was. She skipped toward the house, giddy with her plan.

♫♪♫♪

That night, Gloria drove to the Buchanan gas station. She eased the door of her truck open and slid down. There didn't seem to be anyone around the store at this hour, and Jimmy's old truck sat on the far side under the awning. Gently lifting the buzzing jar, she crept along the hedgerow, her shoes barely scraping on the mulch. Thank goodness the truck was lifted so high it would have easy clearance. She scooted under the engine and quickly spotted the air ducts. With a turn of her box knife, she made a jagged hole and opened the lid. Soon the bees had all flown. She wiggled to reach the tape in her pocket and covered the hole.

She listened for anyone approaching, heard nothing, and then slid out. She sauntered through the bushes and toward her truck, climbed in, and drove the long route around town, just in case anyone spotted her. No one seemed to be following, so she got a cola at the Hardee's and went to her meeting at the food bank. They would chat most of the evening, and no one would recall exactly when she had arrived, a perfect alibi should she need one.

♫♪♫♪

Back at home, Gloria ignored the signal from her cellphone. Anna May's number scrolled across the screen, and she had no interest in what she had to say. Instead, she took out the Courvoisier and filled a glass. After a long swig, she topped the glass and then turned off her cellphone.

Gloria wandered into the living room and dropped back into the chair with a thud, her glass dangerously close to spilling. The twilight sky promised another restless evening. This was her most melancholy time. She took a sip, and as she lowered the glass, the stack of paperwork on the corner of the table taunted her. She would never catch up. There was no such thing as finished, not on a farm. The ache in her right shoulder flared as she leaned back into the recliner. A dark fluffy cat leaped onto the chair arm and eased onto her lap, one foot at a time.

"Hey, Inky. Where have you been all day? Is Smokey outside? You don't care one bit, do you?"

The cat kneaded her belly, then turned into the crevice between her thigh and the chair. The heat from his body was not welcome, but still, Gloria stroked his fur, the rumbling in his chest affirming his approval.

"What am I going to do about this one?" She took another drink, the warmth in her throat catching her emotions as they bubbled up, condensing them into a single moment of dread. What if she did just sell the place? Jasmine could go to school, and Gloria could settle somewhere...where? She was as Southern as a magnolia tree. There was no other place for her. This was home. She and Collette had talked of retiring and maybe getting an RV. Gloria had no interest in seeing the rest of the country. She'd rather have a little cabin in the mountains, right on a creek. She loved the ocean, but a beach place meant tourists, and frankly, she'd had more than enough of being nice to strangers.

Maybe a cabin would be lonely. She was alone now. Unless she let things change. A few tears slid from her eyes. "Damn it, Anna May. Why couldn't you just stay in my past?" Fuck you and your perfect blue eyes. And your laugh. God, the way it runs into my ears. She went to the kitchen and refilled her glass. She had a chance to at least have some company, and she ruined it.

The land line in the office rang, and she hurried to the desk to see who would be calling this late. The number was local but unfamiliar. No reason to answer, the machine would pick it up. After the fourth buzz and a pause, she heard Anna May's voice. "Hey, it's me, Anna May. I just thought I should apologize. For snapping at you and all. You have a beautiful life here, and I shouldn't—"

Gloria snatched up the receiver. "Hey, what's going on?"

"I seem to still have a way of hurting you, and unlike the younger me, I realize it's my fault, and I wanted to say I'm sorry."

"For speaking the truth?"

"Um...it's not my place to say it."

Gloria paused for a moment. "You want to come over? I've got some lemon pie." She hoped Anna May still had a sweet tooth.

"I'm not sure if that's a good idea. I mean, maybe I can meet you for a drink."

"I've already started without you, and I shouldn't drive."

There was a long silence. Anna May startled her. "I'll be there in fifteen minutes."

"Great. See you." She dropped the receiver into the charger. Inky meowed. "You're right. I have lost my mind."

In the bathroom, Gloria ran a brush through her hair. The reflection in the glaring light highlighted every wrinkle. The laugh lines were deepest. The faucet gurgled as she filled the sink, dipping a washcloth in to wipe her face. Maybe I need some of that cream for old ladies. No. This is what hard work gets you, and I've earned this face. She changed her mind and pushed at the corners of her eyes.

Chapter Twenty-one

It was ill-advised, but Gloria had asked Anna May to stop by, and now they sat side by side on the couch. In the quiet of the house, the grandfather clock in the next room clicked, and the chimes for the hour sang out the time. The heat burning in her chest was more than the bourbon. Gloria's heart raced, and her mouth was dry. She brushed her fingers against Anna May's knee, the skin soft over toned muscle.

Anna May took her hand and locked her fingers between Gloria's. "Tell me about your life."

Gloria pulled away from Anna May's shoulder. "I met Collette in college. She was smart, and God, she was funny. We laughed often around here. She had an interest in agriculture, and I owned a rundown farm. A perfect match made in heaven."

She got up and rummaged in a drawer. She handed Anna May a picture and then sat, careful to leave space between them. "This is us the day the adoption became final for Jasmine. She was less than a week old when we were able to bring her home for the first time. She slept so much, I started to wonder if she had eyeballs. Nature or nurture, she's super smart, mechanical things are like giant puzzles to her. She revels in figuring out how things work, why they aren't working, and then how to make improvements."

"Your wife was beautiful."

"I miss her every single day. She died three years ago. Ironically, cancer. All the chemical-free food, and still the genes won out."

"I'm sorry."

"Me too. Jasmine took it harder than me in some ways. She won't leave the farm. I tell her she belongs at school. Instead, she feels like she has to take care of me."

"It is a big place."

"Eh, yes. I could cut back on the most labor-intensive things or just hire more help."

Anna May squeezed her hand. "It may be that she's afraid to lose you, too."

They sat in silence as the grandfather clock clicked with each swing of the pendulum, Anna May's hand still on hers, the palm sweaty and hot.

Gloria asked, "So what about you? Do you have a partner?"

"Ah. Not at the moment. I've had several, you know, over the years. It would start out great, but I never made it past five years. I'm not sure I'm cut out for a forever kind of thing."

"Monogamy sucks?"

"No, well, yes sometimes, but more like I got bored with them, or they got bored with me."

Gloria stiffened. It had been a long time since she'd been with anyone but Collette, and she sure wasn't about to become a play toy for the weekend. "Afraid of commitment."

"Maybe not the right woman to be committed to." Anna May pressed her lips together into a thin white line, her eyes clouded over with a brooding stare into space.

"Maybe not." Gloria lifted her hand and touched her lips to Anna May's fingers, the familiar motion carrying her back in time. Why the hell shouldn't she have a weekend romp? She leaned closer to Anna May, her breath against her cheek. "Sometimes, we end up right where we belong, whether we fight it or not."

"Or not." Anna May responded with a warm kiss, her lips soft and caressing. She increased the explorations until she pressed Gloria back against the cushions, her hands starting to wander.

Gloria had goose bumps as the fire started in her belly, familiar urges driving her to override her hesitations.

Suddenly, Anna May pulled back and settled farther on the couch. "I'm sorry, I was too forward. I just got carried away by the moment."

Gloria gasped. The longing in her heart crushed against her ribs, taking her breath. The debate restarted in high gear. Is this okay? Is it too soon? It's not, we're both adults, well past adults. Practically senior citizens. If we wait, why, wait for what? Wait for her to leave again? Anna May has said nothing indicating she would even stay past the next weekend. Maybe this is foolish. I never do anything impulsive, just willy-nilly. Maybe I should. Dang it, I will. "I'm sorry, I didn't quite hear what you said."

Anna May leaned close to Gloria, the scent of her shampoo fruity and tempting. She whispered, "I won't pretend to know who you are now completely, but I would like to know you."

Gloria mumbled, "Does that work on the ladies in the city?"

Anna May flushed, pulling her hands back as she shifted away. "I'm sorry. I didn't mean it like some pickup line at a bar. I should go."

"Don't be sorry." Gloria caressed the blond curls, sliding a thumb against Anna May's ear, her own body responding to the closeness. She sensed the opportunity slipping away. "Please stay. With me. Here. Tonight."

Anna May answered with another kiss. The moment their mouths touched, Gloria's reluctance melted as the hands stroked her back. She whispered, "Let's get more comfortable." She stood and took Anna May's hand. The dark room popped into view as she flicked on the lamp. The recently painted lilac walls, moonlight sneaking through lace curtains. A cheap printed copy of a handmade quilt, the ecru squares accented with purples.

Anna May smiled.

Gloria couldn't read the expression and hesitated. Was this just another victory for Anna May, or was it a piece of their past flickering forward?

Anna May said, "I don't know why I'm nervous."

Gloria sat and patted the bed. "Don't be," she told Anna May as much as herself. Anxiety increased as Anna May lay on the bed. This was really happening. Gloria curled against Anna May, stroking her arm. "Should I turn the light off?"

"No. I mean, if you want." Anna May brushed her fingers down Gloria's back. "We both look a little different than we did back in the day. But those beautiful eyes—" She pulled even closer. "I feel like you see all the way into my soul."

Gloria squinted. "Like this?"

Anna May tickled her. "Be serious."

Gloria giggled. "Why?"

"Because I am, I don't know. I'm not sure you'll like what you see."

"You talk too much." Gloria kissed her, Anna May's lips opening to allow her tongue access. The taste of Anna May was so different, the wine and the perfume worldly and overpowering as she became lost in the sensations stirring below. She reached for the top button of Anna May's shirt, twisting and releasing enough space to trace against the surprisingly lacy bra. The ache of loneliness bubbling with the urges for connection and pleasure distracted her from the reluctance still looming.

The crash from the porch was a combination of wood smashing and glass.

Gloria struggled up out of the bed, glad to still be dressed. Anna May followed her to the front door. In the porch light, the mischief maker was already gone.

"It was Blueberry. I'm sure of it. The little stinker."

Anna May said, "A blueberry?"

"A goat named Blueberry. I have to find him before a stray dog or a coyote does."

"Isn't that what Luna is for?"

Gloria bit at her lip as she scanned the dark tree line. "I wouldn't take the chance."

Anna May propped herself up on her elbows. "Then let's go find Blueberry."

෴෴෴෴

Anna May was none too happy with the interruption, her back cracking as she stood. They went to the front door. Peering into the dim yard, she didn't see any creatures, great or small.

Gloria stepped into boots and flipped on the porch light. The search was short as Blueberry ran up the steps. Gloria pushed open the screen door. "Oh, no, you don't."

The goat didn't listen, instead flying into the

open space between Gloria's knees and up onto the couch. Anna May stared at the little multicolor goat that had ruined a perfect moment. "I've got him." She lunged and landed on the couch as Blueberry did a pirouette onto the end table.

Jasmine ran into the room, her hair wrapped up in a towel. "What on earth? Blueberry. You little shit."

Gloria hunched at the end of the couch. "Go left."

Anna May shifted, Blueberry followed the movement, then dove the other direction. Jasmine scooped him up. The goat screamed like he was about to be murdered, his legs twitching in the air.

Gloria opened the door. "You want help with the gate?"

"No. This one earned a night in the breeders pen." She looked to Anna May and then back to Gloria. Her expression changed from annoyance to amusement. "Changed your mind, I see." She winked and carried the goat out.

Anna May asked, "What was that about?"

"Nothing." Closing the door, Gloria glanced around the room. "Thank goodness he didn't leave little goat raisins all over. That went pretty well, thanks for your help."

Anna May said, "I'm pretty impressed he knows directions."

Gloria laughed. "What do you mean? You went the wrong way, and he just went opposite of you. He gets out all the time. Besides a shock collar, I'm not sure how to keep him in."

Anna May took Gloria's hand. "Look, I want you to know, well, I really wanted to stay. Maybe this is a sign to wait. I think I should go."

"Oh."

"I mean, I really, really want to...stay." Anna May softly kissed her. "If it's meant to happen, it will."

After a soft kiss good night, she turned and walked out the door, the screaming of a goat audible from the barn. As she raised the fob to unlock her car door, she realized leaving might be the mistake, not staying. It was too late.

Chapter Twenty-two

Gloria watched Anna May shuffle to her car, her pulse racing. What if they didn't have another chance? She pushed open the screen, ran down the steps, and crossed the yard.

Gloria called out, "Wait."

Anna May jumped.

Gloria stopped just short of running into her. "I'm sorry I startled you."

Anna May leaned back against the car. "No, no problem. I'm glad you did. Come here I mean, not scare me." She shoved her hands in her pockets.

Gloria mirrored her actions and then smiled. "Remember that night we went to the lake to watch submarine races?"

Anna May laughed, her eyes sparkling like the stars above them.

Gloria said, "You do. I got grounded for a week for missing curfew."

"I got two weeks." Anna May took out her hands and reached for Gloria, touching her arms. "It was worth it."

Gloria whispered, "Yeah, it was." She leaned toward Anna May and touched her lips to her cheek. "Want to go see if there's any races tonight?"

Anna May snuggled into Gloria and licked at her ear. "Pretty sure I won't get grounded this time."

"The ending might be the same."

"You mean half-dressed asleep in the car?" Anna

May asked.

"I meant the other part."

"Promise?"

Gloria pressed against Anna May and kissed her.

"I can't wait." Anna May lifted the door handle, which didn't work, then searched her pockets for the key. The car beeped as she unlocked the car. She swung open the door. "Your chariot awaits."

Gloria paused. They were a little old to go park, weren't they? The back door screen slammed shut as Jasmine went back into the house, lights flicking off as she moved upstairs.

Gloria said, "We could just stay in the driveway. No one will bother us."

Anna May grinned. "If you say so." She climbed into the backseat. Patting the cushion beside her, she said, "I've never been in the backseat of this car. It's pretty comfy."

Gloria maneuvered past the driver's seat. "This seemed easier back in the day." With a twist, she positioned herself and plopped into the seat. "Hey."

"Hey, yourself." Anna May reached for the top button on her own shirt.

Gloria sucked in a breath as she watched the fingers work their way down the row. Sweat on her face did little to cool her skin. She covered Anna May's mouth with hers, the kisses sloppy and urgent. She braced against the seat as she explored the bra, fishing for the hook. After a few moments, she sat up. "What kind of medieval device is this?"

Anna May laughed as she pinched the clasp releasing the fabric. "I guess some skills get rusty."

Gloria whispered, "Not all of them." She caressed the skin of her breast, rubbing the nipple with her thumb. Anna May lay back, and Gloria moved on top of her, kissing her way down her neck. Anna May writhed against her. Gloria unbuttoned the shorts, nudging the zipper down. Her wrist cramped as she tried to wiggle her fingers toward her goal. Touching the wet fabric, she rubbed as Anna May lifted toward her.

Her own nipples hardened as Anna May bit at her neck, the motions familiar yet new.

Anna May stopped and said, "I need to move my leg. My foot is going to sleep."

"Lose the shorts while you're at it." Gloria tugged at the waistband.

Anna May wriggled. She lifted her phone and touched the screen several times, the soft glow casting a soft pink over her face. Music began to play. "I forgot about the options here."

A song from their days in high school boomed from the little speaker. Gloria whispered, "You won't be able to hear the music in a minute."

"Noisy, are you?" Anna May moaned as Gloria slid her fingers through the short hair.

"If I recall, you were the screamer."

The clatter on the hood of the car brought the actions to a halt. Scratching across the roof indicated another visit from a goat.

Gloria said, "You have got to be kidding me. Damn it, Blueberry."

Anna May cringed. "My paint. I'm really, really sorry to say we have to get him off."

"Somebody should get off, I guess." Gloria shoved the front seat forward. "Fucking goat."

Struggling to get her foot to the ground, she yelled, "Get off the damn car."

Blueberry froze and stared at her.

"Damn it." Gloria lunged and caught a goat horn to the cheek as she grabbed his legs. "Youch."

Anna May said, "Are you okay?"

"Yeah, let me put him up, and I'll be right back." Gloria carried him to the barn, opened the nearest pen, and dropped him down. "You're lucky we don't eat goat."

Blueberry blinked up at her.

"Act like you don't know what I'm saying. You little turd."

She approached the car, and Anna May was dressed and out leaning on the hood.

Gloria said, "I'm so sorry."

Anna May shrugged. "In my experience—"

"Your vast experience?" Gloria teased.

Anna May cleared her throat. "As I was going to say, in my experience, when you get interrupted twice, you should toss in the towel."

"Twice by a goat?"

"That's new, but yes, especially if it's by a goat." Anna May kissed Gloria.

Gloria hugged Anna May, gently putting a hand behind her head, stroking her hair. She whispered, "Are you sure?"

"Yes, but I'm very, very unhappy about it."

"Good." Gloria pulled back.

Anna May said, "I have to get some work done tomorrow. Can I call you?"

Gloria feigned a thick accent like Scarlett O'Hara. "Why, I'm sure I'd be delighted if you would."

☙☙☙☙

The following afternoon, Anna May hunched

over the stale library book, reading the life stories of people who worked in the mill. In a neat column, she'd listed assorted jobs they mentioned, as well as the ages when they started. Her phone buzzed on the table. It was Sho. She glanced around and then headed toward the small lobby to take the call.

"Hey, I got your first draft about the farm. Can you find out how much acreage she thinks you need to make this type of thing work?"

"I reckon."

"Listen to you! That reminds me, I was on Facebook, and I found a cousin who lives in Texas. It turns out, part of my family is from the South, just like you."

Anna May rolled her eyes. "Texas ain't the same kind of Southern."

Sho paused. "I suppose not. Will you be home by the weekend? I've got some comped tickets for Ashley McBryde."

"I'm not making too much headway with Momma, so I guess not."

"Your loss. I penciled your story in for next week. If you can add a couple of inches, that would be great."

"Sure, I recently learned more about goats."

"Did you ever know anything about goats?"

"Not the point."

"If you say so. I have a call coming in."

"I'll talk to you later. Bye." Anna May hung up.

She wanted to see Gloria, but would she think it was another move to get her in bed? Gloria seemed willing. Anna May absently picked at her phone cover. It was time to show that she had matured, too. What if she took Momma to the farm? It would give them something to do besides stare at each other when they visited. She texted Gloria. "I have a follow-up question for you. Can I bring my mom by for a visit?"

A few dots flashed and then, "Sure. Any day after 10."

She tapped her momma's house number. "Hey, Momma, you wanna go have breakfast tomorrow and then ride out to a farm to see the animals and stuff?"

There was a long silence. "Momma, can you hear me?"

"Yes, you don't need to shout."

Anna May took a deep breath. "Right, of course, so do you want to go?"

"How about you come around by nine?"

"Sure, you need me to bring anything?"

"No, just come on."

Anna May hung up and went back to her notes. Did she even know when Momma started working at the mill?

Chapter Twenty-three

The next morning, after a gravy biscuit from Hardee's and several follow-up antacids, Anna May drove her mother out to the Busy Beavers farm.

Mrs. Walker clapped her hands. "What a clever name. Farmers are always busy. Like beavers."

Anna May looked sideways. Who was this woman and what had she done with her mother? "I'm fat as a tick, so I hope we don't have to walk far."

"It's good for you." Her mother waved. "Did you see the llama? He's smiling at us."

Anna May hadn't even noticed the llama. Maybe it was new. Before she could get the car in park, Gloria had the side-by-side next to her car.

"Hey, Mrs. Walker. How're you? Do you remember my grandpa Jackson Paul? He used to work with Ellison. Rest his soul."

"Please, call me Daisy. Of course, we used to get seeds from Jack. My father always had a big vegetable garden. He wasn't much of a church man, but he had a certain spirituality working with the earth. Ashes to ashes, circle of life kind of thing." She adjusted her house dress, blue with tiny white flowers matched to tan running shoes. "I didn't want to ruin my good clothes."

Anna May just watched the conversation, then followed the women to the side-by-side and sat in the back.

Gloria buckled in the frail woman. "I guess I'll be driving Miss Daisy."

"Like the movie. You are so clever." She smiled into the breeze as the cart rolled along.

Anna May envied the easy way Gloria chatted with her mother. She realized she was pouting like a child and instead should be taking notes. "I didn't realize you had a llama."

"I don't, really. He's the neighbor's but hops fences, and I don't mind him helping Luna guard the goats."

Mrs. Walker asked, "What's his name? He smiled at us when we came in."

"He did? He's a charmer. It's the darndest thing. Every day at three, he runs up to the fence when the school bus passes. The driver stops, and all the children wave to him. It's really sweet. Anyway, don't groan, his name is Tony."

Anna May put a hand to her forehead, but her mother cackled.

"Tony Llama."

Gloria patted the woman's hand. "I'm glad you came out to the farm. You are a sweet thing."

Anna May smiled with honest joy. It was true. Her mom surprised her, but it shouldn't.

Her mother said, "The apple didn't fall far from the tree."

Was she nudging them together? Maybe I heard her wrong. Gloria turned her head and winked at her. Nope. Anna May grinned. This was a great idea.

Gloria said, "I still follow the rule to not plant until after Good Friday."

"It seems contrary with the date changing every year, but I swear it works. I haven't had any flowers frosted in decades," Momma agreed. "Do you use the goat manure for fertilizer?"

"Yes, they have three stomachs, so the seeds they eat don't germinate. We actually let them loose in the pasture to help eat down any remaining plants, and they poop everywhere."

"Any time my father planted a tree or a bush, he always put a fish in the hole. I haven't kept that tradition up, but I regret not spending more time in the garden with him. Now, my husband, we couldn't even plant petunias together. He did the garden. I did the canning."

Anna May thought of her hours picking weeds for her family garden, resenting every minute until her row was done and she could ride her bike down to the creek. Traveling for work, she'd never even had house plants. She listened as the women chatted about assorted planting techniques until they pulled up by the hives.

Momma said, "My grandfather had a few hives on the farm. Can we see up close?"

"Sure, as long as we move slow. Let me get you a bonnet." Gloria rummaged in a shed and came out with two wide-brimmed netted hats. "Here you go, ladies."

Anna May asked, "Aren't you wearing one?"

"I usually don't unless I'm moving frames around. I get stung once in a while, but it's supposed to be good for arthritis."

Anna May tugged the string tight on the mesh. "I hadn't heard that."

Momma carefully set the hat on her curly hair. "Maybe that's another topic for your writing."

"Good idea." Anna May stayed ten feet away

from the hives.

Momma did not. She stuck to Gloria's elbow as she lit a smoker.

Gloria said, "This is in case they get grumpy."

Momma nodded. "Pine needles. Good use of natural materials."

"They sell pellets and that, but I use whatever is around. Some things are supposed to help with various parasites, but I'm not too sure about that."

Anna May yelled, "Do you use something to treat the hives?"

Momma put a finger toward her mouth.

Gloria answered, "Just when they need it. Of course, not for hives with honey I'll harvest. I have a whole calendar."

Anna May wished she had brought her notebook. She typed furiously with both thumbs to make comments in her phone.

Gloria lifted the hive lid and set it against the rack holding several hives. "Let me lift a frame so you can see." With practiced hands, she nudged the wooden bars apart and lifted them. Bees covered the entire surface.

Momma peered closely. "Some of them's different colors."

"Yes," Gloria explained. "Some are pollen from different plants, some are honey, and some aren't capped yet. See the honey dripping out a bit?"

"Well, I'll be a monkey's uncle. They are fascinating."

"I don't want to upset the girls, so how about I get you some honey from the shop? Would you rather comb or a jar?" She lowered the frame back into place and returned the lid. "Or you can have both."

Momma's eyes blazed with excitement. "I do love to chew comb. We didn't have gum or anything, so when I was young, that's what we'd chew on."

Anna May waited until the women were closer. "Momma, I didn't know that. I guess I'll need to interview you again for the next story."

Gloria accepted the veiled hats and put them back into the shed.

"You might ought to talk to Gloria again, I'm sure."

"I'm sure I will."

"Good. You've been happier since you two have patched up."

Anna May climbed into the cart. "Why do you think we patched up?"

"You two were thick as thieves, and then you weren't. I didn't have to ask, I really didn't want to say it out loud. But mothers know things."

Anna May opened her mouth and then shut it when Gloria approached.

"You two talking about me?"

Momma giggled. "All good things. What's next?"

Gloria drove between the gardens to the shady fruit trees. "I'm afraid there's not much left except apples."

"Ellison and I brought a few bushels from North Carolina a few weeks ago. I was putting up applesauce when..." Her voice caught. She pulled a handkerchief from a pocket and dabbed at her eyes.

Gloria patted the woman's hand. "I love a dress with pockets."

Anna May wiped a finger over her cheeks. Bubba said he had collapsed at home, but she'd neglected to ask the details.

"He was a good man, rest his soul." Gloria turned the wheel. "Do you like mushrooms?"

Daisy brightened. "Yes. Ellis used to go with his cousin and pick them. I was always afraid they'd get something poisonous and kill us all, so I put a silver dollar in the water to make sure."

"You are kidding me." Anna May grabbed the handle as they went around a corner.

"Nope. It never turned it black, and we never died from the mushrooms." Daisy folded her hands. "Obviously."

Gloria snickered. "Do you like shiitakes and oysters? I have a good crop, and we can pick them right off the logs."

Anna May breathed in the damp air of the woods, glad for the shade.

Her mother unbuckled herself. "Give me a hand?"

Anna May offered an elbow, and they ambled toward the sections of wood laying in a row against a low rail, her mother's tiny hand tight against her. At that moment, she said, "I like spending time together."

Her mother stepped carefully over a rut. "Me too. Now tell me what kind of oyster grows on a log."

Anna May whispered, "It's a kind of mushroom."

Daisy said, "Well, that's a relief. I don't like seafood."

If Gloria heard them, her expression didn't change.

Finally, back in the car, Momma's honey and mushrooms, along with a small bag of apples, were situated in the trunk.

She said, "How about we stop at the Piggly Wiggly? We can make soup."

It was nearly ninety-eight degrees out, and the

woman wanted to make soup.

Anna May exhaled. "Sure, Momma."

❧❧❧❧❧

In the morning, Gloria drove to the orchard with empty bushel baskets. She had filled several, the birds singing to her as she worked. That Mrs. Walker was a hoot. If she wasn't trying to get them together, she'd eat her hat.

Gloria jumped at the shrill tone. It could be some sort of Amber Alert for a missing child, or a Silver Alert for a wandering senior citizen. Maybe Jasmine would set up a tracker on Gloria's phone if she started to get lost. She could have one now and wouldn't know it. She rubbed her hands across her pants and then fished the phone out of her pocket. It was a weather alert. Hurricane Michael had gained some strength but was stalled over the Atlantic. The weatherperson predicted a category two when it reached the outer banks of Georgia before rounding up toward the Carolinas. It would likely completely miss the upstate, other than a few rain bands. It hardly seemed urgent news. She crammed the phone back into her pocket and went back to picking apples.

Chapter Twenty-four

O peration Stinger was a success. Not only would Gloria get her bees back, but Jimmy also paid her to do it. At the gas station, Gloria put on her full bee suit to make the rescue more dramatic. The cash deposit for the job tucked in her pocket, she zipped the front and adjusted the Velcro straps around her ankles. It took a few more days than she thought it might for her to get the call. The other beekeepers in the area didn't do extractions. Jimmy paced near the front door, the sweat darkening his blond crewcut. The sheriff watched as she lit her smoker.

He said, "I do appreciate you coming on so quick. I know y'all don't get on."

"You're correct. But his money is still green."

He adjusted his hat. "He squeezes a quarter so tight the eagle screams. But he says he's allergic. He's been having a fit since I got here."

Gloria flicked the lighter and then pumped the bellows on the small metal canister. "I'm happy to try and help. I've gotten bees out of the darndest places. He must have had something sweet to draw them in."

"I reckon so. Jimmy had loaded trash to go to the dump. He says they swarmed at him when he opened the truck door, so he slammed it. I don't know how big the nest might be."

"Don't worry. I'll take care of it." Gloria picked up a catch box and marched to the truck. Both men stayed twenty feet away as she worked. First, she eased the door open a crack and sprayed in some smoke, the ammonia scent heavy. Normally, she used pine needles, but she added a bit of red oak, and this smoke stunk to high heaven. She waited a few moments, then pulled back the handle enough to set the box on the floor. She watched through the glass as the first bees began to explore.

She straightened and called over, "I'll leave this while I look for the nest."

Using a Maglite, she made a show of searching the entire truck, moving from back to front. Under the hood, she exclaimed, "Well, don't that beat all." She called to the men. "The little buggers settled right next to the air filter. Jimmy, you don't mind if I just take the cover and all. I'll bring it back once I get it cleared off."

Jimmy shook his head. "No problem. Just get rid of the damn bees."

The sheriff nodded. "You're lucky they ain't hornets. Those little bastards keep biting."

He threw up his hands. "Don't even say that."

Gloria carried the plastic tote as she walked past them. "I think I got them all. I'd like to leave a lure box in that tree, in case they have some scouts out."

The sheriff looked at Jimmy and said, "Of course. I appreciate you, Gloria. Thank you."

She unzipped the hood and dropped it back, droplets of sweat beading on her forehead. "If you don't mind, I'll just move along."

In her rearview mirror, she saw the men studying the truck for any signs of remaining intruders. With a laugh, she cranked up the radio.

☙ ❧ ☙ ❧

Back home in her recliner, Gloria watched from across the room as Jasmine tapped away on her phone screen. "I hope you're not on Tinder."

"Maybe you should be, but no, this is Instagram." Jasmine furrowed her eyebrows. "Remember Kendra? She's getting married. We are too young for that."

"I'm glad to hear it." Gloria folded the shirt from the laundry basket at her feet. "You won't find your tribe around here."

"You can't say tribe. It offends Native Americans."

Gloria exhaled. "I do apologize. I've been trying to check my white privilege ever since I started to date Collette, and I'm still screwing it up."

"When you know better, you do better."

"Still, let me try again. You won't find your clan around here."

"Nice. Your pasty white Irish ass is probably mostly Irish."

Gloria cleared her throat. "Language. And although you are correct, the sentiment is the same. You won't find much for engineering projects around here."

"No kidding. All the managers are old white guys. I couldn't even get an internship."

Gloria picked up two matching socks. "You know you have to go back to school."

"There aren't that many women in engineering anywhere, Mom."

"Not that many is still more than zero."

"True." Jasmine went back to her phone. "Maybe you're right."

"I am right."

⁂

At five minutes to ten Thursday morning, Anna May waited outside the door to Pastor Carter's office, the scent of fresh flowers like a funeral home. A clock chimed. She twisted a lock of hair over her ear. Through the tinted window, his figure grew larger until the door eased open.

"Why, bless me if it isn't that skinny champion stone skipper grown into a woman of the world. Come in, come in." He reached for her hands and squeezed them. His cheek dimpled on one side when he smiled, his eyes bright under white eyebrows. There was just a hint of a spicy cologne.

She gently tightened her fingers over his gnarled digits. "Rev. Carter, thank you so much for taking time to see me."

"Certainly. I try to keep up with the hooligans that try to take my son off the path of righteousness." His laugh was deep and joyful.

Anna May settled into the upholstered chair opposite his desk, the room claustrophobic with floor-to-ceiling bookcases jammed with texts and memorabilia. "Do you mind if I take some notes?"

He shook his head and nudged a bowl of candies toward her.

"Let me get right to the point. I'm researching the death of my maternal uncle."

"Dink died?"

"Oh, no, my momma's oldest brother Tillus. He died when she was young. I think it had something to do with the mill, but I'd like to get your opinion."

"How old do you think I am, Miss Walker?"

She could feel the burn on her cheeks. "I thought maybe you'd know the stories."

He laid his hands flat on his desk. "As a matter of fact, I am quite familiar with many rumors around our town. Some have nuggets of truth, some, well, let's just say people have fantastic imaginations."

He reached for a picture behind him. A group of men stood on a loading dock, huge bales of cotton behind them. "This man here, second from the right, is my father. Like the other black men, he worked moving heavy loads for twelve hours a day. Back in those days, they were invisible to the white people running the place, so sometimes, things were said in front of them that maybe should have stayed private."

Anna May clicked her pen and scribbled notes about the image with the massive stacks.

"We lived not two blocks from where we sit right now. Seven of us kids. The boys in one room, the girls in another, and my folks in the back. We didn't have a living room or anything, but we had electricity. My grandparents in the country didn't get power until I was in middle school."

Anna May knew the answer already but asked anyway. "You couldn't move to the mill village?"

"Of course not, they wouldn't rent to us. It was like a two-dollar-an-hour benefit to the white folks."

"That's not fair," Anna May blurted.

His face showed no emotion. "What could they do? You took the job or you didn't."

"It was still bull...crap. Did all your family work at the mill?"

"Oh, no, most of them was working the farm. I liked living in town. There were lots of kids to play with, and they had big block parties all the time. The men would all stand around cooking a big hog. That's when we heard all the best stories." He winked.

"I digress. One time my uncle Hep was saying they should unionize like his brother-in-law who'd moved to Detroit. My father talked about Tillus and how the old man Buchanan had him run off the road. And you know they'd do worse to black men." He paused and closed his eyes.

"I'm sorry, so did Tillus die at the mill or in his car?"

"Yes." He stopped and unwrapped a candy and popped it in his mouth. He chewed for a moment and said, "I heard it both ways. For sure, he was beaten at the loading dock. Late at night. Then either he was run off the road, or they smashed his car and left him in it."

Anna May said, "The newspaper said they found him in the morning, and he'd been dead awhile. They assumed he crashed the night before."

"Who's to say the truth? All of 'em's dead that know. It was a terrible thing. Of course, many terrible things happened around here. Still do sometimes."

Anna May asked, "Why didn't your family move north?"

"No matter where you go, there you are. Daddy said lifting boxes all day the same all over."

"And so is hate." She scribbled a note to investigate current union membership statistics. "The workers at Buchanan never tried again to create a union?"

"After the workers were shot in Honea Path, not many were willing to risk it."

"Wait." She stopped writing. "What?"

"It was back during the Depression. They had a big strike. The governor wouldn't send in the National Guard, so the owner put armed men all around the plant, and they killed about a dozen people in the crowd as they picketed. I'm not sure of the details."

Anna May said, "I'll look into it."

"Funny how we get taught history, and so much is left out."

"Whoever tells the story gets to edit."

He leaned back in his chair. "And picks what stories to tell. They're trying to take all the Klan stuff out of the high school classes. Erasing the past in the books don't mean it didn't happen."

Anna May added to her jottings. "Do you think I can ever get to the bottom of the story of Uncle Tillus?"

"I don't expect you can. Witnesses are dead, and I doubt anyone put anything down."

"It's a story I could tell."

"Be careful, some of the descendants are not going to be too keen about it."

"You mean like they'd be embarrassed?"

"No, more like they don't want anything bad said about their kin. And I note with some irony, they might continue the violence to hide the past violence."

The image of Jimmy in his truck popped into her mind. "I suspect you're right." She thought about her uncle, his knuckles white on the steering wheel, racing for his life. That was if he did. How likely was it that they faked a crash? The way Buchanan ran the town, anything was possible, even probable. She chewed on her pen.

He said, "I hope that I'm not being forward, but it does seem that there's something else on your mind."

"Um, not really. It just seems unfair, the things people get away with." She dared not ask how a higher power would allow that. She didn't have the fortitude for a long discussion on the omnipotence or impotence of God.

"Ah. It's a question people of faith struggle with

often. One day, we will understand, but for now? We try to ease the suffering around us, and if I might add, try to not create more pain for others. In this case, I might say to leave a sleeping dog lie."

"You don't think I should write about Uncle Tillus?"

"I wouldn't go that far. You might could angle it more on the efforts to unionize and not so much why it failed in the South. People still think union is a dirty word."

"Yeah, working only five days a week is horrible." She smiled. "How about we ring Damion and meet him for lunch?"

He patted his stomach. "I can taste Yetty's pie already."

Anna May looked at the time on her phone. She had plenty of time to talk for hours and catch a nap before she went to Gloria's place for dinner. She might not need the rest, but she hoped she did.

Chapter Twenty-five

Anna May turned off the engine and took a deep breath. The butterflies in her stomach caught her by surprise. She'd dated plenty of women. This shouldn't be any different. Somehow, it mattered more. She had to get it right. She checked herself in the mirror and then got out.

Gloria watched at the front door, the fading light casting a warm glow over her face. She raised her arm and yelled, "Glad you made it before dark."

It was an odd expression if she thought about it, but Anna May did not. After all, electric lights had been in use here for almost a century. Cars all had blinding LED headlights these days, you could land an airplane in the beams they cast down the road.

For the first time, Anna May appreciated Gloria for the woman she'd become rather than the older version of the girl she'd loved all those years ago. Flowers in hand, she climbed the steps. The scent wafting from Gloria was different than her usual. Spicier, more alluring. Her earrings glinted in the porch light, matching the sparkle in her eyes. Anna May brushed her lips against her cheek in greeting, a tingle trailing down her arms. Gloria stepped back into the living room, and Anna May followed.

Several scented candles flickered across the mantel, the air still too hot for a fire. The tempting aroma of bread pulled her toward the kitchen. Through the doorway, she could see the table was already set.

She handed Gloria the flowers. "I know you have fields full of them, but these are for you."

Gloria flushed. "Let's get these in some water. They're beautiful."

Anna May bubbled with pleasure. At the kitchen counter, she turned the bottle of wine, a local company. "Shall I?"

"Please. I hope this doesn't suck. I haven't tried their pinks yet."

Did she really say pinks? Not blush or rosé? The country mouse. Am I too much of a city mouse to step back into rural life? Step back. There's my answer. Backward. Yet Gloria occupied most of her waking thoughts and all her dreams, sometimes hot and steamy. The cork distracted her, stubbornly keeping watch over the liquid. With a firm jerk, it relented, and a soft pop echoed in the room. She set the bottle on the counter to breathe.

Gloria put on oven mitts. "Have a seat. I'll just pull this out of the oven."

Anna May smiled as the glass pan with the chicken and rice casserole appeared. Is she trying to remind me of home, or is this just her favorite?

Gloria poured the wine. "I'm not sure who to even ask in this town what would go with this. You know Baptists never recognize each other in the liquor store."

Gloria's giggle was the same, soft, melodious, infectious. Again, Anna May was smitten. Now what? Don't screw it up. That's what.

Anna May scooped the steaming casserole from the pan onto both plates. "Remember that bottle of... what was it? Tickled Pink?"

"Oh, my God, yes. We both had bed spins, and

you threw up the next morning."

"I'm afraid I have learned to hold my liquor like a pro."

Gloria's eyes questioned her, but she didn't ask. "I have tea."

"No, it's fine. I know when to stop." Anna May twisted her fork absently. It was more or less true. She changed the subject. "The years have been kind to you."

Gloria laughed, her head rocking back. "Oh, you are a silver-tongued fox, Anna May." She held up her arm. "This skin is slap worn out from years in the sun, and I've got more scars from wire and ornery critters than I can count."

"That may be true, but that smile hasn't changed one bit." Anna May shifted. "I really am sorry we didn't stay close."

"If you stayed, we'd have found another reason to move apart. Maybe a less dramatic one."

"Maybe less painful."

"Yes." Gloria took a gulp of her wine. "But that which does not kill us, or something like that."

Anna May choked at the pain in Gloria's voice. She'd said it was long forgiven, yet the sting was still here. She whispered, "I'm afraid to even ask if I get a second chance."

Gloria looked her in the eye. "A second chance to what?"

Anna May wavered. It was time for full disclosure, yet she couldn't say that thought of nothing but spending time with her. It sounded ridiculous considering their past. Yet here they were. "You know, be friends."

Gloria leaned back. "We are friends."

"We were friends. You know who I was, not who

I am." Anna May stood abruptly. "Who am I kidding? This would never work out."

Gloria rushed to her side. "Why do you have to think about the future so much you miss what's happening right now?"

"What is happening?" Anna May was afraid to hope.

Gloria put her hand to her neck, her fingers touching the gold chain with a small charm. "What do you want to happen?"

Anna May needed no more encouragement. She reached for her hand, urging her up. She stepped close, their breath mingling together as they stood inches apart. She could stare into those eyes forever, like a galaxy of details to explore.

Anna May stretched her fingers out under Gloria's chin, lifting it up slightly, and then said, "This." The kiss started soft, like a summer breeze at dusk. Hinting more could follow but not promising. Anna May tightened her grip, pushing her pelvis against Gloria's thigh. Gloria responded, her mouth hot and demanding. Anna May let her hands wander, the soft cotton shirt unable to contain the firm nipple as she rubbed Gloria's breast.

In a husky, breathy voice, Gloria said, "Do you want to get more comfortable?"

"If you mean naked, yes."

❧❧❧❧

In the bedroom, Anna May wore just her underpants and socks as she stood locked into the striptease before her. She swallowed, her palms sweaty. One by one, Gloria unbuttoned her shirt, and Anna

May studied the skin as it came into view, appreciative of the lack of a bra as the salmon nipples of the large breasts appeared. The shirt dropped, and Gloria pulled her into a tight hug. The coolness of her skin surprised her. Like the story in her mind, Gloria took the lead, and Anna May was a willing follower. Except this time, Gloria had glorious breasts to push against, and Anna May's muscles twitched with the knowledge of what was to come. Would Gloria let the roles change? Did she want them to?

She sat on the bed and pulled Gloria close. She consumed the left breast with her mouth while her hand cupped the other, her thumb roaming over the nipple. Gloria rocked into the movements, her thighs pressing against Anna May's knees, nudging her legs apart. With a light push, Anna May dropped back, and Gloria lay against her, their bodies grinding together in the familiar dance, only this time, they knew each part to touch and how, not from instinct but years of practice.

Gloria licked her ear before she whispered, "You're still overdressed, and we need to move up or my back will start to spasm."

"You are so sexy, but I hoped to make somewhere else cramp with pleasure."

Gloria opened a drawer and with two fingers unscrewed a bottle. "Roll over."

Anna May quickly rolled on her belly. The oil was warm and got warmer as Gloria stroked across her shoulders. A moan slipped from her lips. Anna May mumbled, "Oh, God."

Gloria rubbed evenly across her spine. "You aren't much of a holdout. You sure you don't want me to stop?" Her hand slid over her butt, teasing into the cleft and out.

Anna May tried to pull her leg over to give access and instead found herself turning into Gloria's body as she moved against her. "Hang on."

Anna May lifted her head to see Gloria pour out more oil. "What is that stuff?"

"Magic juice to make sure everything is, well, slippery." Gloria slathered the oil between her legs, and Anna May shuddered.

Gloria bit at her neck, the nip stinging but then not. Her pelvis rocked up with Gloria's movements, and her eyes closed when the steady motion brought her closer. Closer. She forced her eyes open to look at Gloria's beautiful eyes when the release started, her muscles tight and straining.

Gloria shifted and rubbed her pelvis against Anna May's thigh. Anna May pressed up as she hugged Gloria, surprised as the sounds of her partner's pleasure pushed her again over the waterfall. Holding her tight, the scent of her sweat was sweet and sexy. The ceiling fan whirled above them, a steady clicking inducing her to sleep.

𑁤 𑁤 𑁤 𑁤

Gloria took a deep breath, then blew it out. The moment took her away, but now her nerves kept her awake. They were old enough to be grandparents. Her adolescent image of a sexless old age was naïve and incorrect. She studied Anna May's face, still spotted with freckles across her cheeks. Along her scalp, gray hair peeked from under the hair dye. With her short style, she must spend a fortune on coloring. It was mottled, not white. It would be stunning if Anna May let it show.

Anna May shifted in her sleep, still a snuggler, moving closer. The heat from her body was like sleeping by a bear. Sex was supposed to help you sleep. The insomnia was winning. The CPAP was just in the drawer, but Gloria knew waking up to Darth Vader wouldn't help convince Anna May this was worth further exploration. This what? Relationship? It was a booty call. For all she knew, Anna May would be gone by tomorrow night. The snore rising next to her eliminated any chance to sleep. That woman didn't saw logs, she cleared brush.

Maybe they needed matching hers and hers CPAP machines. How sexy. She considered the shape of her own arm, the muscles strong but the skin still turned lax. Her fingers already twisted; the arthritis held at bay with ibuprofen would surely claim other joints. It's Anna May's own fault she missed the chance to see me in my prime.

Her throat tightened. Collette was the love of her life, and here she lay with another woman in their room. In the dark, silent tears rolled into her ears as she watched another chapter of her life with Collette change forever. There could be a chance for love again, but her life was forever separated into two halves. The time with Collette and the time after she died. Somewhere in her dark thoughts, the glimmer of a life not over pulled her into slumber.

Chapter Twenty-six

Anna May opened her eyes and felt the weight of the arm over her chest, crushing yet comforting. A slit of light came under the blinds, and the urgency of a bathroom trip announced the night was over. After using the toilet, her hand hovered over the handle. Flush and wake her? If the pee didn't rouse Gloria, the water wouldn't. She pulled on her shorts and shirt and shoved her feet into shoes sans socks. She scooted out and touched the door closed. The house was quiet, except for the clock in the living room, a click with each shift in direction of the pendulum.

She stepped lightly across the floor and opened the front door, shuffled out, and eased the screened frame shut. The morning air was still with the bright sun promising another scorcher of a day. She sat on the porch steps, afraid the swing would creak. Putting her elbows on her knees, she leaned forward, resting her head on her hands, the scent of Gloria still on her skin. Anna May was ambivalent about her number of past lovers; should she be embarrassed or proud? She wasn't either. It just was. But with Gloria, it was different. Last night was like finding a forgotten favorite sweatshirt, the fabric soft and warm, the printed image reminding you of happy days gone by. Should you wear it, even with the tiny holes at the wrist, or should you leave it in the drawer?

The goats caught her attention, and she wandered toward the barn. She reached in to pet the dangling ears, and the large dog came to supervise the goings-on. What was her name? Something moon. No, Luna. It was fitting as she was a white dog that stayed up all night. The goat began to explore Anna May's fingers, and she recoiled as the rest of the herd charged the fence. With a move like a gymnast at a pommel horse, Blueberry ran across the paddock and pushed off the back of a black and white goat, flying over the fence. The dog barked at his movements, then took chase. The goat ran in a circle around the yard and veered right for Anna May. The goat rammed her knee and dashed toward the front porch, slipping between the underpinning.

Luna tried to follow, knocking Anna May backward.

"Ahh. Damn it." She caught her balance.

The dog scrambled to the porch, barking the entire way. Luna paused and turned toward Anna May. Her huge mouth opened, the pink tongue hung down, spit flying as she ran straight to Anna May.

Startled, Anna May jerked into motion, sprinting to the nearest truck. With a grunt, she stepped onto the bumper and dragged herself up, using the tailgate as a grab bar. The roll into the truck bed was in slow motion. Shoulder. Hip. Elbow. Knee. Landing on the hard grooves, she was relieved to find it empty and not full of sharp tools or barbed wire or something else deadly. She rolled to her back a little dazed.

She stared up at the sky, soft blue with streaks of white. How long has it been since I noticed clouds? She slid up onto her elbows, then sat. This could have been my life. My family. Would I have been happy here? Her melancholy thoughts disappeared as a thunderous woof echoed in the truck. Two paws hit the side rail, and a black nose followed.

Anna May screamed, certain the beast was going to maul her in the truck. She slid to the other side near the back window. It was the only option. Stepping on the toolbox, she stretched over the roof and pulled up. She slipped and landed hard on her ankle. The instant burning indicated the injury was more than a simple bruise. This seemed easier a few years ago. Wait. A few decades ago. A close bark urged her to move. She took a deep breath and jumped. She lay flat on her stomach; the metal was hot, but at least she was safe. Her foot swelled in her shoe. Damn it. The dog hung on the truck rail and stared at her.

Laughter cascaded from the front porch. "Anna May? What are you doing?"

Anna May turned her head. She fought to sit upright without touching her foot to the roof. If Gloria had any doubts that she didn't belong here, they were cemented now. "Um, well, the dog."

"Luna, come." The dog dropped to all fours, its tail wagging, and ambled toward Gloria. "What happened?"

"I was petting the goats, and I saw how Blueberry is getting out. He's under the front porch right now."

"Are you okay?"

"I think so." Anna May slid to the edge, extended her leg to reach the toolbox, and yelped. "Maybe I tweaked my ankle."

With a spryness Anna May envied, Gloria popped into the bed of the truck. She offered both hands. "Easy."

Anna May fell off the roof into Gloria and her outstretched arms. She gasped. "Yes. My ankle is definitely twisted."

"Can you walk on it? I can get the side-by-side. Hang on." Gloria stepped out of the truck and disappeared into the barn.

Balancing herself with a hand on the roof, Anna May stood on her good foot. The dog barked again, her tail wagging. "Sure, now act all friendly."

The high-pitched engine announced the arrival of her knight in shining armor. Or at least her rescuer in coveralls. Anna May shuffled toward the tailgate, clinging to the side of the truck rail.

Gloria unlatched the tailgate. "If you just sit here, I can help you down."

Anna May squatted, her knees cracking their displeasure. Strong hands grabbed her, and she was swung up onto a shoulder. Before she could protest, she was already seated on a bench. "Wow."

"Lots of bales of hay." Gloria studied the foot. "I think at least some ice is in order."

Blueberry poked his nose out. Gloria shook a painted can with corn in it, and the goat dashed toward the cart.

Anna May drew back. "Is he going to jump on me?"

"I hope not." Gloria strode to the gate, flicked out the corn, and opened the latch. When Blueberry reached the fence, Gloria opened the gate a bit, and the goat raced after the corn. "All right. Let's take a look at that ankle."

❧❧❧❧

Gloria deposited Anna May onto the couch and gave her a pillow for her leg.

She said, "You sit tight, and I'll get an ice pack."

The sight of Anna May sprawled on the roof of the truck was hilarious, but since she'd gotten hurt, Gloria tried not to laugh. In the kitchen, she packed ice into a plastic bag. She grabbed a towel and a bottle of Motrin. This is a fine morning after. Silly goat. As she meandered, she called out, "You should take off your shoe, it'll swell up either way."

Anna May pulled at the laces. "You seem quite versed in this procedure."

"Lots of bumps and bruises on a farm. And a Girl Scout is always prepared." Gloria helped slide off the shoe, her hands touching the swollen foot.

Anna May twisted. "I'm ticklish."

"I remember." She situated the towel and ice. "Twenty minutes."

Anna May set a timer on her phone. "Now what?"

"Well, are you hungry? I can make grits or sausage gravy. You want eggs?"

"Pancakes? They don't have those at Waffle House. And a coffee would be awesome."

"Um, I don't drink coffee, but I have some in little bags. It might not suck too much."

Anna May groaned. "Damn, this ankle hurts. I will admit to my coffee addiction. Yes, whatever you have is great. Thank you."

Gloria put on the kettle and began to fix breakfast. What the hell am I doing? Why shouldn't I? It's not like she was some stranger in a bar and we hooked up for the night. This may have been just one night. She flipped the pancakes, the batter sizzling when it hit the pan.

Jasmine appeared behind her. "I'll finish." She took the spatula from Gloria. "Is this what not dating looks like? Or did her fancy car not start?"

"No. I mean, yes, it would start." Gloria set out a tray and took out plates. The kettle whistled, and she poured water over the instant coffee bag. "Come eat with us."

"I don't want to interrupt."

"Just old friends catching up."

"Sounded like more than chitchat last night. But okay."

Gloria flipped her hair back over her shoulder. "I'm sure I have no idea what you mean." She could feel the heat on her face.

As they came in, Anna May said, "Whatever you have smells great."

Jasmine answered, "Blueberry pancakes in honor of our escape artist and maple sausage."

Gloria sat on the chair nearest the couch. "Anna May says she knows how he's getting out."

"Really?" Jasmine sat on the chair opposite the couch, her gaze flicking between Anna May and her mother.

Anna May said, "Yeah, he's jumping on the back of another goat."

"That little stinker." Gloria offered Anna May syrup. "I'm not sure how we'll break that other than a hotline for a while."

Jasmine agreed. "I'll run it this afternoon."

After they finished breakfast, Gloria asked, "Do you want me to take you to the hospital?"

"No need to go that far. I'm sure it'll be fine." Anna May tried to put weight on her ankle and winced. "Okay, I think it's not fine but not hospital-worthy, either."

Jasmine stood. "I'll get the medical kit from the barn. Mom will get you all patched up. I still have the crutches upstairs from when I sprained my knee in volleyball."

"I'm sorry to be so much trouble." Anna May pressed her lips together.

Gloria reached over. "No worries. Could have happened to anyone." She tried to hide the laugh, but she snorted. "How did you end up on the roof of the truck?"

"I woke up early, I thought I'd take a little walk. The dog chased me."

"Luna's a big old teddy bear. But I am sorry you got hurt." Gloria paused. At this rate, Anna May would never come back to the farm.

"I'll be fine. No worse for the wear."

"All evidence to the contrary. I do apologize for Luna scaring you. Life is a little crazy around here sometimes." Suddenly aware her hand was still on Anna May's knee, Gloria looked her in the eye, hoping she'd get the message she couldn't quite articulate.

Anna May shifted. "It's been an adventure, that's for sure."

Gloria forced a smile. Been. Past tense. There was no way Anna May was going to consider anything more than last night. Rather than leaving her satiated, it left her longing for even more contact.

Jasmine brought in the toolbox full of vet supplies. Gloria thanked her, the intimate moment gone. Just like Anna May would be.

❧❧❧❧

After Anna May left, Gloria settled at her desk to update animal records. She had a new software package, and the old computer in the barn was not much more than a fancy typewriter. A colored matrix popped up. There were boxes for birth dates, inoculations, medicine given, illnesses or injuries, offspring, and several rows one could customize. She selected the species from a drop box and listed the names. At Blueberry, the memory of Anna May on crutches led to thoughts about the activities the previous night. Maybe a city girl liked things a little more exciting. She typed into a search box.

Gloria adjusted her glasses and leaned toward the computer monitor. Thank God Jasmine had gotten her a large one. She looked over her shoulder. The only drawback was now anyone within ten feet could also read the text. She scrolled down. There certainly were a lot of websites selling sex toys. Several claimed to be women-owned. She clicked on the one with sapphic in its name, and a woman wearing only garters popped onto the screen. "Wow. The more things change, the more they stay the same."

She heard the footsteps above her and changed the search box to Anna May Walker. The door to the bathroom shut, and she heard the shower start. She changed the browser window back. Without hesitation, she scrolled down the list of items. Clothing. Well, technically, it was clothing. Her eyes bugged at the categories of vibrators, dildos, and all manner of strap-on items. Her breath caught at the bondage gear, and she quickly clicked and landed on a page of flavored lubes and assorted creams.

She was considering organic choices when she heard the door to the bathroom creak and quickly aligned the mouse to the other page and clicked. Soon Google listed everything Anna May Walker. Numerous blogs were interspersed with articles she'd written.

There were images from a fancy award program in D.C. There was no way Anna May would give all that up for a life on a farm.

An image of Anna May in one particular getup popped into her mind. With a sigh, she clicked off the browser window and went back to the animal records.

Chapter Twenty-seven

A nna May fought with the borrowed crutches, finally yanking them from her car. With the determination of a squirrel hunting a nut and the speed of a turtle on dry land, she approached the front steps. She raised both crutches, quickly realizing that wouldn't work. She lifted the bad foot and set it next to the step. With a hop, she put her good foot up and straightened. She brought up the supports and let her body weight sag onto them. Just one more time. She repeated the process and the crutches slid out as she raised up. In slow motion, she fell to the porch, her hands trapped on the handles so she couldn't block her fall. With a thud, she hit the rocking chair.

Anna May lay there for a few moments. The ankle wasn't any worse, but the left side of her face stung.

Behind her, she heard a voice. "You look like you've been through three wars and a goat chasing."

"Yeah, funny you should mention goats." She pulled up onto her knee, tasting the blood from her lip.

Bubba easily lifted her and took her through the door. He lowered her onto the chair. "Hey, Momma, look what the cat dragged in."

Momma put her hand to chest. "My word, what on earth?"

"I tore up my ankle, and I fell just now on the porch."

"I see that. Let me get a rag with some ice."

Anna May settled back and accepted the crutches

from Bubba. "I had better find some bubble wrap."

"You ain't kidding. Isn't your car a stick?"

She nodded. "I drove the whole way here in third. I can't hardly shift."

Bubba sprawled out in Daddy's chair. "Guess you'll be here a bit longer."

"I reckon. I need more time to talk Momma into moving."

"That dog won't hunt. You might as well give up."

She stuck her tongue out at him.

Her mother returned and handed her the cloth. "Did you eat yet? I've got fresh biscuits."

Bubba nodded. "I'd like some. With honey. Anna May, what's on your foot?"

She looked down at the pink camouflage bandage on her ankle. "It's vet wrap. I was at Gloria's when I tripped. It's all she had."

Momma surveyed the foot. "Bruising a bit. I don't think Doc Brown could do much better."

"I suspect not." Anna May took out her cellphone and typed a message to Shoshanna. "Minor accident/ ankle sprained. Delayed."

Bubba smeared honey on a biscuit. "Did y'all see the weather this morning?"

Momma nodded. "Yes. That storm is rolling up the coast. It'll go out to sea by Savannah. Just a little rain here."

"Well, I thought Anna May might want to get home, but with her ankle, you might ought to stay until it blows past."

Anna May said, "When do you think it will hit the coast?"

"Maybe not until next week. Slow mover. They

say it might hit Jacksonville first and roll north."

"If we're lucky," Momma said. "At least we get a little warning nowadays."

Bubba scoffed. "Just a way to sell batteries and bread. You need anything?"

"I don't reckon. Anna May will stay with me if it gets bad."

"Not sure what good she'll be. That eye's about swollen shut."

Anna May touched her face. I'd be better in the nice sturdy brick hotel compared to this rickety house. Bubba was right. Weather people always exaggerated. "I'll be fine in a few days. Hey, Franklin, will you carry me back to the hotel? Momma, you don't mind if I leave my car here a day or two?"

"Of course, he'll take you, and just leave me the keys in case I need to drive to Atlanta or anything."

For just a moment, Anna May pictured her mother screaming down the highway in her car, the gas pedal pressed to the floor. It was a rare joke from the octogenarian. They all laughed. She leaned to her mother. "Just don't get a ticket."

⚘ ⚘ ⚘ ⚘

Back in her hotel room, Anna May rested her foot on a pillow as she stretched out on the bed. She uploaded the file to her boss, a heartwarming and safe summary of the hardships of life in the South before the opportunities of factory work. She highlighted how the owners agreed to a plan of which factory would spin the fibers, weave the cloth, and sew the garments, shipping materials from place to place. She skimmed over the challenges of the workers actually doing that work. There's another story I have to tell. She cracked her knuckles. After she checked a few facts, her fingers danced over the keyboard.

Awalkerblog

My dear readers,

While in my hometown, I discovered a piece of history, a dark saga, a story I'm embarrassed to admit is true. It happened up the road thirty miles from where I grew up, and I had no idea until recently. To honor the victims, I will share the story with you.

In 1934, there was a massacre at the mill in Honea Path, a small town anchored by the mill just like my hometown. Known as Bloody Thursday, seven people died and over thirty were injured when the managers instructed over a hundred recently deputized men to open fire on the striking workers threatening to unionize for fair wages.

The mill had over 650 workers at the time, and to maintain a profit during the Great Depression, the managers of the mills instituted a "stretch out," meaning that workdays were extended without more pay. Most breaks were banned, workers tended a larger number of machines, and they were fired if they could not keep up the pace. Inspired by President Franklin D. Roosevelt, the textile workers across the country held a strike starting on Labor Day, September 3. Eventually, the walkout reached Honea Path, a town where the houses, the schools, and the stores were owned by the mill.

The manager, Dan Beacham, asked the South Carolina governor, Irba Blackwood, to send National Guard troops. Since there hadn't been trouble in Honea

Path before and the troops were needed elsewhere, Blackwood denied the request. Beacham, also the town mayor and judge, arranged for armed men to take up positions inside the building, ostensibly to protect the mill. He had a machine gun from World War I installed on the roof.

On the morning of September 6, Beacham walked through the crowd of 200 protesters into the mill. On the sidewalk, neighbors began to fight with one another, some wrestling on the ground. A shot was fired. Then another. In the end, all those protesters killed had been shot in the back as they fled the scene.

Claude Cannon had been shot five times. Over 10,000 people attended the funeral, forced to be held in an open field as even the churches were owned by the mill.

Beacham blocked efforts into an investigation. Eleven men were charged, all acquitted. The union leaders were fired. The workers had a choice. Return to work or be forced from their homes. Promise to never speak of the shootings and keep your job or go hungry.

This history was covered up for decades until a granite monument was installed in Dogwood Park on Memorial Day in 1995.

Whoever tells the story selects the narrative. I heard nothing of this in school. What secrets do you know of about your town? Post your answers below.

℞℞℞℞

Anna May shut the laptop. With a groan, she hobbled to the minifridge and took out the refrozen bag of ice. After dropping it to loosen the chunks, she settled on the bed, stuck a pillow under her leg, and rested the ice on her ankle. Her thoughts went to Gloria. She picked up her phone and stared at the blank screen. Damn her luck. How could she ask Gloria out? Where would they go? She couldn't even drive. She gripped the phone as it vibrated.

The message read, "Hi. I've been thinking about you. How's the ankle?"

Anna May considered the message. She could just answer that her foot was fine, although it was still swollen and now purplish. She could be coy and ask what she was thinking. Or be direct and admit she'd been thinking about Gloria, as well. Her finger hovered over the dot. Oh, hell, nothing ventured, nothing gained. She typed, "The ankle is sore. Wondered if we could have lunch tomorrow." Shit. That was too direct. Maybe Gloria wasn't interested in anything more from her. What was more?

The little series of dots flickered on. What will she say? The dots stopped. Then they started again. Is it the signal, or is she trying to get the text just right? The dots stopped. No message. What does that mean?

Anna May jumped when the ringer chirped. "Hey."

Gloria's voice cuddled her ear. "I'd rather hear you than read your messages."

If she was in high school, she would have twisted the cord connecting the handset to the phone on the wall. Now she was forced to just pick at the protective plastic case over the slim box. "I'm glad you called." Oh, come on, what is wrong with me? Where are the mad flirting skills?

"I thought, since your ankle is tore up, I should pick you up. Maybe take a drive around the old haunts. I was going to offer a picnic, but it's too hot, and I don't want you to have to hobble."

"I'd like the tour, and I'll spring for lunch. Is the Mexican place any good?"

"Yes, but I thought you might rather have Vera's."

"Excellent idea. There's a great meat and three near the Metro stop for work, but they lack something in the banana pudding."

"No Nilla wafers?"

"You called it." Anna May looked at the ceiling. Think. Come on. "Um, so I'll see you tomorrow."

"I'll see you at eleven."

Anna May tapped the phone. Is that Southern time or actually eleven? She'd be ready early.

Chapter Twenty-eight

As Anna May predicted, Gloria pulled up to the hotel at quarter after eleven, and now they were cruising around town like teenagers, disco music blasting, each holding a frozen Coke. Anna May moved her leg to try to take the pressure off her ankle. This truck was more comfortable than she thought it might be at first glance. It was easy to get in, and the ride was good.

Anna May asked, "So what's the scoop with the stickers? I was kind of surprised to see the Hello Kitty one."

"You think I let the dogs out?" Gloria snickered. "It's weird. People add them all the time."

"That's hilarious."

"Some are better than others. I haven't had any I had to scrape off."

"So the Deadhead sticker?"

"Mine."

Anna May reached to adjust the vent. "Random people just put stuff on your truck?"

"Yeah, and I'm sorry the air isn't that good. Maybe we should have taken your car. Do you have time to go by the river bridge? There's a new mural."

"Sounds good to me." Anna May spotted a rebel flag flapping out the window of a car passing in the other direction. "I don't miss seeing that."

"That was the only good thing about 9/11. All the flags became American stars and stripes. Now hate flags are all over town, thanks to Jimmy Buchanan and his cronies."

"I wouldn't cross the street to pee on him if he was on fire." Anna May shifted her leg.

"Lovely image, Anna May. They're all stirred up over the Confederate statues coming down. As far as I'm concerned, it's about damn time to get rid of them."

"I have to say, I don't really see what the big deal is about a statue. It doesn't bother anybody just standing there."

Gloria snapped her head. "What?"

"I mean, you don't have to look at it."

"It's a remnant from a war that the South lost, I might mention. Over slavery."

Anna May said, "I thought it was over states' rights."

"It was. States' right to own slaves," Glory shouted.

Anna May swirled the ice drink with the straw. "That was a long time ago."

Gloria gave her the stink eye and took a sharp turn. "I got something to show you."

Anna May adjusted the vent again, the sweat beading on her back. *What the hell did I say?* She sensed it was better not to speak.

They turned down a road Anna May didn't remember. *Surely many new roads had been cut in the last thirty years. No, it was forty. When did I get so old?* Gloria pulled onto a gravel patch under a giant oak tree.

She pointed. "See that bridge there?"

"A railroad trestle. Yeah."

"I never knew this until Damion showed me and

Collette, probably twenty years ago. I'd lived here my entire life, and I'd never been back here."

"Me either. It's not like there's a line painted on the road, but we all knew where we shouldn't go."

"Because you were afraid to be in the black neighborhood?"

Anna May paused. "Maybe."

Gloria said, "I appreciate your honesty. Most people don't look very deep into their own actions."

"It seems I have matured a little bit."

"I'd hope so. Look, it's our job to make sure we remember the history." Her voice caught with emotion. "Until a few years ago, you could see a rope knot up there."

Anna May tilted her head to look closer. "A knot?"

"Yes. It was left so that every black person that passed by would remember their place. Just like those fucking statues. The little old white ladies had them put up starting in the nineteen hundreds. They are there for the same reason the knot was. I can't speak for all black people, but for at least one, each time she passes a tribute to the people who enslaved her ancestors, Jasmine is reminded she is not equal in the eyes of many."

"She's half white."

"But people don't respond to her whiteness, they respond to her blackness." Gloria wiped at her eyes. "Don't mistake these for sadness. Oh, no, I could spit tacks."

Anna May whispered, "I never thought about it."

"You didn't have to." Gloria put the truck in gear and did a U-turn. "I consider myself a strong ally, but even I have the choice to stop thinking about race.

Jasmine doesn't have that choice. And that's my white privilege."

"I don't ask people to treat me differently because I'm white."

"You don't have to ask. They just do."

Anna May said, "I have black friends."

"Do you want a sticker?" Gloria took a deep breath. "I'm sorry, but it's something on my mind a lot. They're planning a rally at the courthouse to protest the removal of statues."

"I heard a couple guys talking at breakfast the other day, but I don't know who they were. Who's doing the rally?"

"Really? Who do you think? The Klan, Anna May. And probably some Nazi skinheads. After Charlottesville, I'm a little worried it'll get violent."

Anna May reached for Gloria's hand and caught herself. "Counter-protesting?"

Gloria nodded, then swiveled her head at the stop sign. "We'll outnumber them ten to one, or even a hundred to one, but they carry guns. Tempers could flare."

Anna May leaned back. Would Bubba be there? "When is this?"

"Two weeks."

Anna May thought about this. Momma wasn't showing any signs of being ready to move. "If I'm still in town, I'll go. And stand with you."

Gloria smiled.

Anna May could tell she didn't believe her. Which part? That she would be in town or that she would protest?

Back at the hotel, Gloria turned to her. "Here you go. Safe and sound."

"Thanks for lunch." She leaned and pecked Gloria on the cheek.

Gloria said, "What? You aren't asking me in?"

⁂

Gloria pushed the door closed and slid the lock over the door.

Anna May held her from behind, her hands already exploring.

"Do you have any plans for the afternoon?" Anna May asked.

Gloria turned around and brushed back a wayward lock of Anna May's hair. If they slept together twice, then it wasn't a one-night stand. Maybe this would be it? Not if she could help it. Something about this woman was addictive. With a tug, Gloria pulled her closer. "Oh, let's just see what happens."

Anna May pushed against her, the heat of her thigh against Gloria's leg amplifying the blood pounding in her ears. With no patience for a leisurely approach, Gloria pulled at the top of Anna May's shorts. The soft cotton boi shorts surprised her but delayed her access.

Anna May sat on the bed and grabbed a pillow. "I should prop up my foot."

"I'll be careful." Gloria lay down and traced her hand along the exposed belly, the skin retracting under her touch. Nudging the shorts, she tickled her way down until her fingers slid into the damp skin.

Anna May raised into the motions, her mumblings indiscernible. Gloria nibbled at her earlobe before settling on her neck. The air unit rumbled to life. Anna May twisted and closed her eyes.

Gloria whispered, "That's it."

Anna May yelped.

Gloria stopped. "Did I hurt you?"

"Not directly. My ankle doesn't like this. It's overruled by my clit."

"Glad to hear that." Gloria pinned Anna May's thigh and shifted. The spasm gripped her lumbar region, rendering her motionless. "Oh, damn."

"That was fast."

"No, no, it's my back." She rolled over. "Give me a minute."

Anna May, "Sure. But I'm not finished with you yet."

Gloria giggled. "I hope not."

☙ ☙ ❧ ❧

Anna May pulled at the pillow and leaned back. "Tell me about your time in college. Was it a big party school?"

Gloria traced a finger down Anna May's arm. "Maybe, but I like to say if there weren't pictures, it didn't happen. Trust me, a lot of things happened."

"Were you out?"

"On campus? Shoot yeah. I had a blast. Bar night twice a week and intramural softball on the weekends. But you should know all about that. Damion said you drank him under the table."

"You know dang well a good Baptist boy doesn't drink much."

"What about you? When did you come out on campus?"

Anna May looked up at the ceiling. "Never."

"How did you meet anyone?"

"That wasn't a priority. Trust me. I made up for lost time once I started working in D.C." Instantly, she knew it was a mistake to say that.

Gloria's face was stone, and Anna May wasn't sure if that was good or bad. Anna May cleared her throat. "I mean, yeah, I guess some of the women on the field hockey team were probably gay."

With a snort, Gloria said, "Ya think?"

Anna May could feel the heat in her chest. "I didn't really ask."

"And they didn't tell? Come on."

"I guess this one time I sort of knew. We were at this tournament in Virginia and all piled into one of the hotel rooms. I was lying on a bed with my roommate when these two players from another team staggered by the window. One of them yelled, 'Which ones of you are the lesbians?'"

Gloria sat up. "No one answered?"

"My roommate shoved me right off the bed."

"Ouch."

"It didn't hurt."

"I meant your feelings. Do you think she knew?"

Anna May studied her fingers. "How would she? I don't know. I thought maybe somehow, she knew. Shit. That was a long time ago."

"And none of the other women were out?"

"I guess not. I mean, I didn't hang out with them all the time."

Gloria asked, "Were you afraid to?"

Anna May heard the words echo. "Yes."

After a long pause, Gloria whispered, "You didn't have to be."

"I just was. Okay. I was afraid. There. I said it. Are you happy? I thought if I stayed away from them,

I wouldn't be..."

"Like me."

"Yes. No. I don't mean it like that." Anna May pressed her lips together to try to fight the unexpected tears. "I don't know what's wrong with me. I'm sorry."

Gloria pulled her closer. "I'm sorry you had to deal with all of that alone."

"It was my choice. I couldn't exactly call you."

"Why not?"

"Who was I gonna get your number from?"

"Anna May, that's ridiculous. A damn phonebook. Jeesh. It's not that hard to find the town dyke." Gloria squinted. "You were afraid to talk to me. Not the bullcrap about how you'd wronged me, just be honest with yourself. Me? I don't give a crap what story you want to spin to the world. I see right through it."

Anna May opened her mouth, then closed it. Gloria was right. All this time, she'd convinced herself it was shame. It was not. It was fear. She wiped her eyes and sniffed. "By the time I came out to my family, it had been too long to just call you out of the blue. I saw you around town sometimes. You always looked happy."

"And you weren't?" Gloria took her hand. "Look, we can keep hashing over this until you feel like the air is cleared, but the only thing I'm sorry about was that we couldn't have been friends."

Anna May kissed her cheek. "Funny thing. I actually still talk to my other exes."

"I was the only one you shunned?" Gloria stared into her eyes.

"You were the one that got away." Anna May tried to pull back.

"Seems that you've gotten that twisted around,

too."

Anna May squeezed her hand. "No, I know it was my fault."

"And it seems I might be back on the hook." Gloria kissed her ear. "Now the question is, are you going to reel me in or cut the line?"

Anna May grinned as she reached for Gloria's breast. "Trust me, you're the one in control."

Gloria whispered in her ear, "I like the sound of that."

Chapter Twenty-nine

Waking up alone, Anna May regretted not asking Gloria to spend the night. Instead of feeling contented, she was horny as hell. If she got her car, she could just happen to drive by the farm. She unwrapped her foot, the bruising now a Van Gogh of yellows and greens with a hint of purple. She eased upright. The ankle protested but no stabbing pain. She grabbed her cellphone, scrolled to her brother's number, and tapped.

He answered, and she asked, "Hey, do you have time to run me by Momma's so I can get my car?"

He sighed. "Yeah. In about an hour if you can wait."

"Beggars can't be choosers, and I can't use Uber."

"What's an Uber?"

"It's a ride-share thing. You post where you're going, and if someone can take you, you pay them, and they come pick you up."

"Like a cab?"

Anna May nodded, even though he wouldn't see. She cleared her throat. "Do you know about the rally to keep the Confederate soldier statues?"

"Well, of course. Who do you think set it up? Santa Claus?"

"Gloria mentioned it, and I thought I would go."

After a long pause, he said, "It's still a free country, thanks to people like me."

"I guess you take more after Papaw than Pops."

"What the hell is that supposed to mean?"

"He was a dragon. Right?"

Bubba raised his voice. "They were trying to keep our way of life. And if you got your head out of your ass and looked around, you'd see it's slipping away."

"Do y'all still go around lighting crosses while wearing a hood to hide?"

"We don't wear hoods."

"But you still light crosses."

"Only in a ceremonial way. We are like-minded folks that want to help our community. We do food drives and everything. Look, I don't want to argue. Do you want a ride still or not?"

Anna May said, "Yes."

By the time he arrived, they had both moved past the fight. She still would have rather been able to call a cab; however, it was the Walker way to just bury it and act like no one had been angry just moments before. He might be a racist pig, but at least his truck was easy to get into. It smelled of mint chewing tobacco and Armor All, the cardboard pine tree on the mirror faded and useless. Eighties rock music drowned out the rumble of the diesel engine.

"Thanks for getting me."

"No problem."

Anna May tapped her fingers. They were almost to Momma's. "Hey, look, I heard on the radio that they think the hurricane will hit the coast head-on. Does Momma need anything done?"

"Nope. It'll just be some thunderstorms anyway. The winds will be high. She ain't got anything out that will fly around."

"That's good." Anna May considered a gesture of goodwill. He was her only sibling. "You need any help getting things ready at the campground?"

"You mean you?"

"My ankle is better, and you're my brother." She studied the mill houses as they rolled through the old neighborhood.

He put the truck in park and looked at her with suspicion. "We're waiting to see how the forecast goes today and decide in the morning."

"Let me know."

Bubba pointed to the shiny car, all the tires flat on the ground. "Gee, girl, who'd you piss off?"

Anna May whipped off the seat belt and shoved open the door. She dropped onto her good foot and limped around the BMW. At least they didn't damage the paint.

Bubba poked at the rear tire with his boot.

Anna May threw up her hands. "What the fuck is wrong with people? Goddamn it."

Her mother came out the front door. "Are you all right?"

"No, I'm not. I'm about to lose my religion. Somebody owes me tires." She spotted the paper under the wiper blade. A flyer for the Klan rally. "Fuck Jimmy Buchanan. I'm going to punch him in the nuts."

Momma said, "Could you be more crass? All the neighbors will hear."

Anna May gritted her teeth. Fuck the neighbors. But she had to try. "Sorry, ma'am."

Her mother tottered down the steps to survey the vehicle. "I'm surprised no one saw this."

"Not me. She probably damn helped him." Anna May shot a glance at Mrs. Wilson peering out her front door.

"Stop it," her mother hissed.

"You'd think if he wanted me out of town, he wouldn't be stupid enough to prevent me from leaving. Where am I going to find tires for this car in Chicora Point?"

Bubba shrugged. "I know a guy."

Anna May put her hands on her hips. Of course he did. "And I might have to sell my kidney to pay for them. You don't want me to have to do that. As your sibling, I'm your walking spare parts set."

"I'll make sure you don't get the stranger in town special. I'll have Luther bring 'em here. He does the semi-trucks. He's got all the stuff in his rig," Bubba said.

Her mother asked, "You going to come in or stay with Bubba?"

Anna May limped past her mother into the house. With a pillow, she propped her foot up and settled on the couch. She fought the tears and lost. "Why do I cry when I'm mad? Son of a biscuit maker." She blew her nose.

"I'm sorry about your tires." Momma handed her a tissue. "It ain't right people damaging your car, but you can't pitch a hissy fit in the street like that. Don't give them the satisfaction."

Sometimes, Momma surprised her.

Chapter Thirty

T he weather forecast was still overly dramatic, in Anna May's opinion. Nevertheless, she and Bubba stood in silence under the picnic shelter at his campground. The river tumbled past them, tidily in its banks under the ancient oak trees. Between the rows of RV spots, pine trees rustled in the breeze. The light blue sky was still clear, but that would change.

She asked, "How far up does the river usually go when it floods?"

He spit out a dark splotch of tobacco juice and wiped at his chin. "Usually? It don't usually flood at all. The last time, it just rose to the top of the banks and spilled over the parking lots there."

"How high was the crest?"

"Three feet."

She nodded. The predictions were always exaggerated, sending residents scurrying for supplies like bottled water and flashlights. Those would be of little help if the crest hit eight or ten feet. "I expect the weather forecasters don't know."

He said, "But if they're right, it'll flood to here."

"Dang. I suppose talking ain't getting it done. What shall I start with?" Anna May pulled her new gloves out of her pocket to show she was serious about helping.

"Stacy printed some maps to show people where they can wait it out. Some of those big rigs are pretty tippy in the wind. I hate to send them off, but some people won't know where to go. Most of the tent campers in the back field left already."

"Well, dang, the forecasters don't even know where it will go."

"I'm going to pass them out and recommend that people drive south. About six hours or so. Should be out of the cone of uncertainty." He bit at his lip.

Anna May knew emptying his park during the prime season was a huge loss. "Maybe they can come back next week."

"Maybe." He cleared his throat. "I need to put up the furniture around the pool."

"I can do it."

"Some will fit in the shed, some you can just stack good."

She watched Bubba climb into his side-by-side and pull off. Math wasn't her strong suit, but just based on the slope, in her estimation, eight feet would cover where she stood. She hobbled to the pool gate. The chairs were light, the blue straps contrasting the white aluminum; it was a good idea to put them up. The lounge chairs wouldn't have much weight, even locked together. The umbrellas could all fit in the shed across the rafters if Bubba helped her shove them up there. The tables were metal, so at least they wouldn't break, but as a projectile? She studied the area around her. The wrought iron fencing should keep them in, right? Maybe the river wouldn't flood.

After she finished with the stacking, she went to the camp office where Stacy was working on the computer. "Hey, what can I help you with?"

Stacy looked up. "I'm backing up the files, of course. I'm unplugging everything, so I'm sure it'll be fine. Can you close the shutters? Just in case a branch comes off the trees and blows this way."

Anna May went back outside and peered at the windows. Turning the bottom brackets, she pulled the blue shutters together and swung down the latch. How Bubba managed to get a crowbar in his wallet to pay for these, she didn't know.

Stacy appeared at her side. "Can you help me at the house?"

"Sure."

As they walked, the caravan of RVs moving out represented every imaginable type of portable home: pop-up trailers, a few fifth wheels, a few C classes, and even a couple of those huge A class rigs that looked like a bus. The most common was the tug behind. Bubba and Stacy were losing a small fortune.

Anna May reset the refrigerator to the coldest setting to keep the food cool as long as possible if the power went out. "What else do you need to do at the campground?"

"Bubba will cut off the power at each site and then the master fuse boxes. Then the water mains at the facility building."

"Do you want me to fill a tub with water?" Anna May asked. What else? Nothing came to mind.

"We're on city water, not a well. But maybe just in case a line breaks." Stacy pulled steaks out of the freezer. "Might as well eat this before the power goes out and we lose them."

Anna May felt her stomach knot. "Do you think it's going to make it this far inland?"

Stacy shrugged. "I pray not. The Lord takes care of those who take care of themselves."

Anna May gave her a weak smile.

❧ ❧ ❧ ❧

The hurricane bore down on the beaches, but in Chicora Point, the cloud cover was patchy and the air close to a hundred degrees. A breeze would be welcome; however, not at seventy miles an hour. Anna May pushed her buggy filled with bottled water and assorted crackers and cookies for her and Momma during the storm. She also bought a Keurig for Gloria. Some things she could do without, but coffee wasn't one of them. She paused. The rebel flag and Donald Trump stickers proved that the truck parked inches from her door belonged to Jimmy. With a huff, she grabbed each plastic-wrapped case and arranged them in the trunk.

The cart return was several spots up. Her ankle ached with each step. It might be better if she just left before he came out. She was not going to let the adolescent stunt of parking her in get to her. She unlocked the passenger door. With as much grace as she could muster, she swung her legs over the stick shift and wiggled to the driver's side. She pushed the button and dropped the windows a few inches to let the hottest air out of the car. A lighter color vehicle would be cooler in the summer, but she loved the midnight blue. A squeaky wheel announced a buggy approaching. She rolled up the windows and started to back up.

The mirror came a few inches from his bumper as she turned. She shifted into first and jumped with the bang on her roof. Her hand flew off the knob, and she caught herself before flipping him off.

Jimmy said, "Hey, look where you're going."

She pushed in the clutch as she touched the

window button. The glass slid down. "I was looking, or I would have hit you."

Sweat stained his shirt, and the ring around his ball cap was white, probably from chugging too much beer. "Right, you wouldn't want to tear up your car."

"True. After I had to get new tires and all." She stared evenly at him. "I bet tires are expensive for a big truck like that."

His eyes narrowed. "You really don't want to make me mad."

"What? Are you the Hulk? Gonna turn green? Maybe that's the problem. You're already green. Your grandfather might have owned this town, but his grandson living in a single-wide with three kids isn't exactly my idea of a dream come true."

"You think you're better than us? Fuck you, and you know what? My name means something around here. I won't let the spawn of lintheads besmirch that name."

"Wow. They put vocabulary words on Skoal cans now?"

He leaned down and rested his arm on the window of her car. He was so close she could smell him as he said, "What a shame about that pretty face."

A chill ran down her back. That was a real threat. He rose and turned back to his packages. She resisted the urge to back over him, but he was right. It would damage her car.

Chapter Thirty-one

Early the next morning, Gloria watched the dark car slow and turn in her driveway. Adjusting her hat, she wondered how fast they could get through the list. She scanned down the items on her green plastic clipboard. The Beemer parked near where she stood. Her pulse quickened. Too bad they couldn't have at least a quickie. There was no time for a distraction.

Anna May stepped out of the car wearing new blue jeans and boots. "I'm ready for duty."

Gloria said, "Hey, girl. I was just looking to see what might be good for you."

"You mean for a city slicker, don't you?"

Gloria smiled. "Yes. Jasmine is already putting straps on the beehives. She won't need any help. Are you willing to try to catch chickens? They need ankle bands."

Anna May shuffled. "Um. Sure?"

Gloria tipped her head. Anna May didn't sound sure. "Let's do it together." Inside the barn office, she grabbed a canvas bag, the straps frayed and stained. She walked toward the largest hutch. "If the storms get bad, we'll let the chickens out. They'll be safer in brush and trees than trapped in the wire frames. They'll show back up when we throw out feed, and I'll need to sort the layers from the retired girls in the next pasture. All these hens will get this pink band." She fished in the bag and held up a plastic, colored band. "I'll catch the chicken and hold it up and you snap this on her leg. Easy peasy."

Gloria caught the first chicken, the other hens running and squawking. Anna May looked pale but carefully attached the marker. Gloria smiled. "One down."

"How many are in here?"

"Only a couple dozen. We lose one every once in a while. Here. Let's get Gertie."

"You name them?"

"Not all of them. Certain ones stand out."

Anna May said, "I don't see any difference between Gertie and the other chickens." She fumbled with the clip, sweat pasting her hair to her forehead. "You would have done this faster without me."

Gloria nodded. "But it's more fun with you."

Jasmine approached the hutch, her netted hood hanging behind her shoulders and the bee suit zipped down, a wet streak down the middle of her shirt. "I'm going to start copying the goat records."

"We'll be down in a minute to help chip." Gloria watched Anna May carefully pinch the leg clip. Maybe she could send her to the store for something. Anything.

Anna May asked, "What's chip mean?"

"Microchip. I don't like to use ear bands, and if they get out in the storm, there's a chance we can get them back if we can identify them. Most are already chipped, but I want to make sure."

Walking down to the barn, Anna May reached over to take Gloria's hand. "I'm supposed to meet Bubba at four at Momma's. She wants her porch furniture put in the shed. Only if it looks like it might get bad." The trees swayed with the gusts.

"I think you might ought to do it. You go on when you need to. I appreciate any help you can give us." Gloria squeezed her hand. An afternoon curled together listening to the rain sounded better.

At the barn, Jasmine held the square plastic box, almost like an old-fashioned TV remote. She waved it over a goat, it beeped, and she made some notes on a clipboard. "Hey, so far, so good. Only Daphne needs a chip."

"Do any need shots?" Gloria rummaged in a cabinet.

Jasmine said, "If memory serves, all the babies got the CD&T. Do you want to give them a booster?"

"I don't think we need to. You sure we got the triplets from last month?"

Jasmine flipped some pages. "Yes."

Gloria took out some plastic tags. "Do you think we should use these?"

"Maybe on a necklace. We could write our number on their nails."

Gloria nodded, her eyes tight. "I hope all this is unnecessary. Anna May, how about you make a list of the names to make sure we got them all?"

Jasmine shook a paint pen, the ball rattling. Under her breath, she said, "Momma, honestly. You're just making up stuff for her to do."

"Don't be ugly." Gloria stroked a little tan goat and lifted its hoof. "Anna May, the first one is Quark."

"How do you spell that?"

Jasmine snorted. "Some writer."

"Any way is fine." She nudged Jasmine with her elbow. "Stop it."

Jasmine said, "Anna May, I just remembered, we should have another copy of their records."

꧁꧂꧁꧂

Anna May pictured herself trying to write on a hoof being waved around by an angry goat. The leg bands were bad enough, the little foot waving with dagger-sharp talons. The goats did have horns, but Gloria didn't seem to have any trouble avoiding them.

To her relief, Jasmine said, "Anna May, would you mind going in the office and making copies of these immunization records?" She handed her a thick manila folder held tight with a rubber band. "There's extra paper in the top drawer on the left."

Anna May clutched the package. The office air was cooler but not by much. The rubber band broke as she tried to nudge it off. To her untrained eye, the forms had a dizzying array of letter codes and numbers. Anna May took each page and laid it in the printer/copier combo and waited as the machine sucked in the paper, made grinding noises, and spewed out the page into a second tray. She would then put the original next to the folder and insert another page. The occasional goat scream and human cursing drifted in from the doorway. At least she didn't have to hold a stinky animal. Once the final page had been copied, she put the originals back in the folder and searched for a fresh rubber band.

Gloria's voice startled her. "What are you looking for?"

"I broke the rubber band," Anna May admitted.

Gloria pulled open a cabinet. "Thanks for making the copies." She took a white pickle bucket and dropped in the papers, snapped on the lid, and pulled a marker from the cup on the desk. In neat letters, she wrote the name of the farm and a series of phone numbers. "In case we get separated from the farm for a while, these will help whoever shows up first."

Anna May hesitated to ask who that might be. Some sort of rescue person? Maybe a neighbor? She followed Gloria and watched as she used a bungee to hang the bucket on the nearest post. "What's next?"

Gloria bit at her lip. "We need to load the angoras into a trailer. If I can get a plywood board in between the two stalls, I might try to put the littlest babies in with their mommas." She glanced around the barn. "And Mr. Jackson's colt."

Anna May asked, "Why only some goats?"

"Simple economics. They are worth the most, and I can pull them wherever we end up going when I get home."

"Where are you going now?"

"The food pantry to pick up supplies and then the high school. We're setting up there in case of evacuations and then we'll feed people." She said this with a calm voice, the way you might speak to a child. "You seem pretty nervous. Don't you have hurricanes in D.C.?"

Anna May shrugged. "Yes, but other than wind and rain, it's not like at the ocean towns in Florida or anything."

Gloria squinted. "I hope they're overstating this storm. But don't worry. You're safe here."

Anna May nodded. "Should I bring Momma?"

"To the gym? If you want. Her part of town hasn't ever flooded that I know of. Those houses have stood through a century worth of storms. But she's more than welcome."

It turned out that loading goats was easy. Jasmine

carried a goat she called alternately Lacy and Shithead into the trailer, and Gloria nudged the rest along to join her.

Anna May swung the door shut. "That was easy."

Jasmine stretched her neck. "We aren't done yet. Let me squeeze out."

Anna May watched the goats explore the trailer while Jasmine and Gloria went to get more goats. They both ran up to her with a momma goat in hot pursuit.

Gloria shouted, "Open the gate."

They both leaped up, and the momma followed. Before Anna May could shut the door, an angry goat charged at her. She fell backward, smashing her elbow on the hard ground.

The soft voice caressed her ear. "Are you okay?"

Anna May nodded, the warm touch igniting desire. "Yeah." Ignoring the urge to kiss Gloria, she simply accepted her help up. "Let's face it. I'm in the way more than I'm helping. I should go on. But if you need me to get anything at the store or that, let me know."

Gloria's eyes wrinkled as her lips turned up into a grin. "I do appreciate you, but I don't want you to get hurt. I'll text you if we think of anything." Lightly, she brushed her lips against Anna May's cheek. "Hope to see you soon."

Anna May caught her breath. Goose bumps popped up across her arms. "Yes, soon. And when this storm passes, let's make some plans. I'd love you to come visit D.C."

Gloria's eyes mirrored the storm clouds overheard.

≈≈≈≈≈

Anna May's boots clomped across Momma's porch as she carried the cushions to the chairs. Inside the small shed, Bubba stacked the rocker onto the other. She laid the cushions on the caned seat. "This seems like a waste of time. These chairs weigh a ton. This old shed will blow away before the furniture inside."

Bubba shrugged. "It makes Momma happy."

Anna May put a hand on the corner of the building, watching as he twisted the lock into place. "I was thinking, speaking of Momma being happy, maybe you could help talk her into moving to D.C."

He turned. "Why?"

"Well, you've got the kids and the business and all. There's a nice apartment near me, and she wouldn't have to get groceries or keep up the house. They have a big dining room and activities and stuff."

He pulled a can from his back pocket and snapped the lid with his thumb. The minty scent was powerful. Black specks stuck to his lip as he stuffed the tobacco into his mouth. "Apartment. Sounds like an old folks' home."

"She is old."

"And she already has a home."

Papers blew down the street as Anna May trailed him to the house. "Please, just think about it. She listens to you."

"I'll think about it." He stopped at the porch. "Don't you think you could just move here?"

She laughed until she realized he wasn't kidding. "I can't even plug in my computer in this house, and isn't moving to another house with me the same as moving to D.C.?"

He shook his head. "Let's talk about this later."

Chapter Thirty-two

Despite her better sense, Anna May huddled with her mother in the Walker living room, taking turns pacing to the picture window to peer out. The rain continued to fall for the third hour. On the TV, the weather people reported the storm from a dozen locations, giddy with the potential floods and power outages. Charleston had new pumps, but the water was still gushing up the drains. Images of boats crashed together alternated with graphics about the wind speeds and the current path of the hurricane. Each prediction showed the path directly toward Chicora Point. Although the eye wall was disintegrating, the clouds were heavy with moisture, and the bands of rain were already pounding the upstate.

"Look at the water going down the sidewalk. It'll flood the driveway before long." Anna May put her hands on her hips.

"No, it won't. It hasn't before, even in 2001, you know, that big storm. What was the name of that one? It doesn't matter. You're safe and sound." Momma kept knitting.

"Speaking of safe and sound, I want to talk to you about something."

"Gloria?"

Anna May snapped her head but stayed on message. "No, I wanted to know if you might come move near me."

"Are you getting a place in Chicora Point?"

"No."

"Then no. I'm staying put. I don't have much time left, and I'm not wasting it packing boxes."

Anna May couldn't argue with that point. "Wouldn't it be nice to not have to cook and clean?"

Momma stopped her needles. "This place an old folks' home?"

"Retirement village, yes. It's transitional. You can have your own place and go to get dinner if you want. If you need more help, they have people that can come in."

Momma started to knit. "I like it fine right where I am. You can't make me go. I can't afford it anyway."

"I would help." Anna May faced her mother. "I worry about you here, alone."

"I'm not alone. I got people that'll take me places, bring me stuff, and I can handle this house. Bubba handles stuff outside, and Stacy comes sometimes to run the carpet sweeper." Momma's voice got an edge to it.

"And what about me?"

"What about you? Seems you run off anyone you bring around here, so I expect you're used to being alone."

Anna May bit at her lip. "I could help you."

"I'll be hunky-dory. This place has stood a hundred years. I expect it to last as long as I'll need it." Momma jumped when lightning struck nearby, the windows shaking. "I hope we don't lose power."

"Want me to get the lantern?"

"Not yet. And you know the roads go both ways. You could move here." Momma looked at Anna May. "Seems you have plenty of work here, and you might even settle down."

Anna May went back to the window, her face hot with anger. Her phone buzzed. "It looks like they're telling people living near the river to get to higher ground."

Momma clamped her hands together and shut her eyes. "Dear Heavenly Father, please watch for our neighbors and keep everyone safe. And keep the power on. In Jesus's name."

Anna May mumbled, "Amen." In her opinion, it was as stupid as asking God to win football games.

They sat in silence for several minutes while Anna May stewed over the comments. This day sucked. Finally, she said, "You want a tea? I'm getting a tea."

"Yes. They'll be putting people up at the high school, I suppose. When it quits raining, maybe we can drive over to help out."

"What?"

"I said, we should go help at the school. The Red Cross will be setting up."

"I didn't know you were with the Red Cross."

"There's a lot you don't know. I mostly put out drinks and that. Sometimes, I read to the children."

"Really? We should both go."

"I wasn't going to swim."

Anna May sat down. Momma was in rare form today. Maybe Gloria would still be at the gym. "Yes, let's go when it stops raining." Things were looking up already.

≈≈≈≈

Gloria watched the cloud formations on her cellphone weather map, the entire South seemed to be in green, the yellow eating the upstate. Holding a hand to her mouth, she watched as red popped up and shifted, the crescents of rotation. She gasped. These hundred-year storms seemed to hit every year now.

"Hey." Jasmine came in and sat next to her on the couch. "What's the plan?"

"I don't know. Most of the worst seems west of us. There are three tornado warnings in Georgia right now. The barn is safer than this old house if one touches down."

They both looked out the windows at the dark clouds and sheets of rain beating the glass like a snare drum. An angry rust-colored stream of water raced through the yard toward the river.

Jasmine studied her phone. "Looks like it will rain at least a couple more hours. You don't think it'll flood here?"

"Well, it hasn't before, honey."

"There's a lot of water in the yard. Might be a foot deep or more. Our own Nantahala River."

Gloria squinted. "Hold your horses. You are not taking out that kayak."

"I wasn't." Jasmine crossed her arms.

"You're right about that." Gloria patted her hand. "I think we'll be fine if we stay out of the runoff. And by we, I mean you. That water would take you off your feet."

Jasmine said, "I reckon."

Another alert sounded on their cellphones. Both women flicked the screens with a finger.

Gloria announced, "Flash floods north of us. I guess we should just leave the trailer in the barn. I should go let the chickens out."

Jasmine put her hands on her hips. "Two steps ahead of you. I already left their door open."

Gloria's phone dinged again. She read the message. "You want to go with me to the high school?"

"Are they setting up a shelter?"

"Yes. Damion loaded some food from the pantry. Those houses by the river are in trouble if the water crests the dam."

"You know, you're not as young as you used to be." Jasmine looked down. "It might be safer for you here."

Gloria cringed. She had hit the age where her child worried about her. "You know, Mr. Rogers always said when you were scared to look for the helpers. I'm a helper."

"I know you are. But isn't there someone else?"

"You could come too. The animals will be all right."

Jasmine watched the water pour over the gutter. "I'm not so sure about that. How 'bout you go on and I'll hold down the fort? I'll come as soon as the storms have passed."

Gloria patted Jasmine's hand. "Good idea. Don't do anything crazy. If it gets bad, you come first."

"I'll be fine. I promise to go to the barn. I'll see you at the gym later."

≈≈≈≈

Gusts of wind pushed her truck out of her lane as Gloria drove. The wipers slapped on high, barely giving her a moment to spot the road before a spray of water covered the windshield. Her knuckles ached as she gripped the steering wheel. The only sound was the beating on the roof as she cut off the radio so she could see better. Jasmine would help any displaced neighbors. Did Anna May have enough sense to stay in one spot? Was she at her momma's or the motel? Did she say she was headed over to her momma's? The old brick building was a better bet than the long-standing mill houses. She probably didn't want her mother to be alone, and I bet Daisy didn't want to be trapped with her grandkids. Bouncing her left foot, she slowed down where she thought the stop sign into the city limit might be. Who would be out? Only other idiots like me.

At the high school, she pulled up past the student parking area toward the band room. The rear entrance to the gym was filling with trucks, several pulling trailers with boats. She jammed the truck into park and pulled her red parka close. When she pulled the door handle, the wind yanked the door open. She climbed out and struggled to shove it closed. With a thud, it surrendered. She ran toward the building, the wind unable to decide if it was westerly or north. Neither was good.

She skidded into the entrance where Damion held open a door. "Come on."

She stomped her feet as if it would knock off the water. "How're things looking?"

"Some power is out, but not too many houses are without yet. It's blasting them in Clayton."

"All that water coming our way, I guess." She clutched his arm. "I'll go check in with your daddy. I suppose he's in charge."

"He wouldn't have it any other way, but he's out driving near the river. David has his clipboard."

After signing in, Gloria hovered outside and watched the trees dance in circles, driving rain pelting her face even under the overhang. Her phone beeped, and an alert message said the Chicora Point high school gym was a safe location for evacuating residents.

Damion appeared at her side. He offered her a cigarette before lighting his.

She gave him an ugly look.

He said, "I know, I know. My nerves are tore up." He pulled in a breath and tucked the Bic in his pocket. The water rushing downstream roared, and they could hear it half a mile away. "You think the river is going to crest soon?"

Bubba Walker strode up. "I'm starting to think that we're going to over-top the dam in the next hour. They've been releasing extra water already, and the banks are breached. The sheriff and some of the men are going door to door recommending residents head here."

Gloria asked, "You think the dam is going to fail?"

Bubba nodded. "I've never seen this much rain so fast, and it's pushed all the way to Georgia."

"All that water's coming here," Damion repeated the obvious.

"Eventually." Bubba adjusted his ball cap. "Please 'scuse me. I'm gonna try and get some fellows to get the rest of my boats from the park. Most of them are rowboats with a trawling motor, but we should be able to use them if we need to."

Gloria shuddered, and her teeth chattered.

Damion closed his eyes. "It's time to pray."

A large white church van with the full AME name on the side pulled up to the overhang. Damion offered his hand as each person stepped out. Damion yelled, "You okay, Daddy?"

The Reverend Carter nodded. "The streets by the

river are flooded over. I'm going to do another sweep."

Gloria said, "I only have my truck. Anyone else have a van or Suburban?"

Damion grabbed his father's arm. "Be careful. Don't try to drive through the water."

"This ain't my first rodeo, and if I don't drive through the water, I ain't going to reach anyone who needs help."

The sheriff pulled up, and a family with three kids got out of his cruiser. "Shackleburg Road bridge washed out. Water rescue is out. Some dumbass in a truck tried to cross and went in the river. Some of the guys are getting ready to launch boats in the neighborhood by the elementary school."

Gloria said, "Can I help?"

"Me too," Damion said.

He rubbed his neck. "Come on. I'll drop y'all by the park to help man the boats."

Damion said, "Don't you mean the river?"

"No, sir, the water is all the way to the park."

Gloria swore she could see his dark face pale as he got in the truck. She whispered, "You can't swim."

"Neither can those other people."

The sheriff flipped on the lights and siren, and they rolled toward the new Lake Chicora Point.

Chapter Thirty-three

A t the picnic shelter in the park, Gloria pulled her rain slicker hood tighter around her face. Trucks with trailers filled the parking lot, and people teamed up to carry each boat to the water's edge. The brown torrent surged where the river used to lazily wander, dragging tree branches and other debris along with it. If they got pulled into the current, no telling how far downstream they might go. Even where she stood, the water crept closer. Most of the homes on the street had water up to their steps, some had already breached the porch. They said not to go in the water. Debris and chemicals. And water moccasins. She shuddered. At least they didn't have alligators this far inland.

"It's time to launch the boats." Bubba Walker handed out life jackets. "We will go in a row, taking people back here, and Pastor will drive them up to the gym. Stay in sight of at least one other boat. Blow your air horn if you get in trouble."

Gloria stepped into the sturdy fishing boat, accepting a hand from Damion. The boat rocked as she moved to the seat, rain droplets like needles against her face. "I'm glad you're with me."

He clutched the edge of the boat and nudged it free from the ground. With a quick step inside, he turned and sat. He checked all his straps on the life jacket and then pressed the button on the small motor. The boat bobbed with the rapids.

Gloria gripped the seat. "Bubba wants us to head to the Greens' house."

"I can see the kids in the window. Do we take their dog, too?"

"I suppose we can't leave it now, can we?"

Damion called over the wind, "I suppose we can't."

Gloria touched the porch rail as they floated nearby. "Hey, now don't y'all be scared. We're taking you to the gym, and they have hot chocolate."

The kids grinned. Their momma lifted them into the boat. "Come on, Apollo."

A yellow lab mix stepped toward the boat and stopped, causing the boat to rock.

Damion shifted back. "Is he friendly?"

Gloria leaned toward his ear and whispered, "Can't swim. Afraid of dogs. You are a brave man, Damion."

"Somebody had to help. Might as well be me." One hand held the motor lever, the other gripped the edge of the boat.

Finally, the kids coaxed Apollo over the edge, and Gloria released her hold on the rail. The rain was an open faucet, and despite the rain jacket, she was soaked to the skin.

The smallest child clung to the dog. "Don't be afraid, Pollo. I got you."

The boat shifted from side to side as the rapids bounced between the houses. Debris floating in the water smashed into the aluminum, the bang barely heard over the rain pelting them.

Damion sang, "I sing because I'm happy, I sing because I'm free."

They all joined in, "For His eye is on the sparrow,

and I know He watches me."

≈≈≈≈

At the high school, Anna May barely had gotten Momma inside the door when the lights in the gym flickered several times before the building stayed dark. Several children started to cry. Flashlights popped on around the room, and Damion asked the children to join him for a story. As he read, the room fell quiet, the adults listening to his variation of the fable about the frightened elephant.

The rumble of the generators soon droned on, the big fans starting to turn. A set of construction lights popped on in a corner, illuminating half the gym. Anna May opened the shrink-wrapped cases of water and arranged them on the table.

Gloria came up beside her, her pants wet to the knees. "What can I do?"

"Seems you have done plenty. There should be coffee, but it may be lukewarm."

Daisy waved. "I'll get you a drink."

"Hot chocolate, thank you." Gloria took Anna May's hands. "How are you?"

"Me? I'm just here to help."

"Tell me, did you coerce your mother?"

"No, it was her suggestion."

Gloria picked up a giant jar of peanut butter and twisted the lid off. "I guess it's sandwiches. You want one?"

Anna May shrugged. "Only if there's grape jelly."

Gloria grinned. "Pretty sure it's that fruit blend you can only get at Waffle House and in gallon jars."

By the time most of the people had food, Anna

May had filled an entire construction trash bag with plastic. Her backache took her mind off her ankle. At least she would have a room of her own to lie down in, unlike these people with flooded homes. A young woman with two young children and a baby came through the line, the infant crying.

Gloria reached over. "May I? I'm pretty good with kids."

The baby lay its head against her shoulder.

Anna May furrowed her brows. "I guess you are."

"Babies can tell when you're upset. This little one is tuckered out." Gloria swayed from side to side, the child's eyes closing for long blinks.

The line had dwindled down. Anna May said, "I suppose we're done here."

"You go on, your mother looks tired. Just go north toward the hotel from her place, not Mill Road. It's not even raining anymore."

Anna May said, "Are you sure?"

"I think I'll stay and help with the kids."

"That's not really my strength," Anna May admitted.

"No, but you came when you were needed. That's what matters."

Anna May shifted, unsure if she should kiss Gloria. "Promise you'll call if you need anything."

"Promise."

In the parking lot, Anna May splashed through the water, the stars bright over the dark town. Chain saws ripped in the distance, people already reclaiming the roadways. With a beep, her car unlocked, and she collapsed into the seat. With the A/C on high and the seat warmer on her sore back, she slowly rolled toward the door to get her momma. She remembered that the hotel room windows couldn't be opened.

"Momma, do you mind if I stay on the couch? I think the power's out downtown."

"That old lumpy thing? Maybe you'd rather go to Franklin's house."

"He's been out in the boat all afternoon. I bet he sure doesn't want to deal with company."

Momma said, "You two still don't get on."

She sighed. "I can only think of one thing we agree on, and that is we both love you."

"I don't know why you just can't let him win an argument once in a while. You two used to play so nice together."

"Hey, it's not my fault. He's the Klan guy, all chock full of family values until he wanted a divorce."

"I think Lisa wanted the divorce first."

"I don't blame her."

"That's what I mean. Always little snide comments. I wish you two could just fake it in front of me occasionally. Pretend you love each other."

Anna May didn't have the heart to tell her they had been trying. "You want music? This radio gets a Broadway musical channel."

"No Christian music?"

"I suppose there is. You'll have to hunt for it. Just push this button." Anna May pointed.

"This one?" Her mother tapped each knob on the dashboard. The monitor flicked between a navigation map, a list of car systems, and assorted comfort settings.

"No, this one. Mash this one." The list of radio stations popped onto the screen.

"Look at the road."

Anna May bit her lip and stared out the windshield as her mother flipped from channel to channel, apparently reading each description before moving on. An old disco song played. Anna May would have never guessed that would be her mother's choice. Maybe she picked it for me.

True to her mother's prediction, the houses in the mill village all stood strong during another storm. The glow from lanterns appeared in a window or two in each home. In the driveway, she parked next to the Buick and listened to the ticks of the engine. Her mother just sat with her hands in her lap. Anna May took the hint and got out, walked around, and opened the door for Momma. Together, they shuffled to the door and up the stairs.

Her momma fished in her purse. "I know I got the key here."

Anna May leaned on the door frame and waited as her mother inspected each compartment one by one.

"Ah ha! I thought we'd be here till Easter. Come on. Don't lollygag."

Anna May grimaced. "I'm going as fast as I can."

"You're stoved up. I got some of that cream I used on your father." Her mother disappeared and then startled her in the dim light. "Pull up your shirt."

Anna May did as she was instructed.

The phone on the side table rang, and Anna May answered, "Walker residence."

"Hey, how's Momma?" Bubba's low voice drawled.

"Good, we just got here from the gym."

"I'm still putting up boats, but if y'all need something, I can come by."

Anna May covered the receiver, "You wanna talk to Bubba?"

She took the line. "Hey, honey, thank you for

checking on us…No, I think we're good. Roads still flooded some, you be careful…Love you, too. Talk to you tomorrow. Bye."

Anna May took the phone. "You helped a lot of people today, Franklin. You should be proud of yourself."

There was a long pause. She thought the phone went dead.

Bubba said, "You got a charger for your phone, Anna May?"

Momma tugged her shirt down and whispered, "You're all set."

"Yes. I can always run the car if I need to."

"I appreciate you watching after Momma and all."

"To tell you the truth, I think she's watching after me. I'll call you later. Bye." She hung up the phone and leaned back into the chair, the cream stinking like the stuff she used in high school after track practice. An aphrodisiac for old lesbians. She smiled. "Momma, you need a drink?"

"Don't you dare open that icebox unless it's an emergency. Bubba put some sodas in a cooler on the counter."

She tried to stand. It was a contest between her ankle and back to see which hurt more. "Momma?"

"Yes?"

"Will you please get me a soda?"

"Of course."

Anna May tipped her phone to shine a light toward the kitchen.

"Turn that off. You're gonna bring in the bugs. You think I can't find my own kitchen?"

She accepted the lukewarm can. "Thanks for the

drink." With a thumb, she tipped the ring, and the can hissed. "This has been kinda nice hanging out today. You ever think you might want to live by me?" She choked down the store brand cola.

The woman scuffled to her chair and eased down. "Of course, honey, I'd love both my kids to be near me."

Anna May opened her mouth and closed it. Without hesitation, her mother welcomed all to her tiny home and shared whatever she had. Right now, there were people sleeping in a gym wondering what their homes looked like. "This drink sure hits the spot."

"I was surprised, too. Only three dollars for a twenty-four case." The click of knitting needles started in the dark.

"Isn't that a wonder?" Anna May didn't need to reflect at all. Momma wasn't going anywhere.

Chapter Thirty-four

In the morning, Chicora Point awoke bent but not broken. Rusty red mud coated the streets, thick and sticky. Broken tree branches jammed the culvert under the main road. Under the bridge, a car joined the debris. There had been no deaths, and aside from the power outage, it would be hard to tell that yesterday, water had risen twelve feet in one day, pounding anything in its path on the race to the ocean.

In the gymnasium, most of the evacuees still slept. Gloria started to boil water for coffee. A tiny transistor radio crackled. The news station reported that over a hundred thousand customers were without power. The city of Columbia flooded downtown as the misery spread downstate, first the storm itself, and now the runoff from the mountains threatened more damage.

The Reverend Carter came in the back door. "Good morning. Why don't you let me take over and go on home? Boiling water is about all I can do in the kitchen, but I think you've done your share."

"Only if you promise to call if you need more help."

"Cross my heart."

Gloria dragged to her truck exhausted from a night helping to settle late arrivals. She brushed back her hair into a ponytail, the morning air still and thick with moisture. The muddy water left a line across her tires. The engine chugged to life, and Gloria eased into gear, the A/C weak but welcome. In the daylight, it was harder to tell if anyone in their area had power. She suspected no. As she got farther from town, there were still branches down across the road, and a few people with chain saws were working on a tree that seemed newly removed from the blacktop.

At her driveway, the fruit stand was still shuttered tight. The house was still. The barn doors stood wide open. She parked in the shade and wandered through the yard.

She called out, "Hello?"

Several goats ran over, ears flopping with each step.

Jasmine's voice came from above. "Hey, I'm up here. The power is out. I'm taking some panels to the house."

"Don't come down. But do explain it to me. Later. Do you need help?"

There was a pause. "No, I'm good. But can you get the goat off the ladder?"

Goat off the ladder. In any other situation, that might be code for something, but here it was literal. Gloria went around the side door, and there was Blueberry, standing with two feet on each rung.

"You stinker." Gloria stepped up a few steps and wrapped the goat with one arm. "Don't jerk and make us fall."

"What?"

"I was talking to the goat. All clear. I'm going to put him with the babies."

"Thanks. I loaned the generators to Mr. Jackson's son. I'm going to take two panels from the barn and hook them to a circuit to keep the food from going bad at the house. The lights won't work in the barn, but at least we can have a cold beer."

"You're not twenty-one."

"Can't blame a girl for trying. Anyway, it won't be near enough to run the A/C, but we should be able to run a couple of box fans."

Gloria said, "Good thing you never put them in the attic because that would be really hot."

"Like Cameron Tucker says, yesterday's lazy saves today's crazy." Jasmine laughed. "Thanks, I'll be down in a while."

꧁꧂

Too tired to sleep, Gloria sat at the kitchen table nursing a glass of water. Through the window, she watched Jasmine crawl around on the roof of the barn. The solar on the house was tied to the power company, so while it saved money, it had to disconnect when the power was off, or it could hurt line workers. They discussed backup batteries, but she didn't want them in the house. Although she had to agree it would be nice if they could run an air conditioner. The barn was on a totally independent system, and somehow, Jasmine was poaching the system to run a circuit at the house. It was brilliant, even if she didn't understand much about it.

With one muscled arm holding some doohickey, Jasmine climbed down the extension ladder and headed toward the house. The song she whistled became recognizable as an old hit from the sixties. Gloria began to sing the words. She was a success as a parent if her kid knew Motown music.

Jasmine stepped through the kitchen door and let the screen door bang shut behind her. She got a glass and filled it with tap water and then plopped into a chair. With one hand raking through her damp curly hair, she tried to release the hair tie without adding to the volume of frizz. She lost the fight, and ringlets surrounded her face. "This hair is making me so hot, I'm ready to shave my head."

Gloria gathered the hair just as she had when Jasmine was a child. "Fine by me. It's your head, but I have always loved your gorgeous hair. Mine just hangs."

Jasmine leaned into the caresses. "Mom, I've been thinking. You know. About school."

Gloria hummed, "Mm-hmm."

"As I was trying to lay out the plan for this cobbled system, I realized that maybe there is a thing or two I could learn in college."

"You think so?"

"I sent in my paperwork before the storm. And if they accept me, I want to start in January. That's the slowest time on the farm, and I can be back by May to help with the first cut."

"Stop. I can get help." Gloria stopped short of adding that she could also cut back the operations. "I'm proud of you."

Jasmine shifted. "I know. Look, I want to get this up and running before dark."

Gloria let go. "Because there is so much solar energy at night?"

"Ha. Ha. It's going to be ready for the morning. Smart aleck."

"Excellent." Gloria's voice raised in pitch, "Can I help with anything?"

Jasmine waited for a beat before saying, "Oh, no. Thanks, though."

"Could I hold the ladder?"

"Thank you but not needed."

Gloria knew it aggravated Jazz when she asked everything three times, but she still asked again. "It's no trouble."

"I appreciate you, but I got this. Love you."

"Love you more." Gloria watched as Jasmine marched toward the furnace room with the panel box. She bit at her lip to prevent a "be careful" from slipping out.

In a few moments, the refrigerator made a soft whir as it limped back to life. Now if only the power would come on. She wiped the sweat from her face.

࿇ ࿇ ࿇ ࿇

The rain had ended, but the cleanup would take another week. To raise funds, several half-barrel smokers ringed the picnic shelter. Men in aprons wielded foot-long tongs preparing a feast. For a five-dollar donation to the rescue fund, they got a hotdog or burger, chips, and a lukewarm soda. Momma settled by Stacy and the kids.

Anna May said, "Bubba, can I talk to you a minute?"

He looked around the crowd and nodded. He moved to an empty table at the back. "Is Momma okay?"

"She's fine. I have a favor to ask you."

"All right."

"I was talking to Gloria about the rally to keep the Confederate statue in the square."

"It's not just ours. It's every town around here and at the statehouse in Columbia. It's an outrage."

Anna May clenched a fist. "Look, people got killed in Virginia. Maybe this isn't a good idea."

"You don't get to waltz into town and start telling me what to do. You wanna run around with the town hippie, go ahead. I have a lot of respect for what Gloria does around here, but I gotta draw the line."

"You gotta march around in a dress and scare black people?"

"That's not what we do!"

Several heads turned in their direction. Anna May lowered her voice. "Franklin, just call off the rally."

Bubba took off his hat and slammed it on the table. "Dang it, you're not even trying to understand."

"So explain it then."

"I've known these guys my whole life. We were in kindergarten together. They're my friends. I like hanging out with them, and I won't give that up. They were the first ones to call me when Daddy died."

"If they were really your friends, they would understand."

"Bullshit. It's who I am. It's who they are. Maybe you should try to understand." Bubba took a Skoal can from his pocket. He popped the lid with his thumb and stuck a big glob in his mouth.

Anna May choked a little. "It's like I don't even know you."

"And whose fault is that?" He snapped the lid shut. "I work hard to provide for my family. I go to church every week, something you might consider for yourself. And I try to help people in this town. What do you do? Write scathing stories hiding behind your computer screen and then spend all your money on good booze and bad women."

"I don't buy women." Anna May failed to keep her hands from shaking.

He squinted his eyes. "Yeah, I guess that's more of a country song, but you get my point. You don't get to tell me how I gotta be. I sleep just fine at night."

She took a slow breath. "Let's just say you quit the Klan. What would happen?"

"I'd go broke. They're my customers. I buy stuff from them. They send people to me. If I'm on the outside, all that is gone."

Anna May shifted on the bench. "I hadn't thought about that. Look, we aren't getting anywhere. Can you promise to think about your kids? Do you want them dressed in little robes screaming obscenities?"

He spit. "I guess not."

Anna May considered that a victory. Changing the subject, she asked, "Y'all got power?"

"Yes, and no, you ain't coming over. Not unless you bring Momma."

"The motel got power back today. Momma's should be on when we get home, or she can stay with me."

He looked around. "Better you than me. Come on, let's go eat."

"Just promise to think about your kids."

"Get off my ass, or OSHA is going to make me install handles with you and Stacy both riding me." Bubba stood with a huff.

Chapter Thirty-five

Gloria was used to the heat but not trying to sleep in it. After two restless nights, she was exhausted. Outside was cooler than the house, so she slowly rocked in the porch swing, a paperback in one hand and a sweet tea in the other. The soft whisper of a breeze caressed her skin. Her shirt was plastered to her skin, droplets rolling between her braless boobs. The sun lulled her to sleep. Her phone played a melody, and she jerked awake. It was her tone for Damion.

"What's wrong?" she asked.

"Hello to you, too, but I will get right to the point. Can you put up a family for a couple weeks? There's a whole block where the houses got flooded with the river water. They need to stay out until they can cut out the wet plaster and sheetrock."

Gloria wiped the sweat from her forehead. "Only God knows what was in that water."

"Besides sewage and trash? Snakes. That's what." Damion paused. "You should see those houses. They already got mold growing up the walls. I feel so sorry for them. It's a nightmare."

"You shouldn't be doing demolition with your back."

"As David reminded me. I got the easy part, finding housing."

"Jasmine jury-rigged some solar panels from the barn. Except for a few outlets, I still don't have power."

"Girl, no one got power."

Gloria did some mental math and said, "I got two bedrooms, and I can pull out the couch. I can do at least six if they don't mind sharing."

"Thanks, darling. Daddy will drive them out in a couple of hours. They're over at Goodwill trying to find them all clothes."

"I don't know what this town would do without you and your family."

"They would find a way." He paused. "Thanks, Gloria. For helping out."

"How's the pantry holding up?"

"Totally decimated. But I put in a few calls. I know who to squeeze when we need instant cash for restocking the shelves."

Gloria said, "Don't tell me who. I'm better off not being a party to this crime. As soon as I get power, I'm fixing to make a big batch of applesauce. I'll bring you some."

"Bring me a bushel of golden delicious, and I'll make you a pie."

"I'll get the ice cream. Talk to you soon." Gloria touched the screen to hang up. She hesitated a moment, then touched the button by Anna May's name.

She answered. "Hey, y'all got power yet?"

Gloria said, "No, not yet. Although Jasmine rigged something that runs one circuit so the icebox is back on. The barn lights won't work, but the cheese cooler hasn't cut off."

"That's good. Do you guys want to come over here? We got A/C."

"You guys?"

"I'm still not completely done with my Yankee words. So y'all come on."

"Where? The hotel or your momma's?"

"Momma's. She's got a kitchen. I don't."

"Your momma won't mind?"

Anna May scoffed. "Hardly. She's a Southern woman."

"I doubt Jasmine will abandon her project, but I'll ask her. See you." Gloria touched the screen. If she went and got cleaned up, would that send the wrong message? What would that be? That Anna May was worth fussing for, or that she still had soap?

Jasmine stomped in. "Hey, is it working?"

"Like a champ." Gloria tried to sound nonchalant. "You want to go with me to Mrs. Walker's and get out of the heat for a while?"

"Yeah, let me clean up a little."

Gloria had a flash of inspiration and went to the cabinet to bring a few jars of honey. As they drove over, they both soaked up the wisps of cool air from the blowers.

Jasmine said, "I hope the air is better at their house."

"It's an old mill house. Hard to say."

"If they upgraded the panel box, they can run a house unit." Jasmine flicked the radio station. "I promise not to say anything."

"You could never embarrass me." Gloria put on the blinker and slowed as they approached the neighborhood.

"I know you think you mean that." Jasmine looked out the window.

Gloria wanted to ask but didn't.

Anna May's face appeared in the window as they rolled up.

Jasmine said, "I think someone is glad to see you."

"Us."

"You. I'm not five. I get how this stuff works." Jasmine opened her door and followed Gloria up the stairs.

Gloria said, "Hey, Daisy, so nice to see you again. Don't get up."

Daisy reached her hands toward Gloria. "I'm so glad to see y'all. Come sit a spell."

Gloria said, "You remember my daughter, Jasmine?"

"Of course. Anna May, get them a drink."

Jasmine perched on the couch. Gloria was certain the empty chair had been Ellison's. She left the decision and headed to the kitchen. "Hey."

Anna May flushed. "Hey, yourself." She peeked at the living room, then gave Gloria a quick kiss. "I've missed you."

"Shh." Gloria looked to the doorway. The sound of Jasmine explaining the solar panel system to Daisy floated over the hum of the window A/C unit. "We can talk later."

Anna May wiggled her eyebrows. "Talk later. Is that what they call it now?"

Gloria smacked her arm. "Stop."

"Who bothers you more if she sees us? My momma or your daughter?"

The heat burning up her neck and face gave her away, but she didn't answer. Her phone chirped. Pulling it out, she said, "It's Damion. Let me get this. Hey. What's up?"

He said, "I appreciate your offer to house some folks, but I found a place with power."

"Keep me on the list if anything changes."

"Will do. Thanks, darling."

Gloria turned to Anna May. "They're finding places for people to stay."

Anna May said, "Any port in the storm. Even without air conditioning."

Gloria shrugged. "Evidently not. Thanks for inviting us. I've been on fire."

Anna May had an odd look on her face but only handed her a glass of tea. Maybe Gloria was reading too much into this. She was too old for this cat and mouse thing.

Chapter Thirty-six

A week later, the social hall at the AME church looked more like an elementary art room. Colorful poster board paper lay on most of the long tables. A rainbow of markers stuck out of jars. Gloria stood with Damion at the front of the room speaking with Pastor Carter.

Anna May pulled out a folding chair and took a seat at an empty table.

The Reverend Carter turned to the group. "Welcome. Shall we pray?"

Anna May dutifully dropped her chin and closed her eyes.

His deep voice resonated across the room. "Our blessed Lord and Savior. Thank you for the fellowship as we prepare to defend our town against the tyranny our people have fought against for centuries. Bring the strength of conviction and may we all remember all things are possible with God. Amen."

Anna May said, "Amen," with the rest of the room. When she opened her eyes, Gloria was next to her. "Hi."

"Hey, thanks for coming out."

"I promised I would." Anna May left off the part about if she was still in town. "Tell me, are the kids here going to be at the rally, too?"

"Sure, they already know they're black."

"Funny. I meant, is it safe?"

Gloria took a pencil and began to sketch on

a large sheet. "Is there anywhere safe to be black in America?"

Anna May also took a pencil. After several moments, she said, "I guess not. That sucks."

"Oh, my dear, it more than sucks. And it's outrageous. But let's focus on the challenge at hand."

They worked in silence, a hush falling over the room as people created their signs.

Anna May selected a thick black marker. With a slow motion, she traced over the pencil marks on the poster board. It was too bad she was here. At her office in D.C., she had a machine that could laminate the signs. The alcohol in the ink saturated the air, quiet except for the squeaks against the paper. She stood to get a better view.

"The Nazis and the Confederates both LOST."

Anna May said, "They would have to get through me to hurt the kids."

Gloria nodded. "Same."

"They drove into a crowd," Anna May whispered.

"I know. A trapped snake strikes." Gloria leaned back. "Hand me the red, please."

Anna May reached for the marker. "I'm not afraid."

"You might ought to be."

"You reckon?"

"If we don't get you back to D.C. soon, you may never recover from that accent." Gloria laughed. "Or you could just stay."

"You want me to? Stay or go?"

"Yes."

Pastor Carter took that moment to begin a speech about his march with Martin Luther King Jr. What had Gloria meant? Yes, she should stay, or yes, she should go? Anna May felt the moment slip away as the crowd listened, mesmerized by the tales. Her throat caught. Somewhere, her brother was probably making signs, too, only of hate. Not a metaphorical relationship, no, her actual brother. She shivered.

≈≈≈≈

The afternoon of the rally, the crowd in the downtown park was sharply divided with a row of construction barricades separating the opposing protesters. One side had fewer than a dozen people dressed in robes, some carrying Confederate and Nazi flags. A yellow "Don't Tread on Me" banner was draped around the Confederate Memorial, which was dedicated in 1902. The inscription read: "The world shall yet decide, in truth's clear, far-off light, that the soldiers who wore the gray, and died with Lee, were in the right."

On the other, hundreds of people collected under the shady oak trees. The signs varied from colorful peace symbols to more graphic language about the KKK. Anna May stood near the front, resting her sign on her foot.

To no one's surprise, Jimmy Buchanan wore his robe and pointed hood. He pressed against the rail and raised his fist into the air. "Fuck the libtards."

Anna May walked closer to him, her hand in a peace symbol, and smiled at him.

His face contorted. "Especially fuck you, goddamn fucking dyke."

Anna May shrank but didn't step back.

Bubba marched over. "What the hell is wrong with you? I thought I said no unnecessary confrontation."

Jimmy spat on the ground. "I guess we don't agree what is necessary. She came over here. This is our damn town. Half those people don't even live here, like your sister. I thought she'd be long gone by now."

Bubba's face darkened. "Did I stutter? No more threats."

"I'm trying to keep our children safe from godless homos like her. You might consider keeping her away from your kids."

Bubba clutched Jimmy at his shoulder, the shirt tight in his fist. "You shut up before I shut you up."

"Big man now. I wonder if we need to throw you out since you are so soft on Communists."

Anna May mumbled, "I wonder if he knows what a Communist is. He probably thinks it means a commune."

Bubba snapped his head. "I heard that. You stop it, too."

"Yeah, you stop it." Jimmy cackled. "You see where your brother's loyalties lie. With the brotherhood. Not with you hippie assholes."

Anna May stepped backward. "Maybe I ought to move to the other side of the street before I kick your ass."

"You and what army?"

Bubba cleared his throat.

Jimmy raised his middle finger to Anna May. He hissed to Bubba, "You gonna be voted out. I'll make sure of it, you traitor."

"Yeah, maybe, but today, I'm still in charge. Cool your jets, Jimmy. I ain't playing." Bubba looked at Anna May. "Stop causing me trouble."

Anna May said, "Oh, this is just the start. If you are on the side of the Nazis, Franklin, you're on the wrong side. You know I'm right." She flashed another peace sign. "I'll pray for you."

His eyes blazed. "Don't mock me. And go on. Please."

"Fine. See you at Momma's." Anna May strolled toward the larger group.

Gloria twisted through the crowd to reach her. "Are you okay?"

Anna May bit at her lip. "I've marched downtown in D.C. about every year for decades. I never felt afraid until today. Here. It's just..."

"Personal." Gloria pulled her into a hug. "It's harder to face people you know. I'm proud of you. You stood up to them." She wiped a tear on Anna May's face. "Tears of anger. It sucks being a woman sometimes. We should tell men the secret that when a woman cries, she's ready to neuter him."

Anna May sniffed. "I'd like to think I'm braver since high school. I'm not so sure."

Gloria stiffened. "Come with me. Jimmy is headed this way."

***

The blood drained from Gloria's face as Jimmy marched toward them. Gloria took Anna May by the arm and steered her toward the back of the crowd.

Anna May said, "I didn't do anything."

"And you wouldn't. It ain't you I'm afraid of showing out." Gloria stopped when they got to her truck. "Get in."

"I don't see why."

"Do it." Gloria looked around.

Damion followed them. "You okay?"

"Not really. I think we should get Anna May away from Jimmy. He seems especially riled up today."

Damion put his hands on her shoulders. "You both go on. Take Anna May's car. I'll call you if I see him leave. Then I'll call the sheriff."

Gloria said, "It must be serious if a black man wants to call the cops."

Damion said, "If I didn't know your heart, I might be offended. I also know you always joke when you're nervous, and if I wasn't afraid for you, I'd be laughing. Go on. Be safe." He kissed her cheek.

"Thank you." Gloria got in and buckled her seat belt. Where to go? Not home. She had her grandfather's old shotgun but didn't even know how to load it. Anna May would freak out if she asked if she could. Thank God the car would be fast. The diesel wasn't speedy or even guaranteed to start. She twisted the key fob in her hand. Maybe they shouldn't have taken the sports car. "How do I start this thing?"

"Put your foot on the brake and push that button on the right of the steering wheel."

Gloria did so. "I can't believe that you just mash a button. Let's get out of here."

Anna May said, "You want a frozen Coke?"

Gloria peeled out of the parking lot and turned toward the Walmart. At the traffic light, her phone buzzed. "Oh, shit." She answered. "Hey." She waited. "I got this, thanks for the heads up. I'm headed to the Jackson back pasture." She did a U-turn.

Anna May gripped the door handle. "What's going on?"

"I think Jimmy is trying to follow us."

"Not trying. Is." She pointed toward the back of the car.

"Hang on." Gloria stomped the pedal, and the car lurched through the red light, the tires screaming behind them. At the high school, she cut behind the football stadium past the boulder wall built a hundred years ago. The tires skidded across the pavement as she counter-steered and the car slid around the corner.

Anna May took out her phone. "Momma. Call Franklin. Tell him his good friend Jimmy is trying to run me off the road." There was a pause. "No, Momma, I ain't kidding. Me and Gloria are in my Beemer." Anna May sighed. "Yes, she can drive a stick. She's driving like she stole it, but would you just call him? Please."

Gloria saw Jimmy's purple face in the mirror, his hands gripping the steering wheel. "How good is your insurance?"

"What? Good. It's good. Why?" Anna May pushed a hand against the ceiling.

"I'm sorry to do this." Gloria pressed down both feet and locked up the brakes. The car shuddered as they collided, then she crushed the accelerator. "Fuck you and your paint job, Jimmy."

He hesitated. His wheels smoked as he sped behind them.

Anna May answered her phone.

"What's going on?" Bubba asked.

"Not a good time to chitchat. Just call off your dog." She bounced as they hit a speed bump.

"Fine. Where are you? Tokers Road?"

"No. Headed west on the old running road." She hung up.

"The running road?" Gloria asked.

"Yeah, cross-country route. He'll know it." Anna May sucked in a breath. "Just in case we die, I gotta tell you something."

"Hush and let me drive." Gloria winked. "Me too. Hang on."

She hit the brakes and again they were sliding left.

Squealing, Anna May put a hand on the dash. "When did you learn to drive like this?"

"Daddy. At the track. You're gonna need a new clutch after this."

"I'll need new pants. Jesus." Anna May paled. "He's caught up."

In the distance, they could hear the wail of a siren.

Gloria said, "I never could tell a firetruck from a cop car."

"What? I don't care who it is just so they stop him."

Gloria shifted. "I'm going to stop him." The car flew as the engine revved, then she popped in the clutch. At the row of oak trees, she slid it into gear and let the transmission shove them faster. His bumper must have been mere inches behind them. She took a deep breath. "Please don't kill him."

"What?"

"Hold on."

Anna May braced herself against the door.

Gloria pushed the brake and clutch just as she pulled the wheel right then left. He passed them, then his brakes screeched. She swerved around him and looked in the mirror and watched as he plowed into a tree. The thunderous boom startled her even as she expected it. "Towanda!" She slowed and pulled to the side of the road.

Anna May craned her neck. "He's still in the truck."

"Is it on fire?"

"No."

"Okay, we'll wait here."

The sheriff's car crested the rise, and he stopped at the window. "You ladies all right?"

"Yes, sir, I think there was a single-car accident behind us."

"Don't go anywhere." He pulled off toward the crash.

Bubba pulled up behind them and ran to the window. "What the hell? Are you okay?"

"Yes, thanks." Anna May waved.

Bubba spit. "He lost his dang mind, I'm not kidding. He could have run y'all off the road."

Anna May said, "It's too bad Uncle Tillus wasn't riding with Gloria."

"You ain't kidding." Bubba tipped his head. "Your new tires ain't looking too good." He spit. "I should at least go pretend I give a damn what happened to him."

Gloria said, "You go on."

A firetruck pulled up beside Jimmy's wrecked truck. Red lights on an ambulance flashed as they parked by the car.

A woman in a navy uniform approached the Beemer. "I'm under orders to check on y'all first."

Gloria read the name tag Coffman and smiled. "Hey, Kim, Jasmine didn't tell me you were working for the fire department now."

"Yes, ma'am. It's nice to see you, but not under these circumstances. You having any chest pains? You know, because then I'd have to stay here."

"Is he okay?"

"Yeah, airbag went off. Dumbass broke his leg." She cleared her throat. "I mean, I need to check your blood pressure."

Gloria said, "Yeah, Anna May is a little shook

up."

Kim wrapped the Velcro and watched the gauge. "Hmm." She adjusted the fit and repeated her steps. "You should be having a stroke about now. You feel okay?"

Anna May said, "Just a little light-headed."

Gloria took her hand. "Maybe we should go to the hospital."

"Nonsense. I'm fine."

"Excuse me, ma'am. Miss Gloria, you sure you're good?"

"Fit as a fiddle."

"I'll be right back with a stretcher." Kim said something into a radio. "I'll have someone pick up Ms. Walker."

Gloria said, "How did you know she was a Walker?"

"She looks just like her daddy, and Jasmine might have mentioned how cute y'all were together."

Anna May said, "Only in a small town."

Chapter Thirty-seven

Jasmine drove the old truck back toward the farm. She turned down the radio. "I'm just glad you're both okay."

Gloria patted Jasmine's arm. "Thank you for driving. I'm still a little shaky."

"No problem. I can't believe that inbred redneck tried to drive you off the road."

"I made my dad proud today, that's for sure." Gloria shifted, her back stiff. "I tell you what, that sports car was sure fun."

Jasmine smiled. "I bet. Never drive faster than your angels can fly."

"I'm pretty sure my daddy is a fast angel if I had to wager."

"I'm sure Anna May will let you drive it again."

Gloria nodded, unsure there would be an opportunity. Anna May didn't mention going home anytime soon, but she didn't mention moving to Chicora Point, either. Frankly, Gloria was afraid to ask. It was one thing to express feelings when you thought you might die and quite another to drop your life to follow your heart. She wouldn't move to D.C., so it wasn't fair to think Anna May might move back to Chicora Point. If it was better to have loved and lost than to never have loved at all, it was rather cruel to have the same woman crush her heart twice.

The air was on when they got home from the hospital. Gloria dropped into bed and slept for twelve hours. She woke to the soft touch of a warm hand.

Jasmine whispered, "Momma? Who you got coming today?"

Gloria struggled to release her body from the sheets. "What are you going on about? Are you hungry? I can make pancakes."

"No, ma'am. I mean, yes, ma'am, I'm hungry, but there's a bunch of people in the yard."

"What on earth?" Gloria wandered out in her nightshirt and shorts. There must have been a dozen cars and more pulling in while she watched.

The Reverend Carter stood at her door. "Good morning, I do hope we haven't woken you. They say the early bird gets the worm."

"It's okay."

Jasmine appeared at her side. "What's all this?"

Gloria said, "I don't rightly know, but I need to make more than a few pancakes."

The Reverend Carter took her hand. "We're here to help with whatever you got that needs done. Damion said your apples are in. I thought we might start there."

She blinked back tears. "With so much everyone else needs—"

"We hired professionals to help with the houses, you know how codes and all are these days. We have at least a day or two until we can get in there. So here we are."

Jasmine stepped into her boots. "I'll show them where to start."

"Rev. Carter, thank you. Would you care for some coffee? Anna May bought me a tiny coffeemaker that makes one cup at a time along with a whole box of fancy flavors."

"I'd be most grateful. Truth be told, I don't get

up as early as I should most mornings." Pastor Carter followed her into the kitchen. "Anna May's not here?"

Gloria felt the heat across her face. "Uh, no."

"I don't mean to imply, I just thought you two were getting on and all."

"I'm not sure what her plans are, to be honest."

His eyes twinkled with mischief. "She just needs to see what she's missing if she goes."

"Oh?"

"I got this one. I can be quite influential, and I know just the person to help her see the possibilities."

☙☙☙☙

The Weary Hiker was packed when Anna May pushed in the front door. A three-piece band played rock music in the back corner. Damion waved to her. Two beer mugs and a basket of chips sat on the table. She pulled out the heavy wooden chair and sat.

"The band is good."

He slid a plate toward her. "Local group. The drummer is from North Carolina. I try to stop in when they're playing."

Anna May sipped the beer. Dancers filled the small area by the musicians. "The lady with the hula hoop?"

"That's new. People stop by on the way back from the trails. Hence the name of the place."

Anna May pursed her lips. "Of course. I'm glad you invited me."

"Needed a drinking buddy?" He winked. "I'd have thought you'd be with Gloria."

"Yes, I mean no. I need some advice."

His brown eyes softened. "I'll try."

"How did you know that David was the one?"

His eyes sparkled. "Anna May Walker, you've dated a lot more people than I have. I'd think you could write a book on romance."

"Romance yes, maybe. Love, not so much."

He dipped a chip in salsa, considering her question. "I knew he was the one when I couldn't imagine any day better than a day spent with him."

She rubbed her arms. "You gave me goose bumps."

"When you write your best seller, remember to use my middle initial in the quote. There are more Carters than Carter has liver pills."

"That's a great line. My grandma used to say that, except, without the first Carter."

"Naturally." He patted her arm. "I have the feeling you've got something big rumbling around that head of yours."

She sighed. "I think I want to stay."

"In Chicora Point?"

"Yes. With Gloria."

He squealed. "Ooh. I love it." He whispered, "I mean, I'll keep your secret, except for David. I have to tell him."

"Naturally." She leaned close to him. "What do you think Gloria will say?"

"You think I know?" Breaking into a smile, he picked up his mug. "She'll be thrilled. Duh."

Anna May squirmed. "You think so?"

"I do, but don't quote me. I don't want her to think I've been gossiping."

"A barber knows everyone's business."

"Maybe." He grinned. "But we aren't supposed to share that business with everybody."

Familiar music blasted from the stage; the funky beat was vaguely like the original song.

She grabbed his arm. "Come dance with me!"

He declined. "I wish I could. My lumbago."

"That isn't even a thing."

"It is, too, but I know when I'm gonna lose a fight."

They worked their way to the middle of the floor and began to move. Soon people shifted away to give them room, and by the end of the song, they were surrounded. Even the band clapped. Anna May brushed her hair out of her eyes as they went back to their table. "I'm not good for much more, but that was fun."

He took her hand. "Save some of that energy for Gloria."

"I'm not seeing her until tomorrow."

He finished his drink and then pointed toward the door. "I may have texted her, and I may have to go now." His eyes flashed with delight.

Anna May turned. Gloria moved toward them, her earrings matching the silk shirt softly clinging to her form. "God, I love boobs."

"Pardon?"

Anna May didn't realize she'd said it out loud. "Um. Nothing, sorry."

"Chill out, it's all good. You two have a good night." Damion hugged Gloria as they passed, and then he was gone.

Anna May held out a chair for Gloria as Gloria tried to grab a chair for Anna May.

Gloria sat and scooted up to the table. "We're going to have to work this kind of thing out. I know the kids are all back into that butch/femme thing, but

I'm still a child of the eighties. Androgyny. We both do whatever we want."

Anna May sat. "Hmm. That's more work than just letting me do the guy stuff."

Gloria laughed. "You're the stud? In white shorts with sandals."

"I can do guy stuff. And you have long hair."

"Ah. It's the haircut that matters." Gloria waved toward the bartender to get a fresh drink. "I should write that down."

"I should tell you I can't cook." Anna May fidgeted with the glass. "I mean, I like to make cookies, but that's about it."

Gloria smiled. "I have so much to teach you." Her hand dropped into Anna May's lap, and she rubbed against her.

Anna May shuddered. "I thought I was the worldly one."

"Doing the same thing with thirty different women doesn't make you worldly."

Anna May burned. "I don't really know I'd say..."

"Fine, forty." Gloria grinned. "Have it your way. I would like to mention that my power is back on, but I can pretend it's not and stay with you tonight."

Anna May jerked as the hand shifted against her. "Okay."

"Okay? I plan to turn you on so much that by the time we get to your room your legs are shaking."

Anna May twisted against the hand, the butterflies in her stomach turning to an ache. "Uh."

"Great conversationalist. Maybe you should consider a career in writing." Gloria accepted the beer and took a drink. She licked the foam off the lip of the mug, and Anna May felt the blood drain from her face to her groin.

Gloria asked, "You all right? Maybe we should lay down."

Anna May's nipples pressed against her shirt as Gloria's lips neared her ear.

Gloria whispered, "Unless you want to order a burger or something." Gloria's tongue lightly touched the skin, and Anna May almost gasped out loud.

Anna May leaned back, rubbing her breast against Gloria's arm as she shifted. Gloria's cheeks flushed, and her pupils dilated. "Yeah, maybe we should eat."

"I agree. Breakfast. Shall I call you or nudge you?"

Anna May cackled. "You ever use that line before?"

"Actually, no." Gloria pulled close to Anna May. "We can go to your car, your room, my truck, I don't care. But if we don't leave right now, I may mount you on this table."

Anna May stopped the waitress. "Check, please."

Chapter Thirty-eight

In the early morning, Gloria left for a farm-related crisis. Sitting in the darkened room, Anna May typed slowly, carefully choosing each word, certain of her decision.

Anna May reread the email, her finger hovering over the keyboard ready to change any offending words or typos. Confident the piece was ready, she hit enter, and the request for remote work was probably already in Sho's inbox. She counted backward from ten, and before she hit two, her phone rang.

Sho said, "What the hell happened to you?"

"I'm sure I have no idea what you mean." Anna May tapped her pen on the table, the ticking sound reminding her of a cheap clock.

"You've been gone a month, and now you're just going to leave D.C.? Why the spur-of-the-moment decision?"

"It's not totally spontaneous. I've thought about it since I got here." Which was true since everyone asked from the moment she arrived in Chicora Point when she was moving home.

"What's her name?"

"Whose name?"

"The woman you met."

Anna May hesitated. At this juncture in time, Sho knew her past, and it was not offensive that Sho would suggest it. And she did have a certain reputation for spontaneity. To be honest, more things went wrong than right. "Gloria. We knew each other in high school."

"Immaterial. Are you going to stay if things go south? Pun intended."

"Yes. And they won't. Go wrong, I mean. Half the country has been working from home since COVID. What difference does it make how far that home is to the office?"

Sho said, "It doesn't. I will miss you."

"I'll miss you, too. We can do Zoom."

"They have enough bandwidth for that in Chicora Point?"

Anna May didn't laugh. "Yes."

"Come on, I'm kidding you. Now spill the beans about Gloria. Is she gorgeous? Rich? Famous?"

"She's got the permaculture farm you sent me to."

"She's a farmer? Did I hear you right?"

"Yes, and I know that seems..."

"Odd for you?"

"Yes. But it's not. She knows everything about everything. Weather, animals, growing stuff, fixing things..."

"All right, all right. I can't wait to meet her. Bring her when you pack up your apartment."

"Good idea."

☙☙☙☙

Momma sat in her chair. Pulling yarn from a new skein, she neatly wrapped it into a ball. Anna May paced the floor.

"Your brother is planning a surprise birthday party for me. Act surprised when he tells you."

"I know when your birthday is." Anna May scratched her head. Had she been gone a month already?

"Not that part, the party."

"Oh, right."

"Sit down. You're wearing out my carpet."

Anna May turned and sat. "I've been thinking. I should move back. Here."

"Here like the town, or here like my house?"

"I haven't worked that out but not here. I mean, you need your space." Anna May rose and began her route around the living room. "I know you're surprised."

Momma folded her hands. "You're right. I am surprised. You didn't ask my opinion before you moved out, and I'm just wondering why you think you need to ask now to come home."

"It's kind of a big change. It might seem sudden. I just thought you might need more help, you know, with Daddy gone and all."

"Mmm." Momma looped the yarn on a needle and started to knit. "I didn't just fall off the turnip truck. You left to get away from something, and you're coming back for about the same reason."

Anna May pulled at her collar. "Is it warm in here? I should check the air conditioner. Maybe the filter needs to be cleaned."

"Sit down." Momma set the yarn down. "You ain't been worried about us all these years. I don't care if you give me some cock and bull story, I deserve that. I haven't been very supportive of your, uh, lifestyle."

"You've been hostile."

"A person can change. For instance, I'm starting to think I shouldn't have voted for Trump the second time."

Anna May winced as the knot in her stomach expanded. She forced a smile. "Only the second time?"

"Don't press it." The flash in Momma's eyes softened. "You're coming back to be with Gloria."

"You reckon?"

"Yes." She picked up her needles and put them in the satchel by her chair. "Let's go to lunch in that fancy car of yours. I suppose you still won't let me drive."

"You reckon?"

"Stop. Now you're just mocking me. Come on. Get a move on. It's peach cobbler day at Yetty's, and they run out by noon."

❧❧❧❧

Thankfully, the mechanic could get Anna May's car in the next day. She could barely shift it in more than two gears, and the alignment was so off it almost pulled into the curb unless she kept the wheel half turned. Gloria had been right. Her car did need a new clutch. And Bubba was right that she needed tires—again. When she asked for a ride, he seemed more than willing to help her out. She was suspicious but grateful.

At the repair shop, Anna May timed the car drop-off so that she could ride along to Momma's surprise birthday party. Bubba pulled up and beeped the horn twice. Carrying a present in a bag, Anna May shuffled out and got in. Bubba wore a striped tie with his dress shirt.

She said, "You look nice."

"Thanks."

"You didn't say I look nice."

"You always look nice, so why should I say it?"

He adjusted the radio down. "I wanted to talk to you before we got to the restaurant."

"I'm all ears."

"Momma says you're moving back to Chicora Point."

"Yes."

He glanced at her. "You know Jimmy got out on bail. He might be on house arrest now, but he might not ever spend another minute in jail."

"He might not be afraid of me, but I think he's afraid of Gloria."

"You got that right. I think he figured out he went too far."

"You think?" Anna May shifted, sweat beading on her forehead. After a long moment, she said, "I hope you and me get along better, you know, for Momma and all."

He cleared his throat. "I thought, well, since we're not so close. I should tell you I'm willing to try."

"You already try me."

"Come on, be serious." He stopped at the traffic light. "I thought about this a lot. And I want you to know that I heard you, you know, about the Klan. I can't just up and quit. I will promise you not to bring my kids in. They don't have any idea, so I'll just keep it that way."

Anna May said, "You don't think someday someone won't tell them they have Grand Dragons in their family tree?"

"Shoot, they can go ahead. I'll just lie about it."

"You lie to your kids?"

Bubba laughed. "It shows you don't have any. Think about it. Tooth Fairy, Easter Bunny, Santa."

Anna May added, "Guy in the sky on a big chair."

"That's not funny."

"You're right. You're making a truce here. I'm sorry. I should respect your beliefs." Anna May pressed her lips together.

"What?"

"I don't know how to say it." Anna May took a deep breath. "What do the kids think about me? I mean, what would you say if I was with Gloria?"

"You could do worse."

"Not what I meant." She tapped her fingers on the console.

"I know what you meant. They don't understand gay exactly, but it's all over the TV and internet and all. Kids today don't care a bit. I don't think we need to explain anything."

"Even if we get married?"

"You're getting married?" He clutched at his chest. "I thought the mighty Anna May Walker could never be broken."

"I haven't asked her yet." Her stomach clenched.

He patted her leg. "Well, sis. I have some experience in this department. I suggest not trying to get cute and hide the ring. I had to buy two for Stacy 'cause I lost the first one in a bale of hay."

"What?"

"Don't ask. Just take my word for it."

Anna May choked up. "Thanks."

He punched her arm. "Any time. Just promise to tell me when you're gonna tell Momma. I want to make sure I have a good seat and popcorn."

"Ha. Ha. So funny." Anna May picked at a fingernail.

"I'm kidding. She likes Gloria."

"Maybe more than me."

"Definitely more than you." He pulled into the parking lot. "Remember, this is a surprise."

When they went inside, Momma was already seated at the head of a long table packed with people. A coned party hat sat on her white curls, but the smile was childlike. Gloria and Jasmine sat between Bubba's current wife and the former. Four kids sat at the other end staring at phones.

Anna May said, "You did good, Bubba. Thank you."

"If my ex-wife can come to Momma's party for our kid, well, I can suck it up and be nice to you." He pulled out the chair by Gloria. "Have a seat."

Putting a hand on Gloria's shoulder, she sat down. "Hey, glad you joined us."

Gloria whispered, "To be honest, I was a little surprised when Bubba called, but your mother is a delight."

Anna May realized this was possibly the first family meal of many, and her eyes welled up. "Yes, she is."

Chapter Thirty-nine

When Anna May suggested she might come by the next afternoon, Gloria didn't think much of it. As she opened the car door for Anna May, the scent of the flowers blasted Gloria's face. A rainbow of roses in every hue filled the backseat.

Anna May said, "I wasn't sure which color was your favorite."

Gloria picked up several bouquets. "I love every color."

Anna May collected several more. "I'm glad."

Carrying the flowers, they walked to the house. "It's a good thing I kept all of Grandma's vases. There's more over the stove if you could reach." As she ran the water, Gloria asked, "Are you hungry?"

"I may or may not have a picnic cooler in the trunk."

"Great. Let's go for a ride in the side-by-side."

The evening breeze hinted of the fall to come, the clouds thickening above them. Anna May seemed jittery, and it was catching. Gloria could feel her heart race. What was this woman up to? At the top of the hill, she put the machine into park and cut the engine. "It should be a nice sunset tonight." She popped out the two camp chairs, setting them facing the west.

"Perfect." Anna May opened the cooler and offered her a drink. "I don't think I can wait until sunset, though."

"Are you okay? You seem uptight."

"Me? Fine. I'm just building up my nerves. I'm not sure what you'll say. I want you to come to visit D.C."

Picking at a thread on the armrest, Gloria struggled to find words. The second shoe had dropped. Gloria could never leave her home. Anna May was going to leave her for the second time.

Anna May said, "I mean just for a week. I'd like to introduce you to some friends of mine."

Gloria tried to sound casual as her eyes welled up with tears. "Sure." It was all she could muster.

Standing, Anna May cleared her throat. She struggled to get something out of her pocket, but Gloria couldn't tell what it was. Then Anna May opened the box and kneeled.

"Gloria, I made a mistake once that I have no intention of repeating. I won't leave you again. I want you to know I'm moving here. This is for you." She held up the ring, the emerald surrounded by diamonds shining in the dim light.

Gloria wasn't sure if she heard her correctly. Anna May wasn't exactly proposing, was she? No, but she was staying in Chicora Point. To be with her. Her senses caught up with her, and she took the ring. "I have to say I'm surprised."

Anna May looked down, and her face turned red. "I hope I'm not overstepping."

Gloria pushed the ring on her pinkie. "Sorry, my hands swell at night." She took Anna May's hand. "It's beautiful. Thank you. And I'm so glad you're moving back."

Sitting down, Anna May almost fell out of the chair. "Oops, I don't know what's wrong with me tonight." She opened the cooler. "I got pimento cheese, egg salad, and tuna."

"And I got Tums at the house. I'll take a cheese."

Anna May opened a wine bottle. Humming, she took out two plastic wine glasses and filled them.

Gloria accepted one. "Here's to making up for lost time."

They sat in silence watching as a family of deer stepped from the woods and helped themselves to the remnants in the field below. Above them, the oranges and purples over the distant trees dipped lower and lower until the stars lit up the inky sky.

Anna May said, "Clemson-colored sky. I hope that bodes well for the football team."

"I suspect so." Gloria waited a few beats. "I have a question for you. I mean, I was wondering, you know. When you move here. Would you want to live here? I mean move in with me."

Anna May turned. The moonlight reflected off Gloria's face, her eyes bright as the day on the beach so many years ago. Her throat got tight. "I wasted so many years, I don't want to lose a single moment I could be with you. Hang on." She rummaged around in the picnic bag. "There you are, you little bugger." She opened a second box, this one holding a diamond ring. "Only if you marry me."

Anna May sat. "Sorry I can't get down on one knee again. It catches." She held the box toward Gloria.

Gloria stuttered, "You bought two rings?"

"To be honest, Bubba said it was good to have a spare."

"That's insane."

Anna May bit at her lip. She snapped the box shut.

Gloria yelled, "Yes."

Anna May jumped. "Jeesh."

"Just wanted to make sure you heard me, old woman." Gloria tickled Anna May.

She twisted but couldn't avoid the hands torturing her. "Stop it. I might drop the box. Stop. I might pee."

"Ah, the perils of age." Gloria settled her hands in her lap.

"I've always had that." Anna May straightened her shirt. She reached out and held Gloria's hand. "I wish I brought a blanket."

"So we can get stuck on the ground without any way to get up?"

"I could get up."

"Prove it." Gloria pushed her down, dove off her chair, and quickly pinned her. "Aren't you going to try and get away?"

Anna May kissed her. "Nope. I'm staying right here."

Chapter Forty

The weather turned cooler over the next few weeks as the first leaves faded from green to yellow. Pumpkins surrounded the front of the fruit stand.

Anna May watched Gloria fill a coffeepot with apple cider. When she bent over to plug it in, Anna May couldn't resist and slid her hand over her butt.

Gloria straightened. "Hey, now. We have work to do."

"Oh, we have a lot we could do." Anna May lifted Gloria onto the counter and stepped between her knees. She grabbed her hips and pulled against her. "Hey."

Gloria reached under Anna May's shirt. "Hey, yourself."

A horn honked, and they pulled apart. Jasmine waved as she pulled up to the fruit stand.

Gloria said, "That's unfortunate, but I'm glad she gave us some warning." She slid down.

Carrying a pumpkin, Jasmine walked in. "Only about a hundred to go."

Gloria pulled on a pair of gloves. "Only a hundred?"

A second set of tires crunched on the gravel as another vehicle pulled in. No doubt they were here for a tour.

"I got this." Anna May touched her arm. "If you think I'm ready."

"I think you don't want to carry more pumpkins,"

Jasmine teased.

Gloria shrugged. "Sure, just don't drive like me."

"Promise."

Anna May approached the car. "Good day. Welcome to the farm. Hop into the side-by-side, and I'll take you around." Three kids piled into the backseat as the mother edged next to Anna May. Driving to the back tree line, she stopped by the field of vines dotted with orange. There was one surefire way to get the kids engaged. "Let's get some pumpkins."

Chapter Forty-one

Awalkerblog

*M*y *dear readers,*

My name is Anna May Elizabeth Walker, named for three aunts, but I use the first two names together. My father, Ellison, and my mother, Daisy, worked at a textile mill in the town I grew up in, located in upstate South Carolina, near the mountains. For most of my adult life, I have overtly tried to disguise this fact. I thought people would think I was as mentally slow as my thick, country accent. There are more layers to it, but it wasn't just me. Even the church leaders of the Southern Baptist Convention, the largest Protestant religion in America, are increasingly dropping the "Southern" part because it's a painful reminder of their historic role supporting slavery.

A wise friend named the Reverend Carter reminded me that wherever you go, there you are. So here I am. My family descends from the Scotch Irish who settled in North Carolina and spread through the Appalachian Mountains with the cold clear rivers, high pine trees, and a dusty mist on the hills. My grandparents left the farm for the village to take a job in the textile mill where they worked six days a week, more than ten hours a day, until they dropped dead from exertion. They were uneducated, racist, and misogynistic. Because of them, I am none of those things.

How do we reconcile the past and the present? We own it, and we roll in it, and we challenge the ideas we have held as truths since we were knee-high to a grasshopper. Black Lives Matter. This is work we need to do, and by we, I mean white people. Yes. I said it. It isn't black people's job to educate us. Educate your own self. You'll mess up. It's okay. Keep trying.

Despite the challenges, I love living in the Southeast. I would crawl on my knees to get to pig picking. If you don't know what that means, come gather with us around a pit fire, grab a plate of pulled pork, and let's listen to each other.

I am Anna May Walker. I am from Chicora Point, South Carolina, where the population recently increased by one.

THE END

If you liked this book...

Share a review with your friends or post a review on your favorite site like Amazon, Goodreads, Barnes and Noble, or anywhere you purchased the book. Or perhaps share a posting on your social media sites and help spread the word.

Join the Sapphire Newsletter and keep up with all your favorite authors.

Did we mention you get a free book for joining our team?

sign-up at - www.sapphirebooks.com

About the author

McGee Mathews won the 2019 Lesfic Bard Award for new author. She is a member of the Golden Crown Literary Society, Rainbow Romance Writers and, formerly, the Romance Writers of America.

Check out McGee's other book

Keeping Secrets – ISBN – 978-1-952270-04-8

What would you do if, after finally finding the woman of your dreams, she suddenly leaves to fight in the Civil War?

It's 1863, and Elizabeth Hepscott has resigned herself to a life of monotonous boredom far from the battlefields as the wife of a Missouri rancher. Her fate changes when she travels with her brother to Kentucky to help him join the Union Army. On a whim, she poses as his little brother and is bullied into enlisting, as well. Reluctantly pulled into a new destiny, a lark decision quickly cascades into mortal danger.

While Elizabeth's life has made a drastic U-turn, Charlie Schweicher, heiress to a glass-making fortune, is still searching for the only thing money can't buy.

A chance encounter drastically changes everything for both of them. Will Charlie find the love she's longed for, or will the war take it all away?

Slaying Dragons - 978-1-952270-67-3

Dani Powell's life had been a series of extreme highs and the devastating lows. Medications and the therapy sessions keep her centered on her art, music, and painting. All a reflection of where her mind is at that moment in time. As she struggles to keep the chaos at bay her partner Andrea Fenwick is her safe port in a stormy ocean

Andrea Fenwick juggles a busy accounting job while trying to keep her partner Dani grounded. Their lives together have had their ups and downs, but Andrea never expect the downs to be rock bottom. She'd determined to keep Dani afloat even if it means her best may not be good enough this time.

Tommie Andrews, a computer whiz and occasional dog trainer, discovers she's developing a crush on her friend and co-worker Andrea. The more she tries to be supportive of Andrea,
the more apparent it becomes that friendship may be the most she can hope for. The timing couldn't be worse. Or could it?

When will things get better for the three women? First, they must define "better."

Other books by Sapphire Authors

Dusty Road Home - 978-1-952270-72-7

Melanie Crenshaw has fallen off the proverbial map. Notoriously private on a good day, the world-famous mystery author has gone dark to avoid any public blowback or scandal from her latest failed relationship. Seeking quiet and solace, she retreats to her rural hometown, hoping isolation will be just the atmosphere she needs to finish her novel. But going back home is never as easy as it sounds, especially when a nosy reporter starts sniffing around.

Pulitzer-winning investigative journalist Pilar Stein has seen people at their worst—and has the scars to prove it. After taking time off to heal from a particularly brutal assignment, she's back in the saddle and ready to reclaim her place among the elite of hard-hitting reporters. Unfortunately, her re-entry story—a profile on elusive author Melanie Crenshaw who has suddenly disappeared—seems to lack the teeth necessary to catapult her back to the top of her game.

Appearances are deceiving, of course, and Pilar soon discovers that what she deems a simple fluff piece might well lead to the scoop of a generation...just not the one she expected.

As Melanie fights to maintain her privacy while Pilar takes a backhoe to her past, the two women find themselves torn between their own professional convictions and their growing attraction to each other.

And no matter which road they take, it's going to be a bumpy ride.

Betrayal (As We Know It Book 3) - 978-1-952270-69-7

Betrayal is the exciting conclusion to the As We Know It series.

The survivors at Whitaker Estate are still reeling from the vicious attack on their community, which left three of their friends dead.

When the mysterious newcomer Alaina Renato reveals there is a traitor in their midst, it threatens to tear the community apart. Is there truly a traitor, or is Alaina playing them all?

Dillon Mitchell and the other Commission members realize their group might not survive another attack, especially if there is someone working against them from the inside. Despite the potential risk, they vote to attend a summit that will bring together other survivors from around the country.

When the groups converge on Las Vegas, the festive atmosphere soon turns somber upon the discovery of an ominous threat. But is the danger coming from within, or is there someone else lurking in the city?

Before it's too late, they must race against time to determine where the betrayal is coming from.

Made in the USA
Columbia, SC
29 September 2022